Forbidden

A Whitmore Elite Prequel

J.A. Owenby

FREE BOOK

SIGN UP FOR J.A. OWENBY'S NEWSLETTER and download your FREE book, Love & Sins. Stay up to date concerning exclusive bonus scenes, updates on upcoming releases, and more. Just click here or visit www.authorjaowenby.com

Trigger Warnings

Please see a list of TW/CW's on my website at https://authorjaowenby.com/about/forbidden-trigger-warnings/

Chapter One

"I can't do this anymore, Shae." Ibrahim shifted in the limo seat across from me, clearly uncomfortable.

My chest tightened with his words, his thick accent rippling through me, coating my skin with goosebumps and causing my thighs to clench. The only reason I was in the backseat of Daddy's limo with his driver was because I needed to get laid.

"What? Why?" Twirling a lock of my long, blonde hair around my finger, I waited for a response.

His dark fingers rubbed his clean-shaven jawline. "You know why. If your father finds out about us, he'll fire me." Worry lines creased his forehead. "Plus, we started fucking when you were sixteen. I don't want to go to prison."

"I'm almost nineteen now, and we've never been caught. Stop worrying about serving time. It was always consensual." I huffed and crossed my arms beneath my perfect C-cup breasts—the best money could buy.

His attention hovered on my cleavage while my lower lip jutted out into an innocent pout, one I'd practiced in front of the mirror hundreds of times.

Ibrahim's resistance was unexpected. I contemplated taking a drink from the stocked mini bar, but it was Ibrahim I was craving, not alcohol.

"Fuck Daddy. Lately he's always working and never around anyway, so how would he find out about us anyway?" I leaned over and squeezed Ibrahim's knee.

"Shae." His voice was deep, throaty, and filled with frustration.

I blinked rapidly, tears filling my eyes. A trick I'd learned when I was young that always helped me get my way. "Ibrahim, I need a grown man, not some silly teenage boy who thinks he knows how to get me off." A tear fell down my cheek, and I glanced away before I wiped my face. If Ibrahim was serious, then my sex life would dwindle too almost nothing. Besides, we had a good thing going, and I had a good thing going. He'd popped my cherry with his thick cock when I was sixteen. The guys my age couldn't compete with him.

Dammit. I wasn't sure if the waterworks were affecting him or not.

I sank my teeth into my perfectly painted red lip, my gaze landing on the bulge in his black slacks.

He massaged the back of his neck, confusion flickering across his expression. "You know I have to send money to my family in Nigeria, Shae. I can't afford to lose this job. I'll never get employed by another wealthy family."

I stared out the passenger window, my hand running up the inside of my thigh, raising my cream-colored mini skirt. I slid along the U-shaped, black leather seat and joined Ibrahim on his side. "Please don't do this." I parted my legs, trailing my nails up my thigh, teasing him. "Besides, I'm only back from college for a few short months." Leaning over, I nipped at his lower lip and softly sighed.

Ibrahim's attention dipped to my thighs, and I lifted my skirt more, revealing my navy, lace thong. "Daddy is in Paris this week and Cole isn't home from school for a few hours so ..." I didn't bother to mention that my stepbrother would be around for the entire summer. I would have to deal with that problem later.

My focus lowered to Ibrahim's erection. "Since Daddy isn't here, how about one last goodbye fuck?" I fluttered my dark lashes at him and inched closer. Little did Ibrahim know that this was far from goodbye. He couldn't stay away from me. We lived for the thrill of the forbidden. For me, screwing around with Daddy's staff was deliciously sinful. Wrong never tasted so good. Hell, Daddy would rather I stick a blade in someone's gut and spill their blood than start a sex scandal that could topple his empire.

"And ..." I closed the gap between us, placing my palm on his muscular chest, then slowly opened the buttons on his white dress shirt. I leaned closer, my mouth grazing his ear. "You took my virginity, so I thought you could be the first to fuck me in the ass." I'd never had anal sex, but I was determined to keep Ibrahim begging for me. I was still nervous, though. I'd heard it was amazing, but I'd also been told that it hurt.

Ibrahim sucked in a breath. "Shae that's ..." He moaned as my hand trailed down his muscular abs, then cupped his cock through his black slacks.

"Do you really want to say goodbye?" With a quick move, I tugged off my navy polo top and tossed it on the floor. I flicked open the front clasp of my bra and slowly slid the straps off my shoulders. My nipples hardened with the caress of the air. "Daddy won't find out." My lips parted, then I flashed him an innocent smile. "I've been a bad girl, baby." I arched my back, my tits grazing his shoulder. Running my long fingernail over his corded bicep, I peeked up at him through my eyelashes. "Very naughty."

Ibrahim moaned. "Fuck." He grabbed my arm tightly. "Do you know what happens to bad girls?" Before I could respond, he bent me over his knees, flipped up my skirt, and revealed my bare ass. The smack against my flesh filled the car as I released a cry. The sting didn't dissipate before he spanked me again.

He rubbed my tender skin before he smacked me again. He moved my thong out of the way, then ran his finger along my slit. "You're soaking wet."

"For you, baby. It's all for you."

Ibrahim fisted my hair and jerked my head back. He could light my body up like a goddamned Christmas tree.

"On your knees," he demanded.

I tried not to smile as I dropped to the floor. He flipped open the button on his slacks, his zipper the only sound other than our heavy breathing.

Ibrahim gripped my chin and rubbed the tip of his cock against my lips, forcing it between my teeth. I licked the precum before sucking slowly, savoring him.

"That's it, Shae. Take it all." He guided my head as he fucked my mouth.

I dug my fingernails into his legs, cursing the material of his pants. This time, I wanted to mark him and leave scratches on his beautiful, dark skin. A click reached my ears, and Ibrahim froze.

With a quick movement, the limo door swung open, the bright sunshine filling the back of the vehicle. Terror twisted Ibrahim's expression, his eyes wide with fear.

Chapter Two

"Sorry I'm late," Matt said, climbing into the vehicle with the soft scent of roses clinging to his sun-kissed skin.

Ibrahim glared at Matt. "Fuck, you scared me." Matt was our gardener's twenty-five-year-old son, who occasionally helped his father look after the estate.

I crawled onto the seat next to Ibrahim and turned to Matt, smiling excitedly. I wasn't sure why he worked for his dad when he belonged on a runway as a model. His sandy blonde hair and hazel eyes soaked my panties every time I saw him. I wiped the corner of my mouth. Maybe working with all those gardening tools had sculpted his arms and chest. Hell, I didn't care how he got ripped, as long as I could run my hands all over the dips and valleys of his muscles. A curl flopped onto his forehead, and he brushed it aside, grinning.

I leaned forward, ready to get back to playing. "Glad you could make it."

Matt closed the door and licked his lips. "Show me your pussy," Matt demanded, tugging on the hem of his black T-shirt, his attention on my slender, toned legs.

Apparently, he wasn't going to waste any time, either.

Since I'd been fucking Ibrahim and Matt, I'd learned something interesting about myself. First, I loved the idea of getting caught. Second, I loved being dominated, which was strange since Daddy made every decision for me. Being bossed around shouldn't have turned me on this much, but it did.

I lifted my skirt and parted my legs enough for Matt to get a glimpse of my thong. Reaching for Ibrahim, I wrapped my fingers around his thick shaft.

"Wider." Matt unzipped his jeans and removed his dick.

Chills shot through me, and I stroked Ibrahim slowly while keeping an eye on Matt. In one quick move, Matt knelt in front of me and pushed my knees to my shoulders, exposing me. A deep growl traveled through him as he moved my thong to the side. He ran his tongue over my slit and grabbed my thighs, his fingers digging into my skin hard enough to leave marks. At least they would be high enough to hide.

"That's it, Matt," I moaned as he sucked on my bundle of nerves.

Matt laid down on the floor, indicating for me to sit on his face. My favorite. I straddled his head, then Matt gripped my hips and pulled me down, his tongue inside me, licking and lapping up my juices.

Ibrahim hunched down in front of me, unable to reach his full height, but he didn't seem to mind. I wrapped my lips around his cock and sucked him as I rocked against Matt's mouth. Desire pulsed through my veins. I loved having both of them at the same time.

Matt dipped his fingers into my pussy, then moved to my ass. Lifting me forward slightly, he shoved his fingers into my hole as he teased my clit.

I stroked Ibrahim as heat coursed through my body. "Oh, God." I ran my tongue around the tip of Ibrahim's cock and peered up at him.

"I need more," I panted, pulling up my skirt to reveal Matt's face. He loosened his grip on me, and I rose.

Matt moved to the limo seat, and I grinned at Ibrahim. "Wanna fuck my ass?" I asked, coyly.

"Oh, hell yeah," Matt chimed in.

I waited for the guys to each roll on condoms, then bent over the seat, placing my hands on the wall of the car.

Ibrahim rubbed his dick along my pussy, then placed it at the entrance of my puckered hole.

"Ready, princess? Just relax," he said, pushing against me. With a quick thrust, he groaned as I screamed. His large palm covered my mouth as he split me in two. Pain jolted every nerve ending in my body while tears clouded my eyes.

"So goddammed tight, Shae." A moan escaped Ibrahim as he continued.

I whimpered against his hand, regretting my decision. I hadn't even noticed that Matt had sat next to me. He sucked his finger, then slipped his hand between my thighs, massaging my clit. "It will be worth it in a minute."

Pain bled into pleasure as Ibrahim fucked me and Matt played with my pussy. My eyes closed as I surrendered, allowing the guys to use my body. Dominate me. Control me. Ibrahim's breathing picked up, then he jerked and tensed, his hand dropping from my mouth.

"Dammit, that was starting to feel good," I panted as Ibrahim pulled out. "Matt ..."

I waited impatiently while the two traded places and Ibrahim zipped and buttoned his pants before he began to play with my throbbing core.

Matt crouched behind me and eased into my ass more gently than Ibrahim had.

"Oh, yeah. Harder." I pushed against him. Maybe Ibrahim had already stretched me out because Matt felt amazing.

Ibrahim shoved two fingers into my wet slit as his thumb stroked my bundle of nerves. I moaned, basking in the sensations coursing through me.

"Jesus, Shae. Ibrahim's right, this ass of yours is fucking tight."

I peeked over my shoulder as Matt's eyes slammed closed, pleasure written all over his handsome face. "Goddammit." Matt fisted my hair and jerked my head back.

Fire ignited in every fiber of my being as I danced on the edge of an orgasm. "Fuck me, Matt."

Ibrahim's mouth parted slightly, his gaze still heated with lust. With a hard pinch to my clit, my world exploded, and black dots filled my vision. Matt jerked and a low, husky sound erupted from him as he came.

"Holy shit, Shae. That was some good fucking right there." Matt pulled out of me, then plopped down on the seat across from us. He grinned like a kid in a candy store, removed the condom, then stuffed his limp dick back into his jeans. I collapsed next to him, my body aching but sated from the delicious orgasm.

"Smells like sex in here. Ibrahim, you probably should air it out and clean it up before Julia needs you to drive her to her book club meeting or wherever." My focus drifted to Matt. "Don't be rude, pick your used rubber off the floor so Ibrahim doesn't have to." I nodded at the used condoms and smiled.

Matt snatched it off the floor and shoved it into his pocket. He glanced at his watch, then at me. "As always, it's been fun, Shae. It's time for me to go." He winked at me, then swung the door open and climbed out of the limo.

I smoothed my hair, my attention falling on Ibrahim who appeared calm and content. I leaned over and placed a gentle kiss against his full mouth. "Just goes to show you that I need real men. Not some egotistical, entitled, rich, teenage asshole who thinks he knows how to fuck." I pressed my lips to his, then let myself out of the car, smiling triumphantly.

The breeze picked up strands of my hair as I strolled to my car. There wasn't a single doubt in my mind that I would get what I wanted from Ibrahim and Matt. Ibrahim could protest all he wanted, but I knew exactly how to play him. Both of them. After all, I'd had three years of practice.

The bright Washington sunshine temporarily blinded me as I walked to my BMW i8. Ibrahim always parked the limo in a semi-discrete location not too far away from the house. It had been our meeting place since we'd started playing around.

Once situated behind the steering wheel, I pushed the start button on the car. Humming softly to myself, I grabbed my Gucci sunglasses and slipped them into place. The car's engine purred as I shifted into drive and headed to the house.

Five minutes later, I eased around the circular driveway and parked in front of the eleven-thousand square foot mansion. The shrubs were freshly sculpted, the stone fountain cleaned, the grass mowed, and hedges trimmed. The early summer ocean breeze whipped through my hair as I exited the car. I collected my tan Hermes handbag and locked up. When I reached the front door, I punched in my code and let myself in.

The faint smell of cleaning supplies tickled my nose as I glanced around. Other than the sparkling marble floors and winding wooden staircase, there weren't any indications that someone was here yet.

I suspected that Cole would arrive in the next few hours. I hadn't seen him very much since Christmas, but that wasn't unusual. Most of the time, he was only home for the holidays and summer vacations. However, he did have a nasty habit of occasionally popping up on our college campus when I least wanted to see him.

Julia, Cole's mom, and my daddy had only been married four years. Cole and I had been at the age to immediately hate that someone new was in our space. Eventually I got used to him, but I wasn't his biggest fan.

My mouth watered as I caught a whiff of dinner. It was Thursday, which meant pot roast. Annabelle, our chef and housekeeper, was absolutely amazing in the kitchen. It was a miracle I wasn't spilling out of my size two clothes.

I hurried up the stairs toward my bedroom, mentally checking off my to-do list before I met up with my best friends. First, I needed a shower. Second, I needed to text the girls about the party that night.

Grunts and moans caught my attention, my ears perking up. I walked down the hall, my heels clicking on the white marble floor. My heart skipped a beat as I heard my name. *What the fuck is going on?* No one should be here except Annabelle.

The only other bedroom on this side of the house was Cole's. Apparently, he'd gotten home earlier than I had anticipated, but what in the hell was I hearing?

As I approached his room, I realized his door was open and peeked in. Cole leaned his shoulder against the wall, his ankles crossed while he rubbed his chin and watched the flat screen television mounted over the gas fireplace, offering me a side view.

He shoved a hand into the pocket of his grey sweats that hung low on his hips. For whatever reason, he was shirtless, and I stared at the collage of tattoos covering his back—a skull with angel wings, a sword, and others I hadn't had time to study. My focus drifted across his rounded shoulders and bulging biceps. It had been a long-ass time since I'd seen Cole without a shirt, and it was clear he'd been working out since last year.

Clothes were scattered across his king-size bed, and a suitcase lay open on the white marble floor. The desk between the windows held a stack of books, and the recliner was nestled in the corner near the gas fireplace. The chair was piled high with jeans and shorts.

Sucking in a sharp breath, I finally identified the sounds and my mouth dropped in horror as I realized what Cole was watching.

Holy shit. How the fuck did he do it? When were cameras installed in the limo?

"You recorded me?" I screeched. "What the hell is wrong with you, perv?" My attention was glued to the screen as I witnessed Matt and Ibrahim fucking me. Storming in, I turned off the television and glared at Cole. "I asked you a fucking question, and I expect an answer." I seethed and folded my arms across my chest, tapping my toe impatiently.

He flashed me a mischievous grin. "How was your afternoon,

sis?" He pushed off the wall and shoved his fingers through his blonde hair. His glacier-blue eyes sparkled against his tanned skin.

I stomped over to him and shoved my finger against the tattoo of a panther that curled around a pec and disappeared around his back. The head of the cat sat on the front of his shoulder, mouth open, revealing its fangs, ready to strike. "I hope you enjoyed the show, asshole."

"Oh, I did. Seemed like you did as well. Can't wait to tell daddy dearest what you do in your spare time." Amusement flickered over his expression.

A burst of anger shot through me. *How fucking dare he try to blackmail me.* With a quick flick of my wrist, I slapped Cole across his face. "Don't threaten me. What do you want and where are the goddamned cameras and recording?" I didn't give a rat's ass how he pulled this off, but no way in hell could he show Daddy or Julia. Julia would insist the situation be handled before someone found out and Daddy had a scandal on his hands. He would cut me out of the will, and I would lose my inheritance.

Cole's nostrils flared as he stepped forward and forced me against the wall. He glowered at me, spilling hate with each breath.

His nose brushed my ear, and his minty breath fanned across my cheek as he wrapped his fingers around my throat, cutting off my oxygen. I dragged my fake nails across the back of his hand while I gasped for air. Cole had a reputation for a short temper, but he'd never pushed me this far.

Cruel and sadistic flashes appeared and disappeared in his eyes. "Keep your fucking hands to yourself. And a word of advice. End it, princess, or I'll show good ol' Dad every second of the recording."

Our gazes locked as I fought against him, clawing at his arm and leaving red angry marks on his skin. Suddenly, images flashed through my mind of Cole thrusting into me from behind while he choked me. *Dammit. What the hell was wrong with me? My step-brother?*

My sight began to fade as he squeezed harder. Jesus. He was going to fucking kill me, and I was aroused.

Cole dropped his hand, and I collapsed. My knees smacked the hard floor as my purse slipped from my shoulder. I peered up at him, coughing and gasping. He sneered at me as he adjusted himself, chuckled, and walked away.

I pulled myself up, dazed and confused about how the limo situation and arguing with Cole had taken a sharp turn. Cole Parker, my asshole stepbrother, had just choked me, and from the looks of him adjusting his dick in his pants ... enjoyed it. More than that, my core throbbed with longing as I recalled his touch and the proximity of his mouth to my sensitive neck and ear. His confidence and domineering attitude rolled off him in waves, intoxicating me. He wasn't the same boy who had left for college. Not mentally and not physically. Instead, he'd returned a goddamned man, and my hormones were the first to notice.

Wobbling on my black Louboutin heels, I placed a palm against the desk to steady myself as I removed my shoes and darted across the hall to my room. I'd disliked Cole before, but after he had just threatened to blackmail me, I hated him now. At the same time, I needed my head checked because his touch had lit me on fire. If he stormed in here, flipped my skirt up, and fucked me senseless, I still didn't think my body would be satisfied. Maybe a night with him. *Jesus, stop! He's your stepbrother, for God's sake.*

Quietly, I closed and locked the door, then rested my forehead against the frame, scrambling for clarity. I had a huge-ass problem I had to stay focused on. One thing was for certain; no one, not even family, fucked with me and got away with it. I was a Wessex. I wasn't a princess. I was a fucking queen. It was time to put Cole in his place once and for all.

Chapter Three

My favorite room in the house was my bedroom. For some reason, it felt safe and secluded from the rest of the mansion. I'm sure it had something to do with the calming light blue, white, and navy color scheme. The bedding, the chair, the rug—everything weaved together with a delicate balance.

Fiery anger ripped through me as I tossed my heels near my desk. Rummaging through my handbag, I located my phone, then dropped my purse on my king-size bed and stomped to the bathroom. If that bastard left marks on my neck, I would destroy him. How dare he film my extracurricular activities with Ibrahim and Matt, then have the audacity to put his hands on me.

Discarding my leather skirt, polo shirt, and lace bra, and thong, I stood in front of my full-length lighted mirror. I tilted my head up and to the left. Red welts glared against my pale skin, but I didn't think it would bruise.

My mind whirled faster than an F5 tornado as I turned on the shower. Within seconds, steam billowed over the top of the glass wall. In my opinion, I had the best bathroom, other than Daddy and Julia's. The vanity counter was the same white and black marble that ran through the sprawling mansion and provided tons of space for my makeup and hair tools.

My favorite feature, other than the double sinks, was the claw foot soaker bathtub near the window that overlooked the neighborhood. In the fall, every tree leaf turned a bright orange, red, or yellow. If I had time, I would soak for hours, sip a good glass of wine, and read a naughty romance novel. I hadn't had that leisure since I'd started at the university last September, though.

Locating a fresh towel, I placed it on the heated holder before I walked under the hot water. Not only did I reek of sex, but this was also the best place for me to relax.

Fear knotted my stomach. Cole had made it clear he would show Daddy the recording, but why would he even care? What was in it for him? It wouldn't mean more money when Daddy died, so what was the fucking problem? Who I fucked was none of his business.

I lathered my long strands of hair, the rose petal scent reminding me of Matt. Unable to stop my smile, my mind returned to my afternoon threesome. My body was sore, but it didn't sway me from wanting Ibrahim and Matt. Next time, I would have to make sure there weren't any cameras around.

Annoyed all over again, I sifted through the possible reasons for Cole's blackmail attempt, but I continued to come up blank.

Once I was clean, I turned off the water before I reached for the warm towel. My cell buzzed with a text. I quickly dried off, moisturized, then collected my phone from the counter. I grinned as I read the message from my bestie, Zoe.

Bitch, don't be late tonight. I know where you live. I'll drag your ass out the door by your hair.

I rolled my eyes at the message, laughing as I texted her back.

I just showered. I'll be ready in plenty of time. Come on over, though. Need to chat.

The little black dots flickered on my screen as I waited for her response.

Let me grab my shit for tonight. Be there in twenty. Btw, this better be something delish to pull me away from Emily in Paris.

I sure as hell wouldn't call Cole choking me delish, but I needed to tell someone about it in case he ever killed me.

You'll survive. See you in a few.

Locking the screen on my cell, I left the bathroom and headed to my closet. My bare feet landed on the plush cream carpet, the silk fibers tickling my soles.

When Daddy proposed to Julia, we moved to this house. Mine and Daddy's previous home was gorgeous, but we didn't need a lot of space. However, with the addition of two more people, Daddy thought it would be best to start fresh. At first, I objected. Loudly. I'd lived in Cherrywood Place since I'd been born. More than that, Mom loved it there. But she was gone, so living in our old house together was just a faded and agonizing memory.

Choking on the painful memories, I busied myself searching for what I wanted to wear to the party. Harrison lived in a mansion on the outskirts of town where the elevation was a bit higher. The ten acres had an abundance of trees and the evenings always cooled off quickly. A dress wasn't the best choice. I ran my finger along the drawers that held my jewelry, lingerie, shoes, and handbags.

The second I'd seen the bedroom with the large bay windows and window seat, I was leaning toward choosing it, but when I saw the closet, it was a done deal. The built-ins included white shelves and dressers, several rows of hanger space, and two full-length mirrors, but the best part was the sitting area with a pink chaise lounge.

It was too early to get dressed for the party, so I selected a burgundy robe and slipped it on. Zoe would be here soon, and I couldn't answer the door undressed. Not with the perv's bedroom right across the hall. I sank my teeth into my lower lip as I realized he could watch me naked anytime he wanted, at least until I deleted the video.

Shit! What if Cole set up a camera in my room? Over the next several minutes, I frantically checked every light, book, corner, under the bed, and any other spot I could think of where he could have hidden a recording device, but I didn't find any. If that son of a bitch had installed cameras in the limo, or had someone do it for him, there was no telling what he would do next. I hated that our bedrooms were so close together.

A quick knock alerted me that Zoe was here. Cole or Annabelle must have let her in. Securing the sash around my slender waist, I hurried across the room, then flung the door open.

"You got here fast ..." Tension coursed through my body as my attention landed on Cole, and I forced myself to relax my shoulders. I would never let him know he'd scared me earlier. "What do you want?" I placed a hand on my hip and leaned on the frame, consciously attempting to appear calm even though I wasn't.

Cole's ice-blue eyes slowly trailed from my lips to my breasts, my stomach, my legs, then returned to my irritated gaze.

"I realize you've seen me naked, but please try to not be so obvious when you check me out."

Cole's jaw tensed, the muscle in his neck popping. I'd hit a nerve. "Didn't it gross you out to see your sister getting fucked? I mean, what does that make you ..." I placed a finger on my chin, appearing deep in thought. "Oh, a fucking creeper."

I grabbed the door to shut it in his face, but he blocked it with the toe of his combat boot.

"Call me whatever you want." He pushed his way into my bedroom, his expression stone cold.

I gulped but held my ground. Cole shot me a menacing stare. "Sterling texted me. He said that you're going to the party tonight."

Sterling, Remington, and Cole had basically grown up together. Anderson had moved to Washington from California. He joined the high school football team and met the guys a few years ago. Although they never got caught, I suspected they were in all kinds of trouble. "Yeah, and?"

"You're not going. If I see you there, I'll have you removed." His eyes narrowed as he peered down at me. His wide shoulders shadowed my petite frame, blocking my view around him.

He'd changed clothes since I'd encountered him earlier. His black T-shirt stretched across his broad chest, his muscles flexing as he moved. My pulse stuttered against my wrist as the scent of his Tom Ford Neroli cologne invaded my senses. Out of obligation, I'd bought him a bottle for his birthday at the beginning of the year.

"You're delusional if you think you can have me tossed out of Harrison's party. It's an annual event to kick off summer vacation. I've attended since I was fifteen." I huffed, irritated at Cole's audacity.

"Not this year, Princess." Without another word, he spun on his heel and left.

I fisted my hands and groaned as he walked away, his designer jeans hugging every curve of his ass and muscular legs. If he weren't such a fucking asshole, he would be panty-soaking gorgeous. *He still soaked yours.* I scowled, then quickly reminded myself that if I didn't want obnoxious elevens when I was older, I had to stop scrunching up my forehead.

Stomping over to the door he left open, I grabbed the knob and prepared to slam it closed when Zoe's giggle reached me. I poked my head into the hall, my mouth gaping.

"Look who's all grown up," Cole said, gently squeezing Zoe's shoulder.

"I'm not the only one. Damn, Cole. Could you try not to look so hot?" Zoe asked, pushing her lower lip out slightly while she tucked a piece of her dark hair behind her ear with a 'fuck me please' expression on her face.

He flashed her a lopsided grin. I'd forgotten how beautiful his smile was because I rarely saw it.

Jealousy reared its nasty head, and I kicked the green-eyed monster to the curb. Why in the hell was I feeling like this? Cole had stomped all over any hope I'd had that there might be an ounce of goodness in him. I clenched my teeth together, pissed that I was having to call out my best friend for practically throwing herself at Cole. "Zoe." My tone was sharp.

Her head snapped in my direction, and she appeared startled, as if I'd caught her with her hand in a cookie jar.

I waved Zoe into my room. Cole tipped his chin up before he tossed me a salute and walked away.

Zoe strolled over to my bed and dropped her brown Gucci duffle bag on it. "Damn, when did he get so gorgeous?" Zoe fanned herself, her manicured red nails catching the light.

I stared at her, befuddled that she was suddenly team Cole. "Just because he came home after his first year of college looking like a God, doesn't mean you get to bang my brother."

"Step, babe. He's your stepbrother. And to clear the air, I'd let him lick and fuck my pussy all damned day."

My nostrils flared. "You're taking this too far, Zoe." I plopped on my bed, pain shooting through my ass. Hopefully, I wouldn't be as sore tomorrow, but that definitely wasn't the case at the moment.

"Salty much?" She quirked a dark eyebrow.

Glancing at the floor, I answered her with silence. I would never admit I was jealous of Cole being nice to her because ... I refused to admit it to myself.

"Hey, what's wrong? You've never given a shit that I thought Cole was gorgeous before." Zoe joined me on the bed, her doe-like eyes searching mine. Zoe was one of the most beautiful females I'd ever seen. Her long, black hair flowed past her shoulders, and she had a slender body with tits and an ass any guy would drool over. Not to mention her perky nose, and a deep tan I had a hell of a time getting myself. She'd been captain of the high school cheerleading squad for three years in a row, which was virtually unheard of, but she was that good. Her parents had put her in gymnastics and dance lessons since she could walk, but she had a lot of natural talent and a fun personality that drew people to her.

Zoe took my hand in hers. "I know that wistful look. Spill."

My head buzzed with my churning emotions, deciding how much I would tell her. Then, the events of the entire afternoon spilled from my mouth. Zoe's expression morphed from shock to irritation to gawking. Once I was finished, she hopped off my bed and paced while she waved her hands in front of her as though she were trying to piece it all together. I assumed it was so she was clear on which part to chew me out about first, since she didn't have a clue about what I'd been hiding. I hadn't wanted to share my personal enjoyment of the staff with anyone. It was much more fun to have a dirty little secret that was all mine. Unfortunately, Cole's recent discovery brought huge consequences, and I needed help from my best friend.

Finally, she turned to me and placed her fists on her slender hips. "What. The. Fuck. Shae Wessex." Zoe only used my full name when she was pissed at me.

"I was afraid to say anything. I'm sorry." I gave her my saddest puppy eyes, hoping she wouldn't be mad at me for long. We had a party to attend. I didn't give a shit what Cole had said.

"How long have you been screwing Ibrahim and Matt?" She shook her head in bewilderment. "If Cole tells your dad ..." She smacked her palm against her forehead.

"Ibrahim since I was sixteen." I cringed, waiting for her to rip me a new one. "Shit. Shit. Shit. Cole *can't* say something to Daddy ..." I flopped onto my bed, wet strands of hair sticking to my back.

Her mouth hung open, then she slammed it closed, her teeth clicking together. "Girl ... I can't even ... You haven't said anything for almost three years?" she squeaked.

"Until now, there wasn't any reason to. I couldn't afford to chat about it. It was too risky."

"Risky? You want to talk about risky, Shae? Cole fucking Jennings recorded you banging your dad's limo driver and the gardener's son. We have to get our hands on the video and destroy it. Then you can cover your ass and make it up to me." Her forehead creased and her gaze narrowed. I wasn't surprised that she was pissed at me. If the roles had been reversed, I would have been upset with her, too.

"It was a bit of fun, Zoe. I didn't mean to hurt you or make you mad. Ibrahim is hot as hell, and he's got a huge cock. He's addictive. He's not a high school boy trying to figure out where the hole is." This was another reason I didn't want to tell Zoe. I didn't want her to scold me like I was a two-year-old that didn't understand my decision or that what I'd been doing was wrong.

Zoe snorted. "God, I actually can't blame you. But fucking the hired help is a big no." Her shoulders slumped forward for a second, then she plopped down next to me. "Promise me no more, Shae. It's not worth losing your inheritance over. Let's figure out what we have to do in order to erase the proof, so you're not cut out of the will. Girl, we have plans, and you can't travel the world with me if you're a broke-ass bitch."

"I know." I blew out a guilty sigh. "Obviously there are cameras in the limo. Cole barely got home for summer vacation, so they had to have been installed sooner."

"I wouldn't put it past him to have talked one of his friends into helping him. But who and why, though?"

Drumming my fingertips on my thigh, I wracked my brain for the answers. Zoe was right. Cole had access to the limo like I did. While in high school, I was constantly leaving a book or my backpack in the car, so Daddy had keys made for all of us. Cole could have easily given his copy to someone.

"Babe, I think you got played. I have no idea why Cole would do that in the first place, but everything that gorgeous, hot, hunk does has a purpose. He's cold and calculating."

"No shit, but I have no fucking clue what he's up to." I covered my face with my hands, wishing I could rewind the events of the day and make different choices. But it was too late. Daddy had always taught me to admit my fuck ups and fix them. I still didn't have an issue playing with Matt and Ibrahim, but my fun was officially over since Cole had stuck his nose where it didn't belong. One thing was clear. I had to get that recording and destroy any evidence before it ruined me.

"Cole said you're not going to Harrison's party tonight?" Zoe asked, pulling me from my thoughts.

"Like I'm going to listen to him." I sat up, sulking that he was around for the entire summer. Shit, he'd only been home for a few hours, and he was already making my life unbearable.

"Of course not, but while we're there I'll keep an eye on him and see if I can steal his phone so we can locate and delete the video. But for God's sake, Shae. Don't fuck Ibrahim again!"

"Shh! Keep your voice down."

"Sorry. I'm obviously still processing and pissed at you." She folded her arms over her chest and glared at me.

I kissed her cheek. "Don't be mad. If it had been you keeping a secret, I would forgive you." I leaned my head on her shoulder.

"Ugh. I know you would, but don't kill my buzz. It's difficult being angry at you, so I'm going to hold onto it for as long as I can and make you suffer."

I giggled. "Love you, Zoe."

"Right back atcha, bitch." She placed her head on top of mine.

Over the next few hours, we took our time getting ready for Harrison's party. Zoe had selected a pair of light wash jeans paired with a black crop top that revealed her belly button piercing, the small diamond winking in the light as she moved. Zoe riffled through my closet and tossed a pair of dark wash skinny jeans, with a plum-colored, off-the-shoulder shirt, onto the chair. I smirked and placed my hands on my hips and tapped my toe against the floor. I wanted to wear something brighter, but Zoe reminded me I needed to blend in since we were on a mission to grab Cole's phone.

I'd messaged Annabelle to bring up some snacks and drinks for us while we analyzed every possibility of how to erase evidence of my sexcapade. Hopefully, Cole hadn't uploaded it to the cloud yet. Unless he'd changed the passcode, I still remembered it from when we were home during Christmas break. He hadn't realized that I was standing behind him with a clear view of his screen when he'd unlocked it. Maybe fate was on my side after all. Butterflies ran amok in my belly with the exquisite thought that I was about to strip Cole of the power that he held over me. Karma was a bitch, but so was I.

***

Once we were ready for the evening Zoe headed downstairs to chat up Cole while I snuck into his room and searched for the recording or his phone. At least it was cleaner than earlier. I wasn't expecting to find anything, but I had to try. I hurried to his desk and glanced around. Nothing. Tugging on the top drawer, I peered inside but only found pens and pencils. I chewed on my bottom lip and pulled on the bottom one. It wouldn't budge. "Dammit. You shit. What are you hiding?"

Zoe and Cole's voices reached my ears, and my heart broke into a gallop. If he caught me snooping, I would be in deep shit. I rushed to his dresser and quickly rummaged through his boxer-briefs. Nothing.

"Wait, Cole," Zoe called out.

"Fuck," I muttered. Not only was I out of time, but how was I going to sneak out of here undetected? I tiptoed to the door and carefully peeked out. Cole and Zoe were at the bottom of the stairs ... holding hands. I clenched my teeth, willing myself to keep my mouth shut.

Cole tipped Zoe's chin up and smiled. *Seriously?* I took a few steps out of his bedroom, leaned against the wall, and folded my arms across my chest, glaring at them. Cole would assume I was irritated with my best friend because I hated him, and he was right, but why did Zoe have to flirt with him? I knew she had to distract Cole, so God only knew why it bothered me. Why did I give a flying fuck that Cole was hot and probably amazing in bed? *Stop!*

Zoe would be thrilled to learn I would need her help with distracting Cole at the party later. The trick was to get his phone long enough for me to unlock and search it. Lucky for us, Cole loved to drink and smoke. After an hour at Harrison's, he would most likely be wrecked, which would make stealing his cell much easier.

Zoe's words continued to cycle through my brain. She was right, Cole was cold and calculating. He was definitely up to something.

Cole and I hadn't been close by any means, but he'd never been brutal and vicious before either. An asshole, yeah, but he'd never laid a hand on me. My biggest complaint about my older brother was that in high school he and his friends had constantly cockblocked me, forcing me to lose my virginity to Ibrahim. I'd been over the moon when the quarterback, Nick Perry, asked me out when I was only a sophomore, and he was a senior. I'd accepted and couldn't wait to shop with the girls for my date. Then, the next day Nick texted and canceled. It wasn't long before the rumors started to circulate that Cole and his friends had told Nick to back off. It hadn't taken me long to realize Nick had no balls if he couldn't stand up to my stepbrother. Every girl wanted Cole, and every guy wanted to be him, so when he said jump ... they jumped, rolled over, and bowed. He still tried to control my life, but I didn't see him as often now that we were in college. Granted, the same one, but it was big enough that we only saw each other occasionally.

The question I desperately needed the answer to was why? What had changed? Little did I know I would seriously regret learning the answer.

Chapter Four

Harrison Swanson's threw the best parties. "Easier Than Lying" by Halsey shook the mansion's walls as we entered the foyer. Current and soon-to-be college kids littered the hallway, drinking and making out. It never failed that someone, usually multiple girls, got knocked up at the summer kickoff event.

Zoe and I started to make our way through the gyrating bodies when a hand gripped my bicep and tugged at me. *Seriously? I barely walk through the door, and Cole sees me?* I glanced over my shoulder, my attention landing on a gorgeous brunette.

"You made it, bitch!" Isabel jumped up and down, her drink sloshing over the edge of the red Solo cup.

I threw my head back and laughed. "When have I ever missed a party?"

Isabel looked adorable. She was one of the few people I knew who could get away with wearing an orange shirt, but her skin glowed when she did. She flipped her hair behind her shoulder, her hazel eyes flickering with mischief before she pulled me in for a big hug, then grabbed Zoe.

Isabel, Dani, Sibyl, Zoe, and I had known each other since third grade. We were the inseparable five. In fact, we were all attending Whitmore University in Oregon together.

"Where are Dani and Sibyl?" Zoe shouted at Isabel over the music. "Amsterdam" by Nothing But Thieves thumped through the speakers.

Isabel shrugged. "Who knows? You know that they love to make an entrance!"

The bass vibrated through my body, and I grinned. A little fun before my mission was in order, since I had no idea if Cole had arrived yet. "Zoe, let's get a drink. I'm thirsty and ready to shake my ass."

"Um, babe?" Zoe tugged on my hand. "Look up."

My gaze traveled over the people, up the winding staircase, and to the level above us. *Well, fuck.* David Graham, the quarterback for Braydon High, was leaning against the railing, his attention zeroing in on me. He ran his fingers through his light brown hair, then tugged on his navy T-shirt. Although the girls liked to look their best, the guys were dressed a lot more casually. Some sported basketball shorts while others wore jeans. David's denims hung nicely on his hips and hugged his muscular legs as he descended the stairs.

I tossed him a wink and waved, smiling at him. David had been asking me out since we ran into each other over Christmas break, but I just wasn't into dating guys my age. There was no doubt he was drool-worthy, but in a few months, we would move back to school in opposite directions. Attachment wasn't in my vocabulary ... playing was.

"Have Sibyl or Dani texted you?" I asked Isabel as David continued to move in our direction, his brown eyes sparkling as a lazy smile eased across his face.

"Not a word. I'm sure they'll be here any minute." Isabel took a drink, then giggled. "The alcohol is in the kitchen. Go grab some."

"Ladies," David said, slipping his arm around my waist and pulling me to him.

I placed my palm on his chest and peeked up. Since Cole had

ruined my summer fun with Ibrahim, maybe I would have to reconsider David. There was no shame in admitting I had a healthy sex drive.

"We're about to get a drink, want one?" I asked.

"Yeah. I need a refill." He raised the red cup to his lips and drained it. "Was that Cole I saw a while ago?"

My heart plummeted to my toes. I had to lay low until Zoe was ready to find him and snatch his phone.

"I have no idea. He's home for the summer, but that's all I know." I gave him a pinched look, not wanting to discuss my stepbrother.

I glanced up, then grabbed Zoe's arm. I pointed to the dark-haired beauty standing at the railing upstairs, Blaire Sable.

The corner of Blaire's mouth kicked up into a sneer and she wiggled her fingers at me in an uppity wave.

"What's she doing here?" Zoe asked, her tone clipped and guarded.

Blaire and I had hated each other all through high school, after her boyfriend tried to sleep with me. Of course, Cole had stopped that really fast, but Blaire refused to believe that nothing had happened. She found it necessary to start slut rumors about me, and in retaliation, I filled her locker with used tampons, and our hatred for each other continued for years.

"No idea. Didn't realize they let the dog in the house."

Zoe and I snickered, then I turned my back to Blaire. She didn't deserve my attention.

Zoe edged closer to me. "I'll see if I can locate Cole."

I nodded and mouthed *"good luck."* Desperation pumped through my veins. My plan had to work. That video had to be deleted no matter the cost.

Zoe snuck off and beelined to the opposite side of the house. If Cole was here, he could be anywhere, including one of the ten bedrooms. Usually, Harrison would keep his parents' bedroom locked and off-limits, so that left nine.

"Damn, look at the people waiting for drinks." Isabel grumbled, pointing to the long-ass line leading into the kitchen, where Harrison had spent a fucking fortune on every kind of alcohol imaginable.

"What do you want to drink, Shae? I'll be happy to get it." David grinned with his offer.

I wondered if he hoped to ply me with liquor, then attempt to get into my pants. "We should do some shots to celebrate our graduation," I replied.

"I know just the thing." David winked at me before he headed to the kitchen.

I scanned the area and grinned as I spotted familiar faces. "Looks like our girls have arrived." Excited to see my friends, I pointed to the white double doors, noting Sibyl and Dani waltzing into the eleven-thousand square foot manor.

Isabel waved at our friends until they spotted us in the sea of people.

Dani's big blue eyes filled with excitement as she located us, and she flipped her blonde hair behind her shoulder. "Wow, this is insane!" Sibyl yelled over the music as she approached us, looking smoking hot in a black, fitted dress that hugged every curve on her body. "Harrison's party gets bigger each year." Sibyl hugged me, then Isabel.

"That's because the graduating class at Hargrove High is the largest they've ever had," David explained as he approached our group, carrying four cups. "Here ya go."

I took one from him and sniffed it. "What is it?"

"Cherry whiskey. You'll like it." His attention stayed glued to me.

A slow smile spread across my face. I downed the shot, the alcohol hitting my throat, burning a trail down my esophagus to my tummy.

Sibyl's emerald-green eyes sparkled as she and Dani laughed, and David handed me another one. She tucked her straight brown hair behind her ear as she studied me.

"It's good!" Tipping my head back, I drank the second one. My body tingled, and a giggle erupted from me. "Are those yours?"

David chuckled and gave me one of the two remaining cups. "You can have one of mine."

"Oh, I want some!" Sibyl grabbed Dani's wrist and tugged her toward the kitchen. "Be right back, Shae."

"Get us a few!" I yelled at her. "When she returns, I'll give you one since you shared." With that, I downed my third. "Damn, that's good." I sighed as the muscles in my neck and shoulders relaxed.

David threw his head back and laughed. "I figured it was a safe bet." He polished off his remaining drink, then collected our cups. Instead of locating a trash can, he propped them up in the corner for the clean-up crew to deal with.

Buzzed and happy, I nudged him in the ribs with my elbow. David was several inches taller than I was and a solid wall of muscle. "Candy Shop" by 50 Cent pounded through the speakers. I raised my palms above my head and began moving to the pulsing rhythm.

David's heated gaze swept over my breasts and my stomach, locking on the zipper of my well-fitted jeans.

"Let's go!" I gripped his arm and led us to the center of the area, where bodies gyrated, and people's attention was roaming across the crowd while others were groping asses. People would start finding rooms and corners to fuck and make out in another few hours.

David placed his hands on my waist as I seductively swayed to the music. He slipped his leg between mine, moving in perfect sync. His fingertips slid up my side and arm. Tingles rippled through my body, teasing all the right places inside me. I hated to tell him he wouldn't get in my pants that evening, but then I remembered that I couldn't go home and find Ibrahim to fuck me senseless. My good mood dissipated as I realized I might have to find someone new over the summer. David certainly wasn't a bad choice, but I would consider my options later. Cole had to be taken care of first. A little harmless flirting wouldn't hurt anyone for the evening, though.

David rubbed against me. His hard-on was obvious. I glanced down, my tongue darting over my lower lip, the alcohol encouraging me to let loose. I turned, backed up to him, and closed the gap between us.

Sibyl and Dani returned, laughing and dancing through the crowd with multiple cups as David slid his arms around me, pulling me closer.

"Here, babe." Sibyl gave one to me.

"David." I held the cup up for him.

Sibyl immediately passed me the extra drink she was holding. As I downed it, warmth flowed through my body, and I continued to move to the music.

Isabel, Sibyl, and Dani danced around us. It took only a minute before a few college guys spotted them and joined in.

David's arm gripped my waist, and he swayed to the beat of the bass. I leaned my head against his chest and allowed myself to relax. It felt damned good to chill. Final exams had been a bitch, and I was ready to have some fun. The alcohol had clouded my mind, but I didn't care. I was tired of thinking.

David eased away, allowing a small gap between us. I arched my back, my ass rubbing against him as I continued to tease him. Realizing he hadn't touched me again, I turned toward him and ran the tips of my nails up his abs. As I looked up from beneath my eyelashes, my blood stopped cold. Cole. He stood tall and rigid, glaring at me, his blue eyes sending ice through my veins.

"What did I tell you about the party, Shae?" he growled.

I backed away, dropping my hands from his stomach. A curious crowd began to form around us. David and my friends were watching as well.

"You can't tell me what to do, Cole, so drop the big brother act." I smirked. *Fuck, if Cole is here, Zoe won't be able to get his phone.*

"You don't want to defy me, Shae. You won't like the results." Cole's brow lifted in a warning.

Seething, I placed my fists on my hips. "You're a straight-up asshole, and I refuse to let you bully me."

Laughter floated in the air, but I didn't care. Cole couldn't push me around.

A malicious grin eased across his face as he stepped back, then cupped his hands around his mouth and yelled. "Don't let Shae fool you. She might act all high and mighty but ..." Cole stared at me and paused. "The Princess likes to get fucked up the ass."

Embarrassment burned up my neck and cheeks as I gaped at him in horror.

"How do *you* know, Cole?" a male voice asked over the snickers.

Several guys were making lude gestures and murmurs of slut traveled through the crowd.

Cole's smile widened. "Normally, I don't kiss and tell ..." Cole tossed up his hands, smirking as though it were all a silly game to him.

"He's lying! I've never screwed—"

"Your brother?" a girl called out, practically cackling with glee.

My chest cracked wide open, and my heart bled all over the floor. How could he have humiliated me in public like this? I had officially met the end of my social life.

Cole looked down at me. "Had enough, Shae?"

"Fuck you. Take your cheap shots, but you will *not* control me. Ever." I poked him in the sternum with my fingernail for emphasis.

"Have it your way, then." Cole bent down, wrapped an arm around my thighs, then tossed me over his shoulder.

My scream split through the music as I slapped him on the back. "Put me down, Cole!"

To my horror, he ignored me and strutted toward the door. The sea of people parted, their snickers and laughter filling the air. Quickly, I checked his back pockets for his phone, realizing this was the perfect opportunity to grab it. Nothing. Both of them were empty. *Zoe must have it, thank God! I knew my girl would come through for me.*

Humiliation washed over me as he stepped outside and onto the front porch. Remington closed the door, and only then did Cole set me on my feet.

I gasped and sputtered as I brushed the hair from my face. "What the fuck is wrong with you? Do you get off belittling people in public?"

The left side of Cole's mouth kicked up in a smile. "I told you I would toss you out if you showed up."

My molars ground together. "What's your problem? You've been a total bastard since you got home. I've not done anything to you, so why do you have it in for me?"

Cole's focus fixated on my breasts, his tongue darting across his lower lip and a spark flashing in his ice-blue eyes. I glanced down. One of the buttons on my blouse had popped open. I suspected it happened when he threw me over his shoulder like a bag of potatoes.

I quickly fixed my top, then returned my attention to him. Maybe I needed to try a different angle. I mustered up as much sincerity as I could. "Listen, I know we've not ever been super close, but we tolerated each other. What went wrong? Tell me, and I'll fix it." *At least long enough to make sure the video is deleted from existence. Then, I'm going to fucking bury you for what you did to me.*

Cole closed the gap between us, his expression stony and unreadable. He ran his hand up my arm, then he tipped my chin up, our mouths so close I could taste the alcohol on his breath. He gripped my side and dug his fingers into my flesh, sending delicious chills over my skin.

I sucked in some much-needed air, my breasts grazing his well-defined chest as heat pooled in my belly. Oh, my God. What was he doing, and why did I like it?

Cole forcefully turned my head, his soft lips skimming my ear.

I whimpered and gripped his toned bicep for balance.

He pressed his hips against mine, and a low moan escaped him, then he jerked away as if touching me had burned him. His features twisted in disgust as he pinned me with his heated gaze. *"You* happened." He dropped his hold on me, then backed off. "Go home, Shae." He spun around and disappeared into Harrison's house.

"Fuck you!" I fisted my fingers, ready to yell additional profanities in his direction, when my phone buzzed in my back pocket. "Finally, Zoe," I mumbled as I removed my cell.

Undiluted fear seized me as I focused on the message, and I stood rooted in place.

Chapter Five

Tapping the screen, I expected to see Zoe's text that the problem had been erased. Instead, my voice came through the speaker, followed by Ibrahim's and Matt's.

I flung the front door open and stopped in my tracks, the cool air from outside drifting into the foyer. Everyone was glued to their phones, then the large flat-screen television in the living room flickered to life. I could literally feel the blood drain from my cheeks as I stared speechless at the scene of Matt eating my pussy as I sucked Ibrahim's cock. Hoots and hollers filled the space, and astonishment ghosted over everyone's expressions. What the hell? Zoe was supposed to erase the video, not send it to the entire fucking world.

Zoe, Isabel, Sibyl, and Dani spotted me near the entrance. Zoe's face had paled, and the other girls stared at me in disbelief. Tears welled in my eyes, and I stumbled backward as they approached. How could Zoe have done this to me? Cole had already shamed and embarrassed me. Wasn't that enough? Zoe knew what was at stake. Even though she said she couldn't stay mad at me, it was obvious she'd planned to pay me back for not telling her about Ibrahim and

Matt when it first started. Other than Cole, Zoe was the only person that knew about the video and what it would do to me.

I spun on my heel and bolted out the door. My best friend had just ruined my life, and my other friends hated me.

"Shae!" Zoe yelled after me.

"Fuck you!" I screamed as I headed in the direction of my car, my heels scuffing against the cement of the driveway.

"Shae! Wait," Sibyl called.

My shoulders shook with sobs as I attempted to locate my BMW through the unwanted waterworks. I glanced over my shoulder, but the girls hadn't come after me. They were standing on the porch, watching me stumble around in the dark.

I retrieved my key fob from the front pocket of my jeans and hit the button, listening for the *beep beep*. There were so many cars, though. Even if I found mine, I might not be able to get out. I tried again, searching for the blinking headlights. Finally, I located my car, but I couldn't go anywhere. I was blocked in. A frustrated scream ripped through me.

Wiping the moisture from my cheeks, I sucked in a deep breath. There was no fucking way I could return to the party. I could either lock myself in my BMW and sleep in the back seat or see if I could find Harrison's guest or pool house. It would be warmer in one of those places, plus I could hide until the crowd started to clear out.

I stepped off the concrete driveway and onto the lush green grass. If I remembered correctly, the guest quarters were to the left of the main home, but the alcohol had messed with my brain, leaving it fuzzy. My heels sank into the soft dirt, and I swore under my breath while I struggled to maintain my balance. Anger and betrayal knotted my stomach. I ground my molars and remained focused on my path. My cell buzzed in my hand, but I silenced it. Whoever it was could go fuck themselves.

Nearing the edge of the tree line on the opposite side of the property, I frowned and studied where I was. Apparently, I'd managed to get lost. I tried to map out the estate in my head, but I wasn't familiar with anything else other than the main house and pool.

Low voices pulled my focus toward a thick grove of trees. It was so dark it was difficult to see. Thank God for the flashlight app on my cell. I held up the phone, spotting a cleared path. The guest quarters must have been nearby. With a spark of hope, I trudged forward. A glow burned ahead, and I followed what appeared to be a light.

Reaching the edge of a large clearing, I slowed. Several motorcycles, including Cole's, circled a group of men, the dark area lit by the headlights. I ducked behind a tree and hoped I hadn't been spotted. The hint of stale cigarette smoke and oil tickled my nostrils. I scrunched my nose at the disgusting smell as I counted eight dudes all wearing a similar leather vest with a burning skull on the back.

My attention landed on a guy on his knees. Blood streamed down his face, and his right eye was nearly swollen shut. *What the hell is going on?* I crouched down and watched in horror as the men simultaneously kicked and punched him repeatedly. The sound of crunching bone turned my stomach, and I grimaced, but no matter how much I wanted to, I couldn't turn away.

Finally, the guy collapsed to the ground, unmoving, and the group parted, allowing me to soak up the rest of the scene. A scream nearly escaped me, and I slapped my hand over my mouth as bile churned in my stomach. Blinking rapidly in an attempt to clear my vision, I stared at the bikers again.

A tall, burly man stroked his chestnut beard before he patted Cole on the back. "We'll take care of the mess, Cole. Don't worry about it. We'll get to the bottom of it all."

Cole placed his hands on his hips, blood trickling across his busted knuckles.

"Let's hope it's in time to protect my family." Cole stabbed the toe of his boot into the ground, staring at the crumpled man in front of him.

My forehead creased in confusion. He clearly meant Julia and Daddy. He'd made it crystal clear that he hated my guts. It was mutual, but now ... now I had something on him. I realized that Cole murdering someone right in front of me could definitely work in my favor concerning the video.

Shivers wracked my body as it finally dawned on me that Cole was standing in the middle of a motorcycle gang. I scanned the area, identifying a bike with a burning skull on the side, matching the leather vests. Shit, Cole was in big trouble. He just killed someone. My stomach churned in horror as I stared at the bloody and broken guy on the ground.

"And Shae?" The burly dude asked.

A pinched expression twisted Cole's features. "She's mine. I'll deal with her." His response was cold and clipped with anger. "Let's take care of the situation before it gets out of control any further."

A lanky man with dark hair spoke. "Get out of here, Cole. We got this."

"All right. Thanks, I appreciate it." Cole hugged him, then hopped on his motorcycle. It roared to life, the sound of the engine splitting through the night.

The burly looking one gave him a helmet, then approached Cole again, but I couldn't hear what was said over the deafening rumble of the bike.

While the noise covered my movements, I removed my shoes and hurried away from the group. If they found out I'd witnessed a murder, I would be the one that turned up dead next. Jesus, what was Cole into? My heart pounded against my rib cage as I broke into a run and hauled ass across the property and back to my car. The soles of my feet ached and screamed as pieces of gravel bit my tender skin, but I couldn't stop. *Cole killed someone.* I had to figure out how to get home before he did and clean up. I couldn't let him know I'd been there and had witnessed him killing a man. A little voice in my head nudged me, reminding me that I hadn't been able to see everything from my hiding place. Maybe Cole hadn't delivered the final blow, but his knuckles were busted, so he'd definitely participated.

Identifying my car, I nearly broke into a fit of maniacal laughter. First, Cole had humiliated me. Second, my best friend shared the video. Third, I witnessed a murder. The fact that my vehicle was no longer blocked wasn't the hilarious part. It was the Audi and Camry in front and behind mine ... they'd been rolled over until they were no longer in the way, resting on their sides. That shit was funny, and I couldn't stop myself from laughing. Someone had decided to help me out even after the video fiasco. I just wish I knew who to thank. A part of me suspected David and his high school football buddies. It would take a team of strong people to move the vehicles.

Using the key fob to unlock my doors, I shoved my feet into my shoes and climbed into my BMW. Glancing around, I started the engine, then maneuvered out of my parking spot and down the driveway. I hoped like hell I could beat my stepbrother home.

The half-hour drive to my place was sheer torture. Not only did I have to get ahead of the video situation, but I had to pretend my life was normal. My heart twisted, leaving a painful ache in my chest. I'd also lost Zoe tonight. I shouldn't have ever told her about the recording, but I'd trusted her—my mistake.

Once I arrived, I parked the car and used the side entrance. I quietly closed the door behind me and listened for any sounds or voices. Although I didn't hear anything, I was on the opposite side of the house from Cole's bedroom. I removed my heels, then tiptoed through the kitchen and into the living area. Multiple lights were on, but that didn't mean shit. Annabelle lived in one of the guestrooms, so I knew someone was here.

I hurried to the stairs and took two at a time. Since it was dark, I realized that Cole hadn't made it home yet, and I heaved a sigh of relief as I rushed to my room. I spotted the doorknob on my bedroom door and made a mental note to replace it. I'd seen what Cole was capable of, and I wouldn't feel safe unless I could lock up from both sides. It would also keep him from snooping or planting a camera. I entered my room and froze.

Chapter Six

I peeked over my shoulder, ensuring no one else was in the hallway, then I closed the door behind me.

"Shae," Zoe shot off my bed. "Please, we need to talk."

My pulse kicked up a notch. I didn't want to discuss a damn thing with Zoe. She'd done enough damage to last a lifetime, and I had more serious shit to deal with. She could wait. "I have nothing to say to you. You leaked the video instead of erasing it. End of story."

Zoe's face paled. "I didn't leak the video, Shae. That's what I've been trying to tell you. If you would just give me a minute and let me explain."

I glanced over at Isabel, Sibyl, and Dani as they sat at the edge of my bed, wearing hopeful expressions. They all nodded in unison, supporting Zoe.

Dani nervously twirled a lock of her long brown hair around her finger. Out of all of us, she dealt with the most anxiety from her picture-perfect family.

"I don't believe you." I folded my arms over my chest, staring at her. "Do you know what you did tonight? Not only am I ruined, but every guy will be trying to fuck me, and every girl will try to slut shame me. Don't even get me started if this reaches Daddy or Julia." I dropped my arms, disgusted with Zoe. Even if we'd been in a huge argument, I would have never betrayed her the way she had me.

"Are you fucking kidding me? How long have we known each other?" Zoe placed her hands on her slender waist and tapped her Coach tennis shoe against the floor.

"Since elementary school," I snapped. "Too long for you to have fucked me over like that. I mean seriously, Zoe ..." My nostrils flared. "We're supposed to be best friends. I trusted you to help me, and instead this is what I get?" My eyes flared in warning, furious with her. She was lucky I didn't punch her in her perky little nose.

"Trusted me? You hid your extracurricular activities for three years!" She held up three fingers in my face like I wasn't capable of counting on my own.

I smacked her hand away, my gaze narrowing. "You were the only one that had his access code and knew the video was there."

"First, you're being a total bitch, Shae," Zoe spat. "Second, you're not listening to a word I've said, so let me say it one more time in hopes I can get through to that thick ass brain of yours." She tapped her finger against her temple. "I did *not* release the video. I couldn't find Cole's phone. I swear. I would never, ever do that to you." She blew out a sigh, her expression softening. "I know what it looks like, but you've known me for years. I've never hurt you on purpose. I've never been that malicious to you, either. Others? Sure, but never you. Please, Shae. You're my best friend. You have to believe me. I wouldn't do that."

Still fucking furious, a little voice inside my head told me to listen to her. Zoe had never screwed me over before. She knew what was at stake. Plus, I'd bailed her out of some shitty situations and naked pictures a few times as well.

My thoughts whirled around, sifting through the events of the party. Rubbing my temples, I realized a critical piece of information.

"Now that I think about it, I didn't see Cole's phone in his back pocket." I stared at the floor, trying to process all of this while my brain was still fuzzy from the alcohol.

"That's because he didn't have it, Shae. After Cole ... escorted you out, I knew my time was limited, so I asked him to dance." She chewed on her lower lip. "I might have run my hands over his ass, checking for his phone. It wasn't in his back or front pocket." A light flush crept across Zoe's cheeks.

"Glad you enjoyed feeling up my brother," I snapped. Chills skated down my spine as I recalled his mouth brushing against my ear earlier ... only half an hour before he killed someone.

"Stepbrother," the girls said in unison.

I dropped my arms, my defenses with Zoe softening. "You really didn't find his cell? He always has it with him."

She shook her head adamantly. "I swear on my Grandma Bess's grave." Her doe eyes pleaded with me to trust her.

I blew out a heavy sigh. "I believe you."

Zoe nearly knocked me backward as she barreled toward me, throwing her arms around my neck. "I'm so sorry, Shae. I feel like shit that the recording got leaked."

I hugged her in return, grateful she hadn't betrayed me. It was almost more than I could deal with. "Me, too. I should check Cole's bedroom for his cell in case it's there. If you see him, please stall him, and talk loudly."

Zoe released me. "I'll keep a look out. Go, go." She shooed me away, hope flickering across her expression.

Hurrying across the hall, I frantically searched Cole's desk, dresser, nightstand, and everywhere I could think of, but there was no sign of his fucking phone.

Defeated, I hurried back to the girls. "I couldn't find it anywhere." I sighed and flung my shoes in the corner, then Zoe and I plopped down on the bed with the others. Isabel tucked her legs beneath her, her gaze filled with expectancy. "Okay, I'm so glad that's over. You two were scary. But now, I need to understand what in the hell is going on since everyone has chilled out again."

"What do you want to know? You all have seen parts of the video, so nothing is off-limits at this point." I grabbed one of my blue-and-white striped throw pillows and propped my back against it.

Sibyl raised her hand. "I want to ask you something. Did the anal hurt?"

I nearly rolled my eyes at her. Sibyl and I had known each other for almost as long as Zoe and I had. At one time, our fathers had worked together, at least until Daddy started his own business. Greg had turned down Daddy's offer to work with him, but I suspected he wished he'd hopped on the opportunity. Daddy had recently been named in Forbes. His name was splashed everywhere. Samuel Wessex, one of the wealthiest men of the year. His company, Weblink, had grown tremendously in the last few years. A swell of pride filled me. I couldn't be prouder of Daddy, but he wouldn't say the same about me if he found out about the recording.

Leave it to Sibyl to ask a question about the sex, not something helpful for me to figure out who had released the recording. "So bad. My ass is still sore, and that video is from earlier today."

Zoe huffed. "Of course it did. Pussy juices aren't enough of a lube. Ibrahim finger-fucked you for a second, then went for it. Lube. Every. Time. Shae." We all knew she and her ex-boyfriend had tried every toy and anal sex the two years they were together.

Sibyl's mouth rounded in an O. "Will you do it again?"

"What she said." Dani pointed at Sibyl.

"I think so." My thoughts traveled to this afternoon with Ibrahim and Matt, realizing it had been my last. "It's not like I can play with Ibrahim and Matt anymore, though."

"I think we should all get on the same page with our story to help, Shae." Dani frowned, appearing deep in thought. "Start with the facts. How did all of this happen?"

Isabel bounced on her knees, excitement bubbling from her.

"Wait, before we get to that I need to know how Cole got so fucking hot!" She fanned her face and pretended to swoon.

I would have laughed if the situation had been different. But my best friends had no idea Cole had killed someone. I toyed with telling them, but I was afraid it would put them in danger. Plus, I wasn't sure if Cole was part of the MC or not. There were too many unknowns to risk their safety.

"What is up with you guys? He comes home for the summer and you're all in heat?" I didn't bother to mask the disgust in my voice.

Zoe elbowed me in the side. "Tone it down, girl."

Isabel frowned, her forehead creasing. "Shae, he's always been hot, but I nearly orgasmed just looking at him when we were at the party." Her brown eyes widened as she pretended to wipe the drool off her chin.

"Ew, Isabel!" I scolded. "He's my brother. Can you chill a little?" I huffed, hating that she was right, and that bastard had strolled back into my life for the summer, looking hot as hell.

Zoe scrunched up her nose. The girl had the most perfect mouth I'd ever seen. People paid good money to have a full and matching lower and upper lip. "Why do you insist on calling him your brother, Shae? You're in no way related, so you should have been hitting that instead of your dad's staff."

An uncontrollable blush crawled up my neck and cheeks. "Zoe!"

The girls giggled while Zoe gave me a half-hearted shrug. "I would totally be down."

"Same!" Isabel agreed.

"Shit, I'd even let him use my body," Dani added, running her fingertips down her side.

A silly grin eased across Sibyl's face. "I say we sneak into his room in the middle of the night, tie him down, and all take turns riding him."

I waved my hands in front of me, tired of Cole's physique dominating our conversation. "Enough." Holy crap. My best friends were talking about gang-raping Cole.

Everyone settled down, then I explained to them about the afternoon with Ibrahim, Matt, and catching Cole watching the video. They might be able to help me think this through.

"Maybe I should tell Daddy before he sees it. It could cause a lot of damage to his company and for Julia, too." I groaned loudly and flung myself backward onto my stack of pillows. "Why hadn't I figured this out? Cole was probably the bastard that leaked it after he saw me at Harrison's party."

Zoe quirked a dark eyebrow at me. "I could have helped you with that. When he saw you at Harrison's, he most likely released it before he hauled your ass out. Maybe he decided to punish you for disobeying him."

I propped my head on my fist. "When have I ever obeyed Cole?"

"When he cockblocked you every time you got asked out in high school," Dani added. "No wonder you messed around with the staff. You were doomed the second Cole showed up in your life." Dani's expression flickered with sympathy.

Zoe reached over and took my hand in hers. "You and your dad are super tight. Even more so since your mom died."

A sharp stab to my heart sent pain rippling through my chest. Daddy and I were close, but so were Mom and me ... until the day I'd excitedly skipped through the front door of our house from drama club late one afternoon and found her dead on the kitchen floor. She'd passed away when I was thirteen, but it felt like yesterday.

I swallowed over the lump in my throat, attempting to control the swell of grief. Later, we'd learned it was a brain aneurism. It was over in a second for her, but for Daddy and me, the pain would last a lifetime. I'd struggled when Daddy sat me down and told me that he was dating someone new. He'd only waited a year before he'd started dating, then he met Julia, and they were married by the time I was fifteen and Cole sixteen.

"Daddy has always told me I have to own my fuck-ups." I cringed.

"Yup, this was definitely a 'fuck' up." Isabel added air quotes for emphasis.

Sibyl snickered. "Sorry, I know this isn't funny. What do you think he's going to do?"

"Cut me out of the will," I replied without a second thought. "Make me work for a humble living for the rest of my life. I'll have to sell everything I own to pay for college, then live in a ..." I shuddered before I ever spoke the word, "dorm."

Isabel's features fell. "Are you sure, Shae? Don't you think your dad did some stupid shit when he was younger?"

I rubbed my neck, exhaustion weighing heavily on me. There was no way I could sleep, though. Each time I closed my eyes, I was afraid I would see the dead guy in my dreams.

"I have no idea. He's never shared any wild stories with me, but he might not have wanted me to get any ideas. As far as him cutting me out of the will ... no, I'm not sure. I've never gotten caught before, but I do know he's going to be super pissed." I smoothed my blue and white comforter, unwilling to make eye contact with my friends.

"If I were in your shoes, I would definitely talk to him first. He'll respect your honesty, and maybe the consequences won't be as drastic as disinheriting you," Dani said. A hint of sadness weaved through her tone.

Isabel shifted, sitting cross-legged. "I agree with Dani."

Sibyl and Zoe nodded in agreement.

"Well, then I better figure out what to say to him because he'll be home tomorrow." Unease pumped through my veins. How in the hell would I have a conversation with my daddy about having sex with two men at the same time ... in his limo ... with his staff? I groaned and hid my face in my hands.

A noise in the hallway pulled my attention away from my thoughts. I hopped off the bed and peeked out to see what I was hearing. Cole walked in my direction, talking softly on the phone, his expression grim.

White-hot anger blossomed to life inside me, and I closed my door so the girls wouldn't hear me confront him.

He jerked his head up, his gaze narrowing as he saw me. I curled my fingers into tight fists and marched into his room.

"I can't do this right now, Shae." He paused at his doorway.

I didn't care what he did or didn't have time for. He owed me answers.

Cole followed me and tossed his phone on the bed. His knuckles were bandaged, and the blood had been washed off his face.

"I saw you," I hissed. "I saw what you did to that man. And you're involved with motorcycle thugs?"

Cole grabbed my shoulders and pinned me against the wall so fast my head spun. He lifted his brow, and I read all the words he hadn't spoken but conveyed perfectly. I had seriously overstepped with him.

"You gonna kill me, too? I mean, you shared the video at the party, so why not murder two people in one night?" I smirked, but my stomach flip-flopped like crazy.

Cole glowed with fury as he pinned me to the spot with a hot glare. He boxed me in, placing his palms against the wall and closing the gap between us. We were toe-to-toe. A spark of electricity flickered through the air, causing me to gasp as a delicious warmth spread into every fiber of my being.

"You have no idea what you're talking about." His voice was calm—the quiet before the raging storm.

"Why did you release the video, Cole?" I couldn't disguise the hurt in my tone.

"Don't worry your pretty little head about it. What's done is done." He trailed his knuckles down my cheek, the same ones that had killed another human being only hours ago.

I sucked in a breath, my heartbeat breaking into a crazy gallop.

"Damage control," I managed to squeak out as his fingertips moved down my neck. Gulping, I tried again. "I have to talk to Daddy. He'll be home tomorrow. You know he's going to come down on you." Did I really just tell him my plan? What the actual fuck happened to my brain when I was this close to him?

Cole chuckled. "I can handle your father." His attention dropped down to my breasts.

I wondered what his mouth would feel like on them. His hot, warm tongue licking and sucking my nipples. *Stay focused on the mission, Shae!* "Why did you do it?"

Cole leaned in, the tip of his nose brushing against my neck. "You make me so goddamned crazy," he whispered. "Seeing you with Ibrahim and Matt ..." He pushed away from me, seething. "How you deal with your problem is up to you." He turned and approached his bed.

Prick! I wouldn't have a situation to fix if it weren't for Cole. An uncontrollable rage rippled through me. As he reached out to collect his phone, I shot across the room and jumped on his back, wrapping my arms around his neck as tightly as I could manage. "You picked the wrong girl to fuck with, you stupid bastard." Before I could throw him to the ground, Cole spun on his heel and flopped back on the bed, pinning me against the mattress. He grabbed my hands and easily peeled my fingers away from his skin. Rolling over, he worked his legs between mine, secured my wrists above my head, and hovered a few inches over me.

With harrowing, intense eyes, he glared at me. "Don't open Pandora's box." His hips lowered against mine, and my mouth gaped when I felt his erection pressing against my jeans. He was getting off on tormenting me. Cole shifted, allowing me to feel the entire length of his cock, his slightly parted lips directly above mine. I sucked in a breath, mentally begging him to rip off my clothes and fuck me. Hard.

Cole shot off me and pointed to the door. "Get out." His steely tone left no room for negotiation.

I rose and adjusted my shirt and smoothed my hair, horrified that he'd played me. Again. "I fucking hate you," I spat.

"Good."

I'd never had hate sex before, but for the first time, I was willing to try it. Composing myself, I tilted my chin in the air and marched out of his room, clinging to what little dignity I had left. I didn't bother closing the door. He could do it his damn self.

"Girl, what happened?" Isabel asked the second I had reached the group again.

"I confronted Cole."

Zoe climbed off the bed and joined me, pity rolling off her in waves. "What did he say?"

"For me not to worry about it. He refused to say anything else." His dick had spoken for him loud and clear, though. He'd loved dominating me.

The memory of his hands holding my wrists, the heaviness of his body against mine, the mattress dipping beneath our weight. *No!* A shiver danced up my spine as I tried to calm my thoughts. No matter how my hormones hummed with need, I couldn't lose sight of the fact that he'd killed someone and humiliated me in public.

Dani stared a hole in me. "That's all? You look flustered as hell."

"I'm fine. I have to pee." I tucked my hair behind my ear and headed to my bathroom, where I could have a minute alone.

After locking myself in, I leaned against the wall and closed my eyes. I didn't understand what had happened with Cole. One second, I was pissed, the next horny and mentally pleading for him to touch me. Shit. Maybe I was bipolar. My emotions and hormones were bouncing around faster than a ping pong ball during a championship match.

I hurried to the sink, turned on the cold water, and rinsed my face. Glancing into the mirror, I noticed sad blue eyes returned my stare. At that moment, I questioned who I really was. I'd never considered the idea I was a bad person before. A bitch, sure, but not an awful human being. Now, I was facing the consequences of my choices. Plus, I'd risked my daddy's respect and trust.

But Cole ... I groaned. My attempt to blackmail him with the murder was a hard fail. I squared my shoulders and reminded myself that I was still a Wessex—intelligent, strong, and courageous. I quickly ran a brush through my hair before returning to my friends and plotting my next move.

I wasn't sure what it was, but something was off about the entire situation. From the video to the motorcycle gang to the murder. How could I have been so wrong about who Cole really was?

There was only one way to find out, and I was up for the challenge. If I was going down, then so was he.

Chapter Seven

Prying my eyelids open, I smacked the top of the nightstand in an attempt to locate my phone. My fingers wrapped around the case, and I peered at the time. Holy shit. It was almost noon.

I bolted upright as the reminder that Daddy would be home soon bitch-slapped me. By the time the girls left, it had been nearly four in the morning. I was exhausted from the drama and had practically fallen into bed with my clothes on.

Tossing the blankets off me, I placed my feet against the soft carpet and stretched. A hot shower would clear my head and help me decide what I would say to Daddy. Knots twisted my stomach as I imagined the look of disappointment on his face. The mere thought of it gutted me. I'd always been the apple of Daddy's eye, but it would change after I confessed about Ibrahim and Matt.

I dragged my feet to the bathroom, my thoughts running rampant. I'd considered telling Daddy about Cole and the gang, but it would come across as though I was trying to get out of trouble and redirect my father's attention to Cole. Honestly, it wasn't a bad idea. This mess was Cole's fault, and I fucking owed him.

Half an hour later, I was clean and had dried my hair. I finally realized what I needed to say to Daddy. Why it hadn't crossed my mind to bury Cole before, I wasn't sure. I'd probably been too shaken up after the party and Cole's activities afterwards.

After I dressed in jean shorts and a soft, pastel pink top that clung to my curves, I applied a light application of makeup, then hurried down the stairs to the kitchen. A double pumpkin spice latte sounded perfect for fueling my revenge plan. I might kiss my inheritance good-bye, but so would Cole. I had no problem taking the bastard down with me. I smirked as my bare feet padded along the marble floors, and the necessary pieces fell into place. I would make sure Cole never fucked with me again. I made my way to the espresso maker, still mulling over my plan.

I grabbed the two percent milk from the fridge, checked the water level on the machine, then selected a big cup from the white cabinet. The best thing about this kitchen was the size. When Julia and Cole were settling in, Cole constantly had his head in the refrigerator, stuffing his face. If the space hadn't been as large as it was, no one else would have been able to nudge their way in. Not that he cared.

Once my latte was ready, I squeezed the pumpkin pie spice bottle, covering my perfectly foamed milk in yummy goodness. I took a sip. "Perfection." No matter what was going on in my life, good coffee always made it better.

I leaned against the black and white marble counter and released a heavy sigh, my ears picking up a familiar voice down the hall. Hurrying to Daddy's office, my heart soared at the thought that he was home … until I remembered the video.

His door was open, and I poked my head in and grinned. He nodded and motioned for me to sit down while finishing his phone call. I pushed the door closed, then settled into the brown chair, the leather cool on the back of my bare legs.

Nervously, I crossed my ankles, then uncrossed them again. I forced myself not to tap my manicured nails against the ceramic mug since Daddy was talking, and I didn't want to distract him.

Tension snaked through my shoulders, and I gave myself a pep talk. I was doing the right thing by telling Daddy, but this fucking sucked on so many levels. Every fiber in my being wanted to bolt out the door and never tell him. However, if it affected his company and reputation, I would never forgive myself. He'd worked so hard, and I was proud of him. I couldn't be the one responsible for toppling his empire.

"Talk to you later." Dad grinned at me, then disconnected the call. He placed his cell on his desk, then stood.

I set my mug down on the end table and ran to him. "Daddy!" I threw my arms around his neck as he hugged me in return.

His chuckle rumbled through his chest. "Hey, Princess. How's my girl?" He released me and pressed a sweet kiss against my forehead.

"Good. Glad to be home for the summer." I flashed him a winning grin, attempting to appear calm and collected, even though I was falling apart inside myself. How was I going to tell him about Ibrahim and Matt? He would be furious with me.

I spotted several streaks of grey in Daddy's dark head of hair. I was most likely prejudiced, but he was handsome for an older guy. He could probably have any woman he wanted, but he fell for Julia for some reason. She was pretty, but not quite his equal, in my opinion.

Sitting down again, I glanced out of the window at the back patio and swimming pool. After I spilled my guts about screwing the staff, I wasn't sure I would even be allowed to live here any longer. A ball of puke wedged itself into my throat, blocking my windpipe. A cold film of sweat covered every inch of my body as it fully dawned on me that I could lose Daddy.

"What's the matter, Princess?" Dad shuffled a few papers on his desk, smoothed his light blue button-down shirt, then folded his hands in his lap and gave me his undivided attention.

I sucked in a deep breath as my knee bounced uncontrollably. Tears welled in my eyes. "I'm so sorry, Daddy." My voice cracked, and my legs started to shake. "I messed up really bad, and then I saw something horrible."

He leaned back in his chair, assessing me. "I'm listening."

I sniffled and grabbed a tissue from the box on the table next to me. "I, umm ... I need to tell you what I did, so you can be prepared in case it hurts you or Weblink." Blowing out a shaky breath, I braced myself for the worst. I stared at my lap, then held my daddy's gaze. "I had sex with Ibrahim and Matt, and somehow it was recorded, then the video was leaked last night. I think Cole did it. When I left the party, I got turned around and walked the wrong way across Harrison's property. I stumbled on a group of men. I'm pretty sure they were a motorcycle gang. They had no idea I was there, but when they moved, I saw Cole beating a man until he actually died. If you don't believe me, he has bandages on his knuckles ..."

A slash of anger flickered in Daddy's grey-blue eyes, and he stared a hole straight into my soul. If he only understood how awful I felt, maybe he could forgive me.

"Please say something," I whispered, muffling my cry.

He stood and turned his back to me, looking out the window and placing his hands on his hips.

"I raised you better, Shae." His voice was low and full of disappointment, which was way worse than if he'd yelled at me.

I also realized he hadn't called me Princess. It was time that I accepted I'd fallen from the throne.

"I know. I'm so, so sorry." I wiped my nose, wishing this was all a bad dream. "You taught me to own my mistakes, and I didn't think it was right if someone else showed you or told you about the video first."

He turned slowly, grimacing. "I found out last night, but I'm glad you had the courage to tell me. I was wondering if you would talk to me or try to hide it. I'd planned on acting as though nothing had happened, testing to see if you would do the right thing."

I gripped the armchairs, hoping like hell he hadn't seen me with Ibrahim and Matt. "How?" I managed to squeak out.

Daddy shoved his hands in the pockets of his black slacks. "I arrived home late, and Cole was waiting for me. He explained about the recording and that you'd caught him in a compromising situation last night."

What the fuck! Murder is not a compromising situation! My pulse quickened, and blood crashed through my ears. *That twisted bastard!* I had to stay calm. I would deal with Cole later. Right now, I had to figure out how to get back into Daddy's good graces.

"I fired Ibrahim immediately. Matt is no longer welcome on my property, and I had a chat with Matt's father first thing today. I also got in touch with my team to manage any press. The video was deleted and removed from social media early this morning, so there won't be any more damage."

My pulse was erratic, my palms pulsing with sweat. *Dammit, Cole.* I didn't even have to say a word to Daddy. It only took a second to realize that I still did the right thing by coming forward. If Daddy already knew about the recording, and I never said anything, things would look much bleaker. They sucked, but I would do everything in my power to make it up to Daddy.

I bit my lip, forcing myself to remain quiet and receive the consequences. I felt awful for Ibrahim, too. After the video was leaked, I was powerless to protect him.

"At first, I was going to remove you from the will, but you showed up and faced the problem head-on. You were honest with me. However, until I see that you're behaving like a responsible adult, your funds are frozen. I'm sorry, Shae. It pains me to make that decision, but you've left me no choice."

My shoulders slumped. "Do I have to move out?"

"No, but your spending limit will be reduced to necessities only, and that includes no more shopping sprees. If Julia wants to take you, that's her decision. You'll need clothes for the school year, but for now, your credit card account is restricted." Disappointment registered across his handsome features.

"I understand." I rose, his painstaking expression trampling my heart. "I'll make this right. I promise." I dragged my feet to the door, then turned around. "What about Cole? He killed a man last night. He's hanging around awful people. Are we safe while he lives in the house?"

Daddy massaged the back of his neck. "Cole isn't your concern, Shae. I've already dealt with the situation."

"The *situation*? So, you didn't cut him off financially?"

"There's more to it, Shae. End of discussion."

If I'd been two years old, I would have stomped my foot and thrown a bitch fit. When *I* had done something wrong, I was punished. However, I just learned an important nugget of information. Cole could do whatever he wanted and not deal with any consequences.

I knew this situation was my own fault. I'd spilled my plan to Cole like I was a dog in heat. The second it had flown out of my mouth, I realized I'd fucked up. I'd meant to threaten him and gain some leverage about the video, but he'd turned the tables on me. I left the office with my tail between my legs—ashamed and embarrassed for being so stupid and thinking I could actually persuade Daddy to give Cole hell.

Suddenly feeling sick to my stomach, I wanted to hide in my room until dinner. Maybe I would crawl back into bed and binge on Netflix.

I moped across the house and up the stairs. Reaching the hallway, I stopped, my ears perking up at the sound of Cole's deep voice. I glanced around, then tiptoed to his closed door and listened.

"Fuck. Are you kidding me?" Cole asked, clearly upset.

I could imagine him running his hand through his blonde hair, rumpling it enough to look sexy as hell.

"Are you sure? If so, we have a huge fucking problem."

My forehead creased.

"Hang on a minute. I've got another call."

I pressed my ear to the door, straining to hear him.

"Hey," Cole purred, his sultry tone sending shivers coasting over my skin. "Yeah, I'll be there." He chuckled. "I won't forget. Bye."

Irritation swept over me. Who was he talking to? Was it a girl? It was well-known that Cole fucked a chick once, then tossed her to the side as soon as he got off. This conversation seemed different, though.

I backed away, tiptoeing to my room and closing the door behind me. Why would I care if Cole was seeing someone? Other than the fact that he had reduced my dating life to nothing. The second a guy learned that Cole was my brother, they practically ran in the other direction even at college. If they had enough balls to ask me out, Cole always managed to find out and cockblock me. I hadn't ever been able to learn why, which bothered me. I honestly wondered if they were scared of Cole. They should be. Hell, I should be. But even after last night, I wasn't terrified of Cole like a normal person should be.

Flopping in the middle of the bed, I stared at the white ceiling. I sent Zoe a quick text and provided her with the details of how things had gone down with Daddy. I asked her to let Dani, Sibyl, and Isabel know as well. I didn't have the energy to chat with them.

Before I put my phone down, I switched on the do not disturb for the rest of the day. Still exhausted from yesterday's events, my eyelids grew heavy. There wasn't anything I could do to fix things with Daddy at the moment, so I might as well get some sleep before my entire life was turned upside down.

Chapter Eight

Over the next four days, my mood took a sharp nosedive, and I hid in my room unless Daddy needed me. The sun had also given me a big fuck you and cloaked itself behind thick, grey clouds. Inviting Zoe over and lounging around the pool wasn't an option without sunshine. I couldn't shop to soothe my nerves, either.

My cell vibrated with a message, and I scooped it off my night-stand and peeked at the time. It wasn't even ten in the morning. Tapping the screen, I opened Zoe's text.

Get your booty out of bed. I'm coming to get you.

Quickly, I typed out a response. *I haven't showered or gotten dressed.*

The tiny dots bounced as I waited for her to reply.

I'm not taking no for an answer, so get your cute ass in gear or look like a bag lady in public. Your choice.

A frustrated groan escaped me, and I dramatically flung the covers to the other side of the mattress. I rubbed my face, realizing my tangled hair would be a mess to deal with. One thing was for sure. I did *not* want to be seen looking like a fucking trainwreck. I'd successfully hidden from Cole as well, refusing to give him the satisfaction of having a front-row seat to my spiraling mood.

I rose, stretched, then made my way to the bathroom.

An hour later, I was dressed in cute black shorts and a red crop top. Even if I was poor for the time being, no one else had to know other than Zoe and our group of friends. I still had a closet full of designer clothes. Plus, Zoe and I wore the same sizes, and we often borrowed each other's jeans and tops.

I gathered my phone and Gucci handbag, then stepped into the hall. Staring at Cole's closed door, I pulled mine shut behind me, the click ringing through the silence. I narrowed my eyes and imagined lighting his room on fire with him in it. To my disappointment, my psychic powers were severely lacking, and the son of a bitch would live another day.

Tilting my chin up and squaring my shoulders, I made my way downstairs and to the kitchen. I halted when I saw Julia sitting on the barstool at the counter. I cleared my throat, waiting for the disapproving look from my stepmom.

"Hey," I softly said as I headed to the refrigerator for something to eat. I removed the fresh turkey breast, light mayonnaise, and cheddar cheese, then grabbed the focaccia bread. My appetite had been next to nothing lately, but it seemed like it was returning. I had to fuel my brain to plot my revenge on Cole, too.

"Hi, hon. How are you doing? You've been scarce since your dad got home." She laid her pen on top of an open notebook, her gaze full of compassion. Julia's dark hair was angled in a bob, accentuating her pretty face. Some of her best features were her blue eyes and cheekbones, but I would kill for her facial structure.

"I guess it's no use pretending that I didn't screw up royally." I rummaged through the silverware drawer for a knife and focused on making a sandwich before Zoe arrived.

"It was a shock, but not the end of the world, Shae. Your dad will forgive you. I know he laid down some consequences, but he was really proud of you for coming to him as soon as he was home."

I glanced at her, tears welling in my eyes. "The worst part is that I hurt daddy and Ibrahim lost his job. He sends money to his family in Nigeria every month ... and now he won't be able to. I screwed everything up."

Julia slid off her seat and joined me on the other side of the island. "Do you want a hug?"

"Why are you being so nice to me?" Julia had never been mean, but she and I weren't close.

"Because I've had my share of mistakes that had big consequences, Shae." She tucked my hair behind my ear. "So has Samuel. Your dad tried to be fair, but he was torn up about it. We never went to sleep after he arrived home that night. Cole was waiting for him, then I woke up when he came to bed. He told me ... everything. We also talked about the stupid shit we did at yours and Cole's ages. I just want you to know that you're not alone. We still love you, Shae. Take the mistake and learn from it."

My chin trembled as I hugged her. "Thank you. I want to make this right."

Julia returned my embrace, then released me. "Get out of the house today and get some fresh air. It will help." She offered me a kind smile.

My cell lit up with a message from Zoe.

I'm outside.

I grabbed a sandwich baggie and stuffed my food into it. "I'm going out with Zoe for the day."

"Good. Have some fun." She patted me on the arm.

I wanted to tell her that I couldn't shop or have a spa afternoon, so I doubted it would be much fun, but I was just pouting. Zoe and I had spent tons of days together, not spending money.

"Thanks." I pulled a napkin from the holder and walked toward the front door.

"Oh, Shae?"

I glanced over my shoulder at Julia.

"I'm sorry you had to get tangled up in Cole's problems. Maybe stay clear of him for a while. He's a bit ... moodier than usual. He has a lot going on." Guilt flickered across her features.

"Sure." I should have felt guilty for lying, but I didn't. What was such a big deal that justified Cole killing someone and treating me like shit? Honestly, I didn't give a rat's ass about whatever issues he was dealing with. All I cared about was making him pay for what he'd done to me. I left the house and spotted Zoe's red convertible. She hadn't lowered the top, which worked for me. I wasn't in the mood to try to manage my hair after it had been wind-whipped.

I climbed into the front passenger seat and buckled up.

Zoe shook her head. "Girl, you look sad as fuck."

"Thanks, Zoe. Your pep talk is exactly what I need. And to think I was about to say that your yellow shirt looked hot on you." I quirked a brow at her, irritated. I placed a hand on the door handle. "If our day together is going to be full of encouraging words, then I'll pass."

Zoe slid her sunglasses up on top of her head. "Thanks. The shirt is new. And I'm sorry. It surprised me is all. I mean, I know you've been in a funk, but I didn't realize it was this bad." She smoothed her white shorts, then shifted the car into drive and rolled out of the driveway.

My attention landed on the limo parked to the side, and my heart skipped a beat.

Zoe looked at me from the corner of her eye. "Don't go there, Shae."

"Go where?"

"Beating yourself up for Ibrahim getting fired. He had a lot of fun with you over the last few years—by choice. He was well aware of the risks, so Samuel firing him is on Ibrahim. Not you. You have your own mess to fix."

"I still feel guilty, though." I shifted in my seat, staring at the abundance of pine trees as we drove into town.

"Good. I would be worried about you if you didn't. But, unless you need to talk about it, I say let's get our nails done, buy some ice cream, then head to the liquor store."

I gave her a wistful expression. "I can't. My credit card is frozen, remember?"

Zoe batted her dark eyelashes at me, then blew me a kiss. "Bitch, what are best friends for?" She giggled, then took my hand in hers. "It's going to be okay, Shae. I know it doesn't feel like it now, but it will."

"Thanks." As long as I had my girls and my relationship with Daddy was repairable, I believed her. I absolutely had to stay away from Cole. Anytime I was around him, my intelligence dribbled right out of my ear and onto the floor. When he was near, I was a stupid, hormonal mess. That wasn't who I was, and if he held that kind of power over me, I would pretend he didn't exist until I was able to form and implement a plan. Sweet, satisfying revenge was the balm I needed to soothe my soul.

Over the next several hours, Zoe did everything possible to cheer me up. She even had me in a fit of giggles at one point. It was a relief to think about something else for a while. My fingers and toenails looked good again, and it was nice to relax and have a mimosa while we made plans for the summer. Zoe had reminded me that, even though Daddy had restricted my funds, I had four very wealthy friends who loved me and that our vacation wasn't ruined.

Once I discussed the situation with Zoe, she was on board with the idea of a new doorknob for my bedroom and happily stopped by the store. We agreed that I would feel better if I could lock the door from the outside when I left the house. Fortunately, I'd had enough emergency cash on me to make the purchase, which was a huge relief.

After we picked up takeout at P.F. Chang's, Zoe eased to the edge of the restaurant's parking lot, and my heart jumped into my throat.

"Wait!" I grabbed Zoe's arm. "I'll be right back." I opened the car door and hurried to the side of the street. After looking both ways, I jogged to the other side.

"Ibrahim! Wait!" I weaved through the afternoon crowd, hoping to catch up with him. Ibrahim had been walking in the opposite direction when I'd spotted him. I had to know if he'd found work or if he was so angry with me that he never wanted to look at me again.

He peered over his shoulder, then came to a stop, waiting for me to reach him. My sneakers smacked against the sidewalk as I grew closer.

"I'm so sorry. Ibrahim ..." I slowed a few feet ahead of him. "Are you okay?"

A sarcastic smile eased across his face. At times I forgot how tall Ibrahim was until I was next to him. His six-foot-four frame towered over my five-foot-seven. His dark eyes flashed with anger. "Although I'm furious, I'll be fine."

"Ibrahim." I reached for his hand. "I had no clue about the video. I swear. I would never hurt you ... hurt us like that."

He glanced around nervously, then returned his attention to me. "What happened?"

At least he was willing to hear me out. "Apparently cameras were in the limo ..." I pressed my mouth into a thin line, a rush of guilt squeezing my chest. "I had no idea. Please believe me." Zoe's words rang through my thoughts as I pleaded with him. She had said the same to me the other evening. "While I was at a party to kick off summer vacation, someone leaked the recording." Memories of everyone laughing, pointing, and gaping tortured me. I wasn't sure I would be able to move past it.

I gulped, trying to assess where Ibrahim's mind was at the moment, but his expression wasn't revealing his feelings. My cheeks and neck heated with shame. "Then someone cast it to the big screen television. Our afternoon was on full display." I looked away from him, anger rushing to a boil inside me. "So, I will be slut shamed or laughed at for the rest of my life, but even worse, you lost your job." My chin trembled with my confession. "This mess is all my fault, and I just wanted to tell you that I'm sorry."

Ibrahim's brows knitted together. "I've never heard you apologize before—to me or anyone else. Hearing those words means a lot to me, thank you."

"I should go. Zoe is waiting for me. I kind of jumped out of her car and left her up the street." The corner of my lips turned up in a small smile. "I just wanted to try to talk to you."

His eyes softened as he raised his hand to my cheek. "This is for the best. You're my kryptonite and I could never refuse you. I have work already, though. Don't worry."

My heart lit up with the news. "You do? Is it with a good family?"

His gaze flicked to the floor, then back to me, seemingly uncomfortable. He nodded. "They're very kind people. I'm sure we will see each other on occasion. We can keep it friendly."

I had a feeling Ibrahim was hiding something from me, but I had no idea what.

"Okay, that helps me feel a little better. The entire situation blew up, and I didn't have time to warn you. I'm not even sure how the video got leaked." I leaned into his touch, relieved the conversation was turning out better than I'd anticipated.

Ibrahim dropped his hand, and I immediately missed the warmth of his palm. "You should go. Take care, Shae." He bent down and pressed a sweet kiss to the corner of my mouth. Suddenly, Ibrahim jerked and spun around. A loud crack filled the air, then Ibrahim's body lurched, and his arms flailed as he struggled to keep his balance.

"Ibrahim!" I scooted to the side of him, trying to see what the hell was happening. A fist landed in Ibrahim's face, and he crumpled to the sidewalk, blood gushing from a gash over his eye. His nose bled, and at a glance, I realized it was most likely broken. "Ibrahim!"

Ibrahim grabbed his head, moaning in pain. As I started to kneel to help him, a black boot caught my attention, and I slowly looked up. *What the fuck?*

Chapter Nine

Fury rolled off me in waves. I was doing my best to lay low, then this motherfucker had to mess up a sincere conversation.

"Let's go." Cole quickly grabbed my wrist and practically dragged me behind him.

"Stop it, Cole! Let. Me. Go!" I dug my heels into the pavement, pulling him backward.

"I don't have time for this, Shae," Cole growled as he glowered at me.

My nostrils flared, and I fast-talked myself out of punching Cole in his nose. Unfortunately, it wouldn't do me any good since he was stronger than I was. "You hurt him. What the hell is wrong with you?"

Cole flashed me a searing look. "Now."

A thick tension swirled in the air between us. He tugged on me and took off in the opposite direction, pulling me along with him. I looked over my shoulder, realizing a crowd had formed around Ibrahim. *Shit.* Suddenly, the toe of my shoe caught on a raised crack on the cement, and I tumbled to the unforgiving ground, the pavement ripping open my knees and palms.

"Shae!" Hurried footsteps sounded behind me. "Oh, my God. Are you okay?" Zoe asked while she placed a hand on my back.

She must have been looking for me once people started to gather. My long hair covered my face, and embarrassed, pain-filled tears gathered in my eyes.

"We have to go. Zoe, she'll call you later." Cole scooped me off the ground and into his muscular arms. It took everything inside me not to hang onto him and hide from watchful eyes. I was beyond horrified, and my knees stung like a son of a bitch.

Cole set me down a block away, and I attempted to brush off the few pebbles that were stuck to my palms.

"Get on." He climbed on his motorcycle then started it. The engine roared to life right before the police sirens wailed through the air. He handed me a helmet, and I slid it into place, numb and in shock from how my apology had turned into Cole pummeling Ibrahim in public. I wouldn't have ever pegged Cole as a street fighter, but maybe he was. Every cell in my body burned with guilt and a desire to help. What he'd done to Ibrahim was awful and entirely uncalled for.

He glanced over his shoulder, his eyes cold and hard. "I'm not going to say it again. Let's go."

My need to get out of downtown and away from the crowd outweighed my desire to tell him to fuck himself. Not to mention, the cops would be here any second. If I stayed, then I would have to testify against Cole, and Daddy would have another mess to deal with. I didn't care about my stepbrother, but I did care about my father.

I carefully lifted my leg over the seat, my knees stinging with every movement. Once I was settled in behind him, I folded my arms in front of my chest. He looked at me before he gripped my wrist and wrapped my arm around his stomach, holding it in place. The bike lurched forward, nearly sending me flying off the smooth leather. It only took me a second to realize that I had to hang onto him if I wanted to live.

Giving in out of sheer terror, I grabbed his waist and held on for dear life.

Cole swung a quick U-turn, then weaved in and out of traffic until we reached a sideroad. With a hard right, my pulse kicked into high gear and I tightened my hold on him. It was clear Cole was comfortable on a bike, but I'd never been on one. My legs clamped against his as he picked up speed, avoiding the potholes on the side streets.

The realization of the events minutes ago hammered my brain. I'd apologized to Ibrahim, then he'd been beaten to a pulp and left on the sidewalk as Cole pulled me away from the scene. What really pissed me off was that I'd been in the process of making things right with Ibrahim. The thought of Cole's vicious outburst made my stomach tighten, and I shuddered, accidentally hitting my helmet against Coles.

He leaned into a curve, and I followed his body, pressing against his back. I wasn't sure when, but we'd taken a backroad with winding curves and steep hills. For a moment, my thoughts calmed with the wind against my skin. Was this what freedom felt like—speeding on the open road, embracing the danger, and witnessing the beauty of the trees?

A rush of calm enraptured me. All my life, I'd been on display. I had to be good enough, rich enough, beautiful enough. But at this moment, none of that mattered. I was truly free. My anxiety melted away as I fell into a rhythm with Cole, feeling his muscular body against mine and for a split second ... trusting him.

Within minutes, Cole pulled into a gravel driveway and slowed, the rocks crunching beneath the tires. The sound reminded my stupid brain about reality once again, and my anger kicked up a gear as I replayed the events that had occurred in downtown Spokane in front of the world. The cops would be sniffing out this bad play like a terrier looking for a cow patty to roll in. Cole hadn't bothered covering his face, so there were plenty of eyewitnesses to the attack. Confusion clouded my mind. Nothing about this situation was acceptable by any means, but I didn't understand what was behind Cole's actions. Julia had asked me to stay away from him, and I'd happily obliged. Maybe she should talk to her son and not me. *I wasn't the problem.*

Cole parked and cut the engine in front of a gorgeous, modern rustic home. An abundance of trees surrounded the house, and I released a sigh. This place was peaceful and quiet with no expectations ... yet.

My stepbrother climbed off the motorcycle and removed his helmet. He held his hand out, offering to assist me off.

I placed my palm in his and sucked in a sharp breath. A spark of electricity traveled up my arm with his touch, igniting the air around us as I hopped off. Removing my helmet, I set it on the seat of his bike. Cole's gaze fell to my knees. Blood had streamed down my shins and dried. Pain shot through my legs as I followed him up the steps and into the house.

"Where are we?" I asked softly, not wanting to disturb the monster currently sleeping inside Cole.

He met my question with silence as he unlocked the front door and waltzed in. I gasped, soaking in the comfort and safety of the blonde, redwood floors and open plan. A cozy stone fireplace begged to be used. The worn-in brown leather couch and chairs complimented the living room that opened to the dining and kitchen area. I noticed the staircase to the left and wondered if the bedrooms were upstairs. The minute I'd stepped into the fortress, I realized I never wanted to leave. Even though I was here with Cole, the home felt safe and inviting.

"My place. I inherited the place from my grandpa," he mumbled as he released my hand and dropped his keys on the brown and white granite counter. He ditched his jacket and tossed it onto the kitchen island. "Let's get you cleaned up."

My attention darted around, trying to assess the situation as I followed him into the bathroom. It was small but easily held a shower, single sink, and toilet.

"Sit." He lowered the lid, then pointed to the commode.

I did as he instructed, overwhelmed by the environment and the shock of how I got here. "I need to text Zoe, but she has my phone."

"She knows you're safe with me."

"Not sure safe is an accurate word," I quipped.

Cole ignored my jab as he located a washcloth from the cabinet, wet it, then knelt in front of me. He gently cleaned around the ripped-open skin on my left knee.

I sucked in a sharp breath and flinched, trying to keep my leg still.

He dabbed at my shin with the cool cloth. "It's worse than I thought."

I peeked at him, not wanting to look at the raw and bloody wounds.

"I didn't mean to hurt you," he said so softly I almost didn't hear him. He glanced up at me, his blue eyes softening.

"Okay." I was afraid to say anything, because I wouldn't shut up long enough to give him an opportunity to provide me with some much-needed answers.

Cole remained quiet as he continued to take care of me. He located the hydrogen peroxide and poured a bit over the wound.

The bubbles foamed, and my leg jerked. I released a groan while I clenched my fingers into tight fists. "Son of a bitch, that stings!"

"I know."

Finally giving into the whirlwind of thoughts in my head, I blew out a sigh. "Why, Cole? Why did you beat the shit out of Ibrahim, then haul me off like a little kid in trouble? I don't understand."

Cole began working on the opposite leg. "I ..." He paused and held my gaze. In a heartbeat, his face changed, and his stony, unreadable expression slipped into place.

"First, why did you leak the video?" I figured if I was going to make any progress, I needed to dumb it down for him. One topic at a time, like our parents did when we were little.

"I didn't."

What?

"You're lying. You were the only person that had access to the recording. I assume you had a copy on your phone, then when you saw me at the party you shared it to make a point."

Cole poured peroxide on the second ripped-open knee, and I gripped the sides of the toilet, releasing a scream. Tears welled in my eyes as I glared at him, willing knives to stab him a million times. "Fuck. You." I stood, forcing myself to walk away from him.

"You assumed wrong."

I looked over my shoulder. Cole leaned against the bathroom door frame, crossing his arms over his chest. As if he realized he wasn't comfortable, he strolled into the kitchen, and I followed.

"What do you mean?" I grabbed a barstool at the island and eased onto it, holding my breath from the pain shooting through my shins. "If it wasn't you, who was it?"

Cole opened the fridge and removed two Coronas. He popped the lids off, then placed one in front of me. I eyed it grudgingly. "Don't suppose you have anything stronger?"

"I do, but you're going to be on the back of my bike again, which means I need you sober so you don't get crazy and cause me to wreck. Samuel would be pissed at me."

Finally, more than a few words!

I wrapped my fingers around the cold bottle, then tilted it up and guzzled it like one of the good ol' boys. I smirked at him as I set the beer down on the granite with a thud.

"Who leaked the recording, Cole? And don't give me a bullshit story. I know you were behind it."

Cole took a pull from his drink. "It was my fault, but I didn't leak the video. There was a period of time my phone was unlocked and unattended, so I'm not sure who did it." His tone was calm and cool, and I wanted to crack his hard exterior in half to see if he was actually human. Nothing seemed to bother him. Ever. I fucking hated it.

As much as I despised his overall attitude, I was secretly relieved that he hadn't released the video. There was a possibility he was lying, but that wasn't Cole. He might be aloof or not answer me, but I'd never caught him in a lie. Key word being caught.

"Why did you let me think it was you, then?" I tapped my nails against the countertop, already growing tired of his games.

He gave me a half-shrug. "It didn't really matter who you blamed. The damage was done."

I would give him that one. "Who did you kill? Was it self-defense, and that's why you told daddy?"

"That's between your dad and me." He pushed off the counter and checked the time on his phone.

"Ugh. You're infuriating! You act like you don't give a shit about anyone except yourself."

Cole approached me, grabbed my legs, and pulled me to the edge of my seat. "You're not going to get the answers you want, Shae, so stop asking." His attention traveled down to my breasts as his tongue darted over his lower lip. "Stay away from Ibrahim."

My cheeks flushed with his proximity, and a newfound heat coursed through my body. I hated that he had this kind of effect on me. Where I lost my mind and wanted him to fuck me until I couldn't walk. I definitely needed therapy. Something was very wrong with me.

"I'm grown, Cole. You don't get to boss me around." Crossing my arms and blocking his view of my boobs, I glared at him.

His fingers dug into my hips, shooting pain through me and mingling with the throbbing sensation in my knees. "Nothing is what it seems. Do what I tell you." He sneered, a slight wobble to his voice.

Cole had never sounded unsure of himself, and my curiosity kicked up a notch. I glanced down at the small space that existed between our bodies. Excitement and fear battled for control within me as I focused on the bulge in his jeans. My gaze traveled to his, and goosebumps peppered my skin. "What do you want, Cole?" I whispered.

Cole fisted a handful of my hair and gave it a harsh tug, causing my chin to tilt up, our eyes locking. "You're playing a dangerous game, Shae. I'm not fucking around with you. Stay away from Ibrahim."

"Or what?" Apparently, the fact that I'd witnessed him kill a man wasn't enough for me to back down. My hormones had shifted into full throttle. Cole could have bent me over the kitchen counter and fucked me senseless, and I wouldn't have fought him.

He pressed himself against my core, and I whimpered. The tip of his nose brushed my neck and traveled up to my ear. I grabbed his bulging biceps in order to steady myself.

"Do you want to know, Princess?" His soft lips moved against my jaw.

Oh. My. God. What was he doing to me? "Yeah."

Cole released my hair, then picked me up. I instinctively wrapped my legs around his waist, ignoring the "fuck you" my knees gave me.

He carried me to the other side of the house, then kicked a door open. Butterflies broke loose in my belly as I realized it was a bedroom. A king-sized bed with a navy comforter hugged the wall. Cole set me down near the pillows that were propped against the headboard. His eyes darkened with need as he stared at me. "Just remember that I know how you like it." His voice was low, and I quivered next to him.

My nipples pushed painfully against my bra as I willed him to free them. The thought of his tongue on my body, licking and sucking. *Oh, God.* I was going to hell for wanting to fuck my stepbrother. Not even a priest could absolve me for the dirty thoughts I was having.

Cole grabbed my wrist and tugged it to the headboard. I sucked in an excited breath as he removed a pair of handcuffs from his nightstand, then secured me to the bedframe. *Oh, shit, this was hot.*

His fingertips glided over my arm, then down my side. I stopped breathing as he touched the bare skin of my stomach and lingered at the waist of my shorts.

Cole's lips hovered over mine, and my pulse stuttered against my wrist as I willed myself to stay still and let him make the first move.

He straightened slowly. "That should occupy you for a bit, Princess." With that, he turned on his heel and strolled out of the bedroom, shutting the door behind him.

My mouth dropped. It took a second for me to comprehend that Cole had played me. I tugged on the handcuff, the metal digging into my wrist. "You fucking pussy! Just admit you want me!"

An angry scream escaped me when he didn't return or answer.

"Fuck! Fuck! Fuck!" I pulled harder on the cuffs, then frantically searched for a release button like the ones for sex play. Nothing. I leaned over, searching under his pillows for a key. My heart sank as I realized there wasn't one nearby. Hopping off the mattress, I bent down and peered under the bed. Dammit. Not even a speck of dust existed beneath it.

I stood, my arm hanging in the air from being tied to his headboard. I berated myself for considering the idea that he was serious about messing around. Our parents would freak out if they suspected we wanted to fuck each other. Not that we did, but ... Ugh. How could I have been so stupid?

The rumble of motorcycles reached my ears, and I fell silent. Spindles of fear snaked through my stomach as the cold, harsh reality dawned on me.

My shoulders sagged, and I sank onto the edge of the bed. This whole time, I'd dared to hope he had a shred of humanity, but he only wanted to turn me over to the MC gang he was involved with. Cole had probably told them I witnessed the murder, and they were here to shut me up. Permanently. A sob escaped me, and I slapped my hand over my mouth. How in the hell I'd ended up here was beyond me. I was so excited about summer vacation and being home for a few months. Now, here I was about to be turned over to an MC to what ... rape me? Hold me for ransom? Kill me?

The sunlight filtered into the dark room as the sun shifted to my side of the house. I mentally told Daddy how sorry I was for getting myself into this mess. Also, I was sorry that he hadn't listened to my warning. Cole was, in fact, a monster without a conscience.

I curled into a ball the best I could and gave into the hot tears that streamed down my cheeks. My life would never look the same. I would be used and abused or tossed into the river, never to be seen again, all because I'd witnessed a murder.

My cries finally settled down, and I curled up on Cole's pillow. Deep, low voices traveled through the house, but I couldn't tell what they were saying. Heavy footfalls sounded down the hall, and I froze. Fear seized me as I waited to see if they were coming for me.

Chapter Ten

The door creaked open, and a head poked through. "Shae, right?" A tall, lean guy with sandy blonde hair and a well-kept beard stepped into the room.

I stared at him, trying to remember if I'd seen him the other night when they'd all beaten a person to death. Maybe, but it had been dark. Plus, I'd been more focused on the fact that Cole was with them.

"I see Cole's been messing with you." He grinned, then strolled over to me.

As hard as I tried not to, my body betrayed me, and I started to tremble. The guy reached into his front jeans pocket, then produced a key. He inserted it into the tiny hole, then with a quick turn, the cuffs clicked, and I was set free. I pulled away and rubbed the sensitive skin on my wrist. "Thank you," I whispered.

He stepped back before he folded his arms over his chest, his black vest bunching beneath him.

"Nice vest," I said quietly, appreciating the leather for a moment. The only hope of getting out of here with him guarding me was to try to connect with him as a human being.

A huge grin split his face. "It's called a cut, and thanks. I'm King. I'm the prez of the MC."

"Oh, sorry. I didn't know it had a particular name." *President.* That would explain why his presence was overwhelming. There was no doubt in my mind that this was a powerful man in front of me. He was probably a force to be reckoned with, like Daddy. They just didn't dress or act the same.

Drumming up a bit of courage, I forced my chin up. "What do you want?"

"We need to chat but come with me and meet the guys." His hazel eyes landed on me, then he motioned for me to follow.

Once he'd left, I rose on shaky legs, steeling myself for what was about to happen. Daddy had always taught me to overcome my fears, but this was worse than I'd anticipated. I trudged down the hall and into the living area, my palms sweating with every step. My eyes widened as I swept the room. At least five men, all wearing jeans and black leather cuts with a flaming skull on the back, stood around, laughing and drinking beer. Cole chuckled, then his heated gaze fell on me. He nodded, indicating for me to join him. If I was in a room filled with devils, he was my safest choice no matter what.

I slipped through the group and joined my stepbrother.

"She's pissed at you, man. Handcuffing her to the bed was low," a short, burly guy said. "I'm Snake. It's good to meet you at last." He held his beer up to me and nodded.

My forehead creased in confusion. Then it dawned on me that Cole had told them that he'd cuffed me to the headboard. How else would King have known where to find me?

"This is Hawk, Taco, Rigs, Brute, and Snake already introduced himself." The room filled with the sound of the guys greeting me.

I tentatively raised a hand. Apparently, MC members were friendly to their prey before they pounced. I peered up at Cole, unsure why I was here.

He cleared his throat. "I had to detain you for a bit. You left me no choice."

"What the fuck is that supposed to mean?" I placed my fist on my hip, feeling overly confident.

"Means we had some business to discuss, and we couldn't take any chances of you eavesdropping," King said, taking a swig of his beer.

I rubbed my face, not following what was happening. The fact that these men acted as if they were here regularly was concerning. Plus, they were being nice to me when I'd seen them firsthand kill a man in cold blood. They weren't good people. Neither was Cole, yet here I was fighting the urge to mind my socialite manners, offer them dinner, and ask if they'd had a nice day. The absurdity of the situation nearly made me laugh.

"Cole said you saw us having a business meeting the other night." King shifted from one booted foot to the other.

A couple of the guys snickered, then grew silent when King shot them a dirty look.

"Um, yeah. I didn't realize it was business, or I would have left." I tapped my temple. "I had too much to drink and got lost. Fuzzy brain. I actually don't remember anything."

King chuckled. "Cole says otherwise, and I'll tell you now, pretty lady, I'll take his word over yours all day long."

Dammit. It was worth a try. Maybe honesty would keep me alive longer. "Okay, fine. I saw a group of you. The motorcycles provided good light for me to see. But I had no idea what was going on until it was almost over. When some of you moved out of the way, all I saw was a guy dropping dead on the ground. I didn't see anyone else do anything." I pointed at them and shook my head just in case they'd misunderstood what I was trying to say.

"That's what he said." King stroked his well-trimmed beard as I uneasily leaned against the back of the couch.

"I'm going to take a wild guess that you're here to silence me, so I don't rat him out." My tone was ruder than what I'd meant. *Fucking nerves.* I rubbed my arms, pretending I'd caught a sudden chill.

Cole chuckled, and my head snapped up. "You sick fuck, you actually think this is funny."

"You were right, Cole. She's definitely feisty," Snake said, grinning.

"Great. Now I'm here to entertain everyone." Exasperated, I tossed my hands in the air. "Fuck my life."

"Get this girl something to drink before she worries herself to death, for God's sake," Taco said.

Within seconds, someone gave me some whiskey. I tipped that bad boy up and drained the clear shot glass. "Shit." I shuddered, holding it out for a refill. If I was going down, I would get as numb as I could, so I wouldn't understand what was happening. I finished the second drink and held it out again.

"Enough," Cole said, snatching the glass from my hand. "I need you sober, Shae. There are some things you have to know."

The alcohol tickled my senses, lulling me into a fake sense of calm. "I already know that you're a fucking douche. You choke me, blast my sex video out to the world, talk to me like shit, and handcuff me to your bed without even an orgasm."

The muscle in Cole's jaw ticked, then he burst out laughing. The rest of the room followed suit.

My cheeks burned from my overactive chatty moment.

"Fuck, Shae. I didn't realize you were such a lightweight or I wouldn't have given you a refill," Snake said.

I folded my arms, my lips curling into a sneer. "Thanks to Cole, I haven't eaten anything today. He also found it necessary to throw me down on the ground and bust my knees open." I pointed at the swollen, raw flesh.

"Fucking Ibrahim." Cole rubbed the back of his neck, fury rolling off him in waves. His mouth curled, and I was suddenly distracted by how badly I wanted to punch him in the nose.

Irritated, I glared at my stepbrother. "Can someone tell me what the hell his problem with Ibrahim is? He won't. Will any of you?" The men stared at me as if I spoke a different language. "I mean seriously, Ibrahim is a good guy and didn't deserve Cole's temper. He's been Daddy's limo driver for the last five-and-a-half years. He has family in Nigeria that he sends money to …" My eyes landed on Cole, irritation crawling over my skin. "Not to mention, Ibrahim was a *really good* fuck."

Cole twitched with my words, then he clenched and unclenched his fingers before he rubbed his jaw.

Pure, delightful gratification swelled in my chest as I watched Cole's temper flare.

"Damn," Snake said, shaking his head. "You're a little spitfire."

The men laughed, then a heavy silence blanketed the room, and I glanced at each of them, attempting to understand what they knew that I didn't. Their silence was thick with secrets.

I tossed my hands up, frustrated as hell that no one would explain what Cole's problem was with Ibrahim. "Okay, well, guess Cole is just up to his typical shit, then."

"Why don't you sit down, Shae," King said, patting the back of the couch. "I need to talk to you about someone else."

For some reason, I already respected King. Plus, it was probably in my best interest to do as he suggested. I had a bad feeling about what he wanted to discuss.

I sank into the soft leather, wishing it would suck me in and I could simply disappear.

"What do you know about Greg Hampton, Sibyl's father?" King asked.

Why in the hell were they asking me about Greg, Sibyl's dad? "He and Daddy have known each other for years. When Daddy started his company, he asked Greg to be his business partner, but he didn't take the offer. He seems like a good guy. Other than that, I don't know him well. He was very good to us when Mom died, though." Grief punched me in the stomach. If Mom were here, I would curl up next to her while she smoothed my hair and rubbed my back. My throat tightened with the memories and longing for her. Shoving the ball of emotions aside, I focused on the matter at hand. "Why do you care about him?" I wasn't sure what game they were playing, but I was over it. "I don't understand what this is all about. Other than being an eyewitness to your 'business meeting,' I have no clue why I'm here." My shoe tapped against the floor, indicating I was growing impatient when I was actually super nervous. Unfortunately, when my nerves were frayed, I talked too damn much.

King stood next to me while Cole stood between two of the bikers near the fireplace. His gaze burned through me, and I squirmed in my seat. Then, I noticed the guy named Taco next to my stepbrother for the first time. Holy hell, he was hot. He had sandy blonde hair and hazel eyes. He was taller than Cole, with broad shoulders, and his jeans hung low on his hips and conformed to his toned thighs.

"We're trying to narrow down possibilities, and looking into anyone who knows your family, including your father's friends. It's precautionary until we have more information. Hopefully, you can help us. The man at our business meeting ... Someone is after Cole and they sent a rookie to try to do the deed," King said, rocking on the heel of his black combat boots. "The son of a bitch tried to hurt your man."

I cringed with King's reference to *my man*. Cole definitely was a lot of things, but not that. However, the fact that someone tried to hurt him caught my attention. "Who is after Cole?"

King tugged on the silver chain that hung from his jeans pocket. "Not sure yet, but we're keeping an eye on anyone around him, including you."

I stared at my stepbrother, my eyes narrowing with disdain. "So, Cole gets into some trouble and that justifies you taking a man's life?" My brain spun out in multiple directions as I muddled through what this meant. Bile swam up to my throat. If Cole was in danger, then so was I. My father had always warned me about the company I kept. Little did he know he'd allowed the devil to stroll right into our home a few years ago.

I focused on Cole, attempting to read him but, as usual, failing.

Seconds later, it felt like a nuclear bomb detonated in my head as the truth crashed down on me.

"That's why cameras were in the limo. You're keeping tabs on me," I said, my tone accusatory.

Cole nodded. "I gave King my key, then he had someone install them for me."

Fury stomped all over the fear, winning out as I hopped up from my seat and marched over to Cole. "You mean to tell me that I got caught in *your* mess and *I'm* paying for it?" I jabbed him in the chest with my teal-colored nail. "I'm sure you fucked someone over, but it cost *me*! I could have lost everything!"

Cole closed the small gap between us, his eyes flashing with anger. "Let's not twist the facts, Princess. You shouldn't have been screwing the staff. What went down is on you. Not me."

I reached up to slap him, but before I made contact, he grabbed my wrist. He leaned down, his lips against my ear. "You're playing a dangerous game, Princess. Don't even fucking think about hitting me again because you won't like the way I deal with you."

I sucked in a sharp breath, my skin burning from his hold. I should have been disgusted the more I learned about Cole, but I wasn't. There was a flame deep inside me that I couldn't extinguish. Even though I fought against it, an attraction was blooming to life, growing without my permission.

"Maybe you like dangerous. Maybe you're tired of sitting on your throne being a pious bitch." He released me and stepped back, his attention falling to my hard nipples that pushed through the thin fabrics of my bra and top.

"Fuck you." My heart pounded, and my throat felt thick as I glowered at him. The nagging voice in my head told me I'd just woken a beast inside Cole that I wasn't sure I could tame.

Chuckles filled the air, and I shot the guys a scathing look.

"Let's get back to business," King said, silencing the room. "Cole received a death threat, Shae. The man you saw that night was involved. We were protecting one of our own."

My eyes widened. "Cole is in your MC?"

King pulled on the collar of his shirt. "No. He's never prospected or patched in even though he could if he wanted. Everyone here would be cool with him joining because we've talked about it."

"Patched in?" I asked, unclear of the term.

"It's when a guy pledges for up to a year, then the club votes to see if we want him or not," King explained.

I nodded, eyeing Cole, completely baffled that he led a double life.

"So, the dead guy ... did he try to hurt Cole or ... kill him?" I wasn't sure I wanted to hear the answer. Maybe remaining naïve would be the best way to handle the situation.

"It's a long story, Shae. What happens in the club stays in the club, but here's what I can tell you. The cameras in the limo weren't there to watch you. Your dad has meetings, clients, and staff in the car. It was a good place to learn who might be involved. It's clear that they know Cole pretty well. Other than college, his family was the easiest to start with. It's a process of elimination at this point."

"But an innocent man lost his job. Ibrahim didn't deserve to be caught up in Cole's mess, either." My stomach dropped to my toes at the thought of Ibrahim losing his income and reputation.

"I don't know Ibrahim personally, Shae. All I can say is that you two were in the wrong car for your afternoon romp." The corner of King's mouth twitched, and I suspected he was trying to hide his smile.

"Shit. Did Cole show you all the video?" I glared at Cole. If he had, he'd be a nut short after I was finished with him.

King threw his head back and laughed.

"I tried to talk him into sharing it, but it was a no go," Snake said, smiling. His perfectly straight white smile made him appear friendly. From the rumors I'd heard about motorcycle gangs and what I'd seen, I highly doubted he was a good guy.

"We all knew it went viral, but none of us saw it, Shae. It was taken down before we had access to it," Taco explained as he shoved his fingers through his blonde hair.

"Girl, you need to wake up and see what's in front of you. No way in hell would Cole have allowed anyone to see you in a compromising situation. Even if they'd wanted to." King gave his men a pointed look.

Cole loudly cleared his throat, then muttered, "None of you fuckers will ever see it."

Holy shit. Cole had just protected me. Confused, I wasn't even sure what to do with what I'd heard.

King rose from his seat, grinning like crazy. He placed a gentle hand on my shoulder. "Back to the business meeting. Even if you went to the cops with what you saw, no one would believe a word of it. You were drinking and it was dark."

"I wasn't going to go to the police. Even though I can't stand Cole, I didn't want him to go to prison. I just don't want him to be a controlling asshole. Besides, he would look horrible in orange."

Chuckles filled the room.

"Now that you know I'm not going to rat him out, are you done with me? Can I go home?" My pulse raced while I waited for King's response.

"That's not fucking happening. There's other shit going on, which means you're stuck with us." King released me, compassion in his expression.

Frowning, I placed my palm against my chest. "I don't understand."

King cracked his knuckles as though he were headed into a fight. "Cole's already talked to your Pop. He knows what's going on."

I huffed. "Just because Cole pissed someone off and now they're threatening him doesn't mean my life has to come to a screeching halt."

"Yesterday, Cole received an anonymous message," Taco chimed in.

A heavy hush fell over the room, and I glanced at Cole. For the first time ever, I saw sincere fear flicker in his gaze.

"Cole?" I asked softly. "What is it?"

Chapter Eleven

"They threatened to hurt you and our family, Shae," Cole explained. His mask of indifference faltered for a moment before it slipped back into place.

The room tilted on its side as his words sank in. Within a few days, I'd gone from being a spoiled, wealthy girl tucked away in a sheltered world to living in reality full of lies and danger.

My attention swept the group, searching for a smile or someone attempting to hide their chuckle, but everyone remained solemn. I tossed my hands up in front of me. "Okay, the joke can stop now. I am absolutely nothing to anyone except my daddy."

"That's not true." King shot Cole a look, then he focused on me again. "Cole needs to talk to you about everything else, so I'm gonna shut my mouth now. Just know you'll be seeing a lot more of us."

"My father and Julia are in danger," I whispered as tears clouded my vision, and I mentally begged them to tell me all of this was a sick joke. If they were hurt—or worse—because of Cole, I would make it my life's mission to bury him alive.

Warm fingers wrapped around my biceps, and I peered up into Cole's eyes. Regret and sorrow flashed in his face. My stomach twisted into knots. "Samuel wants to hire a bodyguard. He'll take care of them. I'll take care of you and so will the MC."

A cry escaped me, and I smacked a hand over my mouth, attempting to regain control over my emotions. Finally, I turned to King. "Can you protect my family?" My voice trembled with my question. I had no problem breaking the law if it meant the people I loved most were safe.

"Yeah. But we gotta know who we're dealing with. We have a few leads, but nothing solid yet. All of Cole's associates are under suspicion."

I squared my shoulders. If I was asking an MC for help, I needed to show them I was capable of keeping my shit together. "If you keep Daddy and Julia safe, then you have my loyalty. I'll never mention the business meeting again, nor will I ever tell anyone if you choose to use ... unsavory methods to protect my dad and stepmom."

King peered past me, then nodded. "Consider it done."

I wasn't sure why King had agreed so quickly, but I suspected it had to do with Cole and the gang being close. It was finally dawning on me that I was in danger and safe at the same time because of the man that stood next to me—my stepbrother.

"I think I need some air." I wrapped my arms around my waist, trying to hold myself together as this new information crashed down on me. A heavy weight settled on my chest as I opened the front door and hurried down the sidewalk to the gravel driveway. Heavy footsteps reached my ears. Glancing behind me, I spotted Taco approaching his motorcycle.

I wondered if he might provide some helpful insight. "Are you leaving?"

Taco mounted his ride and pulled his helmet on. "Yeah, I gotta be somewhere. It was good to meet you, finally."

I chewed on my bottom lip. "Cole talks about me?"

Taco coughed into his hand, attempting to hide his smile. "He's mentioned your name every once in a while."

I nodded and stepped closer. "I like your bike," I said, tracing my fingertips along the blue and white flames that traveled over the side of the fuel tank. "Maybe you can take me for a ride sometime." I glanced at him, assessing his body language, but I couldn't get a read on what he was thinking.

"As much as I would love to have you on the back of my bike, I can't. You're Co—"

"Shae." Cole's tone was clipped as he quickly walked through the front door to me. He grabbed my hand, scowling. "Get inside." I didn't miss the dirty look he shot Taco.

Taco tipped his chin up. "It's all good, man. Later." With that, he started his motorcycle, the rumble echoing through the property.

"Why do you have to ruin everything?" I attempted to jerk away from Cole, but he tightened his grip. "Cole, learning about our family being threatened ... it was a lot to take in. I just wanted a ride to take my mind off things for a while." My chin trembled against my will. I couldn't fall apart in front of him.

Cole towered above me, then gently tucked a strand of hair behind my ear. "I know. I'm sorry you got pulled into this mess."

Completely taken off guard by his moment of humanity, I reminded myself that the monster inside him would return in seconds, and not to get my hopes up that we could meet on common ground.

"Please don't let anything happen to Daddy and Julia." A lump clogged my throat at the thought of losing them. I'd already lost Mom. I couldn't lose them, too.

Cole tilted my chin up, our eyes connecting. "I'll do everything in my power to protect Mom and Samuel."

Silence filled the space between us. "So, these guys." I nodded at the house. "Are they into some deep shit? Illegal stuff?"

Cole massaged the back of his neck. "Yeah. Yeah. The Blue Angels are a one percent club. They're good men, though."

I gave him a questioning look. "I have no idea what a one percent club is."

"They're outlaw bikers. They're a brotherhood who don't care about the same rules as everyone else, they live by their own laws. They're loyal as hell to the members." Cole squared his shoulders. "I trust them with my life, and that's all you need to know."

"How did you get involved with them, Cole? You have a good home, people who love you, and money. I don't understand."

Cole stared behind me with a faraway look in his eyes. "Don't worry about it."

I bowed my head, my shoulders trembling with anger. After a moment, I looked at him again. "If my life is really in danger, I at least deserve some answers, dammit."

Cole focused on the ground and kicked at the gravel with the toe of his boot, now covered in dust from the ride here.

I released a weary sigh. Cole was wearing my patience down. "Fine. Don't tell me. When can I go home? I want to speak to Zoe." I didn't miss the disapproving look on Cole's face. "I won't tell her about the threats. But if the MC is going to be around, then she will meet them eventually. She's my best friend. I can't hide this from her. Plus, I need someone to talk to. This shit got intense really fast."

Cole hesitated before he answered. "Honestly, I don't want us to go home. I have no idea if it's safe or not, but we have to pretend that life is normal right now, or we risk tipping off whoever is trying to hurt me."

From the outside, I probably appeared calm and collected, but I was struggling not to fall apart on the inside. "That doesn't make me feel better, but it makes sense."

Cole led me back into the house. I half expected the guys to be staring at us, but they'd replenished their beers and had settled in at the table to play a game of poker. I couldn't help but giggle as they talked shit to each other. Unfortunately, it would be the last time I laughed for a while.

A dull ache pounded in my head. I was ready for another drink and some food. I had no idea how long I would be here, but I figured I might as well make the best of it. Grabbing a beer, I sat down with the guys and watched them play. Even though I was physically present, my thoughts were elsewhere. My attention landed on Cole, who had joined us. He laughed at the jabs and bullshit the men said to each other, appearing perfectly at ease with men who broke the law.

There was no doubt that Cole was an asshole, but maybe he would actually prove that he would protect the people who were important to him. My pulse jumped. If I was here, it meant he actually did care about me. There was that, at least. I just wished I could ignore the pull to him. It was as if every nugget of information revealed his sinister side. It was calling to me, lulling me into a false sense of security with him.

Over the rest of the afternoon, I witnessed a different side of my stepbrother. One that I thought I could get accustomed to. Dark, dangerous, and with more layers than I ever imagined possible. The more I processed what I'd learned about Cole, the more I wanted to dance in the dark with him.

After the MC left, Cole and I cleaned the house. The guys had been good about tossing their beer bottles in the recycling bin and throwing their trash in the trashcan, but that many people in a small house made a mess. Cole wiped down the countertops while he pointed me to the vacuum for the hardwood floors. He hadn't asked me to, but I also scrubbed the bathroom. It had been a hot minute since I'd scrubbed a toilet, since Daddy had a housekeeper, but I managed. Oddly enough, as we took care of the house together, our silence felt comfortable, like we had shared a space all the time.

With a racing heart, I almost admitted ... I refused to finish the thought. It had been a long-ass week, and I suspected PMS was playing havoc with my emotions. Maybe a different type of birth control pill was in order. Maybe.

"Thanks for the help," Cole said, running his hand through his blonde hair.

I hung the cordless Dyson vacuum on the charger, then made my way to the kitchen.

"Sure. I ... uh. I appreciate you and the guys looking after Julia and Daddy. Helping around here is the least I can do." I looked at my knees. The skin had grown tighter over the last few hours, and I figured the ride home on Cole's motorcycle would be uncomfortable, but I would live.

Cole's lips thinned, and the muscles on either side of his jaw pulsed. "Whether we like each other or not, we're family, Shae. I will always protect family, unless ... unless they don't deserve it." Pain etched itself into Cole's forehead, and he looked away quickly.

Since Cole was trying to keep me safe, I assumed that in his opinion, I deserved the help. That revelation should have been what I focused on, but it wasn't. Who hadn't earned Cole's loyalty? I wondered if this was part of what Julia had mentioned before.

Cole spoke and interrupted my thoughts. "Let's head out. There's a chance of rain, and I'd rather not take you home drenched. Samuel might not appreciate it."

"Since when do you care about what Daddy thinks?"

Cole's dark gaze swept over me, then landed on my eyes. We stared at each other, completely transfixed as unanswered questions and tension crackled in the air between us.

Finally, Cole spoke. "Samuel is a good man, Shae." He tore his attention away and looked out the window. "The storm clouds are rolling in. We should go."

Silently, he followed behind me, locked the front door, and walked to his bike. He handed me a helmet. I slipped into place, then waited for him to hop on.

"She's a beautiful motorcycle." I pointed to the blue and white flames on the side of the fuel tank, then leaned closer when I realized a woman's face was woven into the fire. A crease dented the smooth skin in-between my eyebrows. Surely, I wasn't seeing this correctly. Maybe the alcohol was still messing with me, and I hadn't noticed it.

"Cole, what's her name?" I ran my fingertips over the artwork, warmth spreading through my chest.

Cole started the engine, the rumble cutting off my question. I climbed on, and this time I wrapped my arms around his waist and pressed myself into his back. He eased down the driveway, the gravel crunching beneath the tires. Sadness tugged at my heartstrings. For whatever reason, I already loved Cole's house. He was different here, and if I were truthful, most of the man I'd seen today, I could like. But I wasn't ready to be honest because the other part of me didn't trust him. Now it seemed as though I no longer had a choice. Confused and tired, I pushed the thoughts out of my mind and enjoyed the ride. At least for a few minutes, I could feel free. It was just Cole and me against the world, and I no longer felt quite so lonely. Funny how everything changed so quickly.

Chapter Twelve

Fat drops of rain fell from the grey sky as Cole pulled into the driveway of our house. The downpour lasted long enough to drench us before we made it inside, then stopped as quickly as it had started. Once Cole had parked his motorcycle in the garage, we climbed off. I smiled at the puddle that was accumulating at my feet.

I glanced up at him. His tongue wet his bottom lip as he became transfixed on my shirt and stomach. The thin fabric was soaked through, revealing my hard nipples and flat tummy. Cole had seen me in a bikini a ton of times, but that was before he'd witnessed me fucking Ibrahim and Matt on the video, so he was now familiar with what was beneath my clothes. But the look in his eyes was different. Instead of neutral, it was possessive and hungry.

My cheeks flushed, and a newfound heat coursed through my body. I cleared my throat, breaking the spell between us. "I need to shower and change."

Cole tore his gaze away. "Do whatever you want. I'm not your keeper." He placed his helmet on the bike seat, then stomped off.

Great. Asshole Cole is back. I traipsed after him through the garage, but before I could follow him through the door, the bastard slammed it in my face. I gritted my teeth, refusing to give him the satisfaction of seeing me pissed off. It was clear that Hyde was home, leaving Jekyll outside.

Grumbling under my breath, I let myself into the house. Hopefully, I wouldn't run into Daddy or Julia until I was cleaned up and had bandaged my knees. I wasn't up for any questions. Besides, Cole would probably fill Daddy in on the day's events. He seemed to have his nose up my father's ass. Attempting to smooth my ruffled feathers, I finally realized my phone was with Zoe. I would have to use the landline to see if she could drop it off.

With no sign of anyone, I hurried to my bedroom and closed the door, ignoring Cole's presence across the hall. I shucked the wet clothes and tossed them in the sink in my bathroom, then took a hot shower. The rain and ride home had chilled me to the bone, but I'd been so focused on Cole, I hadn't realized it until the water soothed my skin and burned my wounds.

An hour later, I had fresh bandages on my knees. I dressed in soft black yoga pants and a clean purple tank top. I made my way downstairs and to the kitchen. There wasn't a real need for a landline other than Daddy's business calls, but I was grateful for it. I located the phone on the counter and called my best friend.

"Girl, I've been waiting for you to call! What the fuck happened?" Zoe gushed without even saying hello.

I stared out the window. "I would have texted you, but I left my cell in your car. Any chance you want to bring it over and hang?"

"I'm already getting my shoes on. See you in fifteen."

Before I could say goodbye, Zoe hung up. I decided to wait for her under the covered entrance. Maybe it would help me clear my head for a few minutes. Sneaking outside undetected, I closed the door and sat on the bench. A chill skated down my spine, and I rubbed my arms.

The smell of the fresh, early summer rain soothed my nerves and brought back memories of Mom and me watching thunderstorms from our covered deck when I was a little girl.

A distant rumble of thunder told me the weather would clear any minute. Seconds later, the sun peeked through the remainder of the clouds and began to dry the wet pavement, causing small billows of steam. Lost in my thoughts, I almost didn't realize Zoe had driven up the driveway. I rose from my seat and met her at the car. She climbed out, eyeing me as she waved her hand over the door handle and locked the convertible.

"Hey," I said, squinting at her through the bright sunshine.

"Bet you felt naked without this." She held my phone up, then gave it to me. "And this." She gently shook a brown paper bag.

"Oh, shit. I forgot all about it. Thanks." I took the items from her. As soon as I had the doorknob installed, I wouldn't be so paranoid about recording devices in my room.

"You're welcome. Also, you have a text from Cole." Zoe removed her sunglasses and pressed her lips into a thin line. "No, I didn't read it. Well, I did when it flashed on your screen."

"What did he want?" I asked, pocketing my cell instead of looking at the message. I didn't want to appear too eager in front of Zoe. Plus, he'd pissed me off the moment we'd arrived home. Needless to say, I wasn't too keen on seeing what he wanted.

"Something about keeping your mouth shut when you saw me." Zoe slipped her arm through mine. "What's up, Shae? You seem different, and the shit that went down with Cole today ... I swear I won't say a word, and no judgement. Ever. But it's clear the dynamic between the two of you has changed."

We reached the entrance, and I paused. "We can talk quietly in my room, but I want to search for recording devices first."

"Fuck, I forgot about that. You need that doorknob on, like, yesterday." Zoe dropped her hold on me and frowned, making the lines in her forehead prominent.

"Zoe, stop frowning or you'll get wrinkles early. Ever since the limo fiasco, I've checked for cameras, and it's getting old. Maybe it would be better to leave until I have time to change the lock. No one even knows I'm home other than Cole. Julia thinks I've been with you all day." I flipped over my cell and opened the back of the case, checking for my ID and what cash I still had.

"Let's get out of here. We can grab some dinner and go to the river. I'll put the top down and we can absorb some vitamin D through the golden orb in the sky." She laughed, then worry flashed across Zoe's expression as she squeezed my shoulder. "Remember, I'm here for you."

"Thanks." I hugged her, then we hopped into her car and left.

There were very few times I'd seen Zoe's face pale, but with the update about the MC, the fact that someone was threatening Cole, and then me, she'd turned ghostly white.

"Shae, this is serious shit." She nibbled on the end of her French fry and stared at me. "I don't even know where to begin. First, Cole is sending you hella mixed signals. Dude needs to knock it off. I mean, what's his deal with Ibrahim?"

I gave her a half shrug and took a bite of my hamburger. I hadn't realized how hungry I was until the smell of the yummy carbs tickled my nose. My mouth had started to water before we even parked at a quiet spot near the river. At least we could talk openly without being concerned someone might overhear us. Cole had told me not to discuss the danger or the MC club, but I wasn't about to listen to him. Maybe it was a stupid decision on my part, but I couldn't manage all of the chaos on my own.

"I'm guessing that something happened between him and Ibrahim, but I don't have a fucking clue what. Maybe he felt like Ibrahim was taking advantage of me since I was younger. I'm pretty sure it was the other way around, but it doesn't matter anymore."

Zoe removed a napkin from the brown paper bag. "And I thought for sure Cole released the video, too. So, he simply forgot his phone, and someone picked it up and saw it, huh?"

I nodded. "My guess is that it's one of his friends, Remington, or one of the other guys. They would totally pull shit like that, but I'm thinking they'll pay dearly if Cole finds out who did it. Maybe he never will."

Zoe's nose scrunched up in distaste. "He should! I want to know who did you dirty like that, Shae."

I plucked off a piece of the hamburger bun and nibbled on it. "Honestly, I'm not sure it's even worth it. Daddy had the recording removed, so hopefully that's the end of it. Besides, I have other shit to worry about."

"Yeah, and the end of your social life as long as Cole is around. Not only are you stuck with him this summer, but I doubt he's going to leave you alone at college again this year. He certainly has a habit of making sure you don't date anyone." Zoe's big brown eyes cut to me. "Babe." She reached over and smoothed my hair. "It's time you consider another idea."

"What's that?" I grabbed the Dr Pepper that I'd bought with my dinner and took a sip.

"I think your stepbrother is into you." Zoe's tone was gentle, as if she were consoling a small child.

Spewing the soda from my mouth, I immediately broke into a coughing fit.

"Oh, shit. I'm sorry!" Zoe picked up the remaining napkins and began soaking up the drink that had landed on the leather seat.

Once I'd regained the ability to breathe correctly, I faced her, dumbfounded. "You're wrong." *Was she?*

Zoe raised her hands in surrender. "I'm just saying that you shouldn't dismiss the idea is all. Cole has literally cockblocked you since your dad and Julia got married and he strolled into your life. He's rude as fuck to you, humiliates you, and is practically obsessed with who you're with and talk to." She tilted her head, studying my reaction.

I pursed my lips. "Nope. No. And hell no. There's no way. Did you hear what he said to me at Harrison's party? Then he tossed me over his shoulder and carried me out of the house not half an hour before he *murdered* someone, Zoe. Beat a man to *death*."

Zoe folded her arms across her chest and gave me a pointed look. "And he told you why. He was protecting you and the parents."

Wide-eyed, I slapped my palm against my forehead. "Oh, yeah. How could I forget? That makes everything okay ... and legal." Sarcasm dripped from my words.

"I mean, to have a hot as hell badass protect you, yummy. I'm not sure about you, but a guy being a fuckwad to everyone except the girl he loves ... we all want that. It's why we love the bad boys. Think about it, though. Damon from The Vampire Diaries, Chuck Bass from Gossip Girl, and that serial killer, Dexter."

I blew out a sigh. "I get it, but that's not the real world."

Zoe arched a brow. "Yet, you spent all day with him and the motorcycle dudes. And I want to meet Taco. If he's as gorgeous as you described him to be ... that's probably why Cole barged out of the house and jerked you away ... ya know, before Taco licked your snatch." Zoe burst into giggles. She nudged my arm. "Get it? You're supposed to eat a taco, not the other way around." A snort escaped her, and she laughed harder, holding her sides.

Dismayed, I shook my head. "What am I going to do with you?" A grin almost broke free, but I was emotionally too tied up in knots at the moment.

"Several of the bikers were hot, but that doesn't mean I need to drag you into that world with me. You're my best friend, Zoe. I get the impression they're loyal as fuck to the people they love and care about, but other than that, life is a different game to them."

"Does Cole know that you were going to talk to me about the MC?" Zoe turned in the seat and propped her elbow on the armrest.

"I told him I needed to talk to someone about the situation, and he seemed like he was fine with it at first. But then his text said otherwise." I rolled my eyes. "In my mind, I've nicknamed him Jekyll and

Hyde. I never know which one I'm going to get. The man or the monster."

"I have an idea about that." Zoe wiggled her brows at me. "I think he's confused about his feelings for you. You're his stepsister and off-limits or some bogus bullshit like that."

"Well, he's not wrong." I groaned. "Can you imagine the look on Daddy and Julia's faces if we got together?" I barked out a maniacal laugh. "I could kiss away any chance of Daddy reinstating my funds. Fucking the stepbro wouldn't be a show of my maturity in his opinion."

Excitement flickered in Zoe's expression. "I bet Cole is so damn good in bed." She sucked on her bottom lip and moaned. "If you sleep with him, I want all the deets. Every. Single. Inch of the details." She squealed and grabbed my arm. "Oh my God, this is going to be epic."

I pried her fingers from my biceps. "Aren't you forgetting that you're speculating, and in reality, Cole isn't interested in boning his sister?"

Zoe pretended to barf. "*Stepsister.*"

"You, Dani, Sibyl, and Isabel are the only people to see us as stepsiblings. Didn't you hear all the lewd remarks at Harrison's party?" Humiliation burned through my body as I recalled Cole's words, implying that he'd fucked me. "When he gave everyone the impression that we were sleeping together ... why would he have done that?"

"Ugh, Shae! I'm trying to tell you. He wants you. You might be taboo to him, but he let every guy there know you were off limits and that he was in your pants. Wake up, babe."

Butterflies flip-flopped in my belly. "If, and let me be clear *if,* you're right ... do you think that's why he's so mean to me?"

Zoe tapped her chin with her finger, a sign that she was pondering my question. "Honestly?"

"Always." I inhaled the fresh air in an attempt to slow my racing pulse.

"This is only my opinion based on the four years he's been in your life, okay?"

"Out with it, Zoe." I rubbed my sweaty palms along my yoga pants, unclear why the conversation was stressing me out. Just because Zoe shared her thoughts didn't mean she was right.

"There's no two ways about it. Cole is an asshole. But ..." She lifted her hand to stop me from interrupting her. "I think he's battling some demons that we have no idea about. Not that it justifies him treating you like he does, but I do think there's more to it. I think he's conflicted about his feelings, and on top of it, someone is threatening him, and now you." Zoe's attention darted around us. "Shit. I forgot about that part, and here we are out in the middle of nowhere."

I glanced around nervously. *Shit.* The realization hadn't crossed my mind, either. All I was interested in was a safe place to talk. Shuddering, I realized I might have put us in danger without meaning to. "Let's go to my house. We can sweep the room for recording or listening devices."

Zoe looked a bit perplexed as she barked out a sarcastic laugh. "Do you realize we sound bona fide crazy and paranoid?"

"Yeah, but Cole hid cameras in the limo, so this girl isn't taking any more chances." I patted my chest.

"I don't blame you." Zoe pushed the button, and the car engine purred to life.

I rode the rest of the way home in silence, weighing Zoe's words with Cole's actions. The idea of Cole sent my pulse racing, but hell if I knew when it had started. He'd always been hot, but he was my stepbrother—possessive, overprotective, and moody. Maybe Zoe was right. And maybe, just maybe, I had to admit that I had feelings for my stepbrother. *Shit. Shit. Shit. I'm going to hell.* The real question, though ... was Cole going with me?

Chapter Thirteen

Zoe and I had conducted a thorough sweep in my room, closet, and bathroom for cameras but didn't find anything. It made me wonder if Cole had told me the truth and the recording in the limo hadn't ever been about me.

After more speculation and talking about how much life had changed in the last week, Zoe left a little after midnight. Worn out from sharing all the secrets and speculating about who might want to hurt Cole and my family, I was ready to get some sleep. I grabbed my phone, opened Spotify, and turned on a new playlist I'd made before the vacation began. I'd been so busy that I hadn't had time to listen to it. "Devil" by Two Feet began to play, and I sent it to my Alexa Show. The speaker on the device was pretty sweet, and the sound easily reached me when I was taking a shower or bath.

The thump of the bass filled my ears, and I walked into my bathroom, where I shed my clothes, tossing them into the hamper. After I brushed my teeth, washed my face, and moisturized again, all I wanted was to find some pajamas and crawl into bed. "Nothing Holy" played as I strolled into my room. My mouth gaped in horror, then a scream tore from my throat.

"What the fuck, Cole? You terrified me." I covered my breasts, realizing I was standing in front of him with only my light green G-string on. "Don't you knock?"

Cole leaned against the doorframe, watching my every move. "Don't you lock your door?" He smirked, his eyes not leaving mine even though I was practically naked.

"I thought I did." I tapped my bare foot impatiently, raking my attention over him in a derogatory manner. "What do you want?"

Cole remained silent, his calculating gaze raking up and down my body.

"Fine. Get out. Don't come in my room again." Out of spite—and if I was honest, a little curiosity—I dropped my arms.

Cole focused on my tits, his Adam's apple bobbing up and down as he swallowed.

I strolled over to him, stopping a few feet away. "Is this what you wanted? To see me practically naked?" My voice sounded confident and strong, but inside I was shaking. I refused to cower to him, though. If he wanted me, then he had the opportunity to do something about it instead of hiding behind a facade.

Cole pushed off the wall and moved toward me. "What are you doing, Shae?"

He growled as he drew closer, and I stepped backward. The back of my knees hit the edge of my mattress, and I fell on the bed. I scrambled to the top. A flutter of nerves and excitement filled my stomach.

Cole wedged one of his legs between mine and parted them while he hovered over me. He pinned me with a heated stare. "Do you think about me, Shae? Do you think about my cock buried deep inside you, making you moan?"

I gulped, unwilling to answer. He'd played me before, and I wasn't sure where this was going. A shiver danced up my spine as I released a soft breath, and Zoe's words whispered through my mind. If Cole was into me, then I was about to find out.

He lowered a little more, my breasts only inches from pressing against his chest. A shadow of conflict coasted over his face.

I swallowed over the dryness in my throat, willing him to touch me.

"Tell me, Shae."

I nearly melted into a puddle, the way my name rolled off his tongue. Sexy and haunting all at the same time. Chills peppered my skin, and my pussy clenched, begging for him to bury himself inside me.

"Which vibrator do you use when you imagine me fucking you? I've thought about tasting your pussy, licking and sucking your clit while you're sitting on my face. The thought of your head back and eyes closed while I slide my tongue into you makes me almost come by itself. My name would roll off those pretty, pouty lips of yours, then I'd shove my dick in your mouth until you fucking choked on it. Tears would stream down your cheeks as I cut off your air. But that's not where I want to come, baby. No, I want to slam my cock into you until your pussy clenches around me. I bet if I touched your cunt right now, you would be drenched."

Oh. My. God. Cole didn't need to touch me. All he had to do was talk to me in that deep, sultry voice, and I could have repeated orgasms.

He rolled to his side, and my breath stuttered in my chest as his fingers moved down my belly and eased into my G-string. He didn't waste any time as he spread me apart and shoved a finger into me.

I whimpered as he stroked the fire burning deep inside me. He removed his finger, then pressed it against my lips. "Suck."

Blindly obeying, I licked and sucked my juices off him. "Crazy in Love," Beyonce's remix, filtered through the speakers, adding to the already sexually charged mood.

Cole's touch lightly grazed over my neck, then to my breast. He rolled my hard nipple between his fingertips, then pinched it. I yelped. "I want to come all over your tits. Would you let me, Shae?"

"Yeah." My voice cracked, betraying how much I craved him.

His head dipped lower until his mouth latched onto my sensitive bud. Losing any self-control, I arched into his touch as his hand cupped my other tit. I wanted to grab his hair, but I was afraid if I touched him, he would stop, and I desperately needed him to continue.

His fingers wrapped around my throat, but he didn't squeeze. Cole pressed his lips against my ear, his breathing calm and in control. "You should run from me, Shae. I'm not good for you. I'm a monster. I've already put you in danger, but I can't walk away. I'm obsessed with you. You're my poison, but I would gladly drink every last drop you had to offer."

Good God. Zoe was right. Cole has feelings for me. "Cole," I whispered. "Please ..." I closed my eyes, realizing this was all a bad idea and that I was mostly naked on the bed ... with my stepbrother, and all I wanted was to fuck him until I couldn't walk. "I need you inside me." My heart rate was erratic, and my palms were damp with sweat. I'd never needed anyone so much in my life.

"Make no mistake, Shae. When I come inside you, in that moment, I will mark you as mine. Are you ready for me to own you?"

Cole tightened his hold on my neck. Instead of being afraid of him, I craved him as I inhaled the narrow stream of air he allowed me to have.

Suddenly, he released me and ripped my G-string off. He moved down and pushed my legs wider apart. His hand smacked my pussy, and a cry escaped me. "I don't think you understand what it will be like if you're mine." He slapped me again. Pain shot through me, but I wanted more. I wanted him. His breath grazed my soaked core, and a shudder of pleasure rippled over me. Cole slipped his arms under my ass and pulled me to his mouth.

Bunching the comforter in my hands, I moaned as he sucked my clit, his tongue licking my slit before he pumped me with two fingers. My back arched, and I shook with anticipation, humming with need.

His ice-blue eyes glanced up, locking with mine.

"Cole." My chest heaved as desire licked every inch of my sensitive skin. My muscles tightened. He released a harsh growl, grabbed the backs of my thighs, and dug his nails into my flesh as a soul-obliterating orgasm pulsed through my body, and I touched the edge of heaven. Reveling in his touch, I savored every blissful second until I came down from my high. "Oh, my God." I peeled my eyelids open when I felt the mattress shift beneath me.

Cole's gaze darkened, and his snarl sent chills skating down my spine. He looked like the devil—a dark, murderous expression on his face—and terror pumped through my veins.

Without a word, Cole threw the door open and stalked out of the room, slamming it closed behind him. Shame reared its ugly head, and I swallowed the rejection like it was cheap alcohol—bitter and stinging all the way down.

Holy shit. What did I just do?

The bright morning sunlight woke me the following day. I stretched and peered at the clock on my phone. It was nearly ten.

I blinked a few times, reveling in the fact that I didn't have a class to attend for several weeks, then reality slapped me. *Cole.* I still wasn't sure how we'd ended up on my bed last night, but after he'd given me the best orgasm of my life, he left like a whirling dervish. The memory of his face tied my stomach into a million knots. I tossed my blankets off and sat on the edge of my mattress. I needed coffee, and a lot of it. I had to sort through what we'd done before I saw Cole.

Collecting a pair of shorts and a T-shirt, I brushed the tangles out of my hair, then collected my phone from the nightstand. I cautiously peered into the hall. To my relief, Cole's door was closed. I tiptoed down the hallway, then to the kitchen. Daddy and Julia were sitting at the little table in the breakfast nook.

"Morning." I waved and smiled at them. For the first time this summer, Daddy wore some navy shorts with a white polo that fit his well-defined shoulders and chest. Daddy was in great shape for his late forties.

"Good morning, Princess." Daddy stood and hugged me. He had no idea how much I needed his comforting embrace. He kissed me on the cheek. If I didn't know any better, I would have thought I wasn't in any trouble with him at all, but my black American Express card would say otherwise. At least it wasn't super tense between us. Maybe he would be able to forgive me soon.

"The pool will be ready this afternoon," Julia said, then tucked a dark strand of hair behind her ear as I made my way to the espresso machine. "It's going to be eighty-five today." She offered me a genuine smile. I was convinced that Julia never ate or drank anything that would stain her teeth, but I knew better. My guess was that she paid a lot of money for those pearly whites.

"Sounds like a good day to work on your tan." I grabbed a ceramic mug and placed it under the spout, then turned the machine on.

Disappointment flickered in her eyes. "I was thinking maybe we could get some sun together and catch up. I realize you've only been home for a week, but summer will be over before you know it and you'll be off to school."

My coffee finished brewing, and I sipped the hot liquid. "True. Cole will be gone again, too. It probably gets lonely without us here at times."

Julia's forehead creased.

"What is it?" My attention bounced from her to Daddy and back to Julia.

"You don't know?" Julia asked cautiously.

"Know what?" My fingers tightened around the cup as I anticipated bad news.

A wistful expression twisted Julia's features. "Cole left. He won't be back, Shae."

"I don't understand. He lives here." I massaged my temple, my defenses quickly building bricks around my aching heart.

"Shae, Cole packed last night. After he spent some time with Samuel and me early this morning, he moved out."

I physically flinched as though she'd struck me. The hurt of Cole's abandonment had carved out a hollow hole inside my chest. I could no longer fight the battle of emotions that ripped through me, shredding me into scraps of nothing. I thought things were changing between us after yesterday. My nostrils flared, angry at myself for being vulnerable. He'd used me, then stomped away without a word like a child throwing a temper tantrum. Zoe was wrong, I meant nothing to him, last night proved that. He'd also broken his promise to keep Daddy and Julia safe. I slammed my cup down in fury, coffee spilling over the edge. I knew where he lived. He might have left without saying goodbye, but no way in hell would I put up with his moodiness any longer. Mentally, I punched his face until he was black and blue.

I swallowed the lump of betrayal and lifted my chin. "At least I don't have to share the upstairs with him anymore."

"I'm sure you'll see him at school, Shae. It was a difficult decision for him," Daddy added. "He didn't make it lightly."

I stared at the floor as tears pricked my eyes. "Why did he leave?" Finally, I looked up at them.

"He didn't say, but he did mention that you're up to date on the circumstances. Honestly, I suspect the threats have something to do with it." Daddy rose from his seat and approached the espresso machine. "Regardless of what you think, Cole cares about you, Shae. He always has."

Confusion clouded my mind. Daddy had no idea what he was talking about. He and Julia had no clue what had happened behind closed doors just hours ago.

"He does," Julia said, joining me. She took my hand in hers. "Cole isn't good with his feelings, but I know my son. He's worried and scared. He's in new territory and needs space to make some big decisions."

I clenched my molars, fighting the swell of emotions threatening to overtake me. "What does any of that have to do with me?"

"Everything," Daddy wrapped his arm around my shoulders and pulled me to him.

"You're talking in code, Daddy."

"I'm trying not to betray Cole's confidence, but you're my daughter, and your happiness means the world to me."

I burst into tears, hiding my face in his chest and wrapping my arms around his waist. "I'm so sorry I messed up. I'm sorry I hurt people. I thought I'd lost you for good." If anything or anyone had the ability to break me, it was Daddy. He was my entire world.

"Princess," he kissed the top of my head before he continued, "just because I was disappointed with your choices doesn't mean I don't love you and want the best for you. Part of parenting is hoping I've done well enough that you want to make good decisions and are able to consider the repercussions."

"We've all made mistakes, Shae. Just because the consequences are in place doesn't mean we think any less of you. Samuel and I were actually impressed when you talked to him about it. You were honest and showed concern for Samuel and the business," Julia said.

When my crying slowed, Julia handed me a tissue from the box near the refrigerator. I released Daddy and wiped the moisture from my face. "Thanks for telling me about Cole. I just wish he would have told me himself."

"I suspect he'll be in touch, honey. Try to give him some time," Julia encouraged.

Frowning, I looked at her. "From the way both of you are talking, you know something." I looked up at Daddy. "About Cole and me." I gulped while my stomach churned, realizing I was taking a risk.

"We saw Cole change around you this last year, Shae. Samuel and I have talked about it. I've tried to ask Cole what's going on, but he refuses to admit anything. However, we have eyes in our head and we're not stupid. We know that Cole has feelings for you."

"Wh-what?" My cheeks burned with the revelation. Cole had

admitted as much last night, but the words coming from Julia were an entirely different game.

"Cole also knows that if he acts on those feelings, then he needs to be honest with you about what he's lived through," Julia explained.

Tension snaked between my shoulder blades, and I massaged my neck. I was well aware that we all had a past, but maybe Cole's had crippled him in some way. At least, that was what I was taking away from Julia's comment. "Daddy? Do you know what she's talking about?"

He rubbed his jaw, concern flickering in his gaze. "Yeah. Cole and I have had some long talks."

"About me?" I squeaked, embarrassed.

Daddy glanced at Julia, then back to me. Apparently, everyone in the family knew what the hell was going on ... except me. "You, his background, and the threats. He's a smart kid and he has some valuable people in his life. I trust he will make the right decisions."

I snorted. "Those valuable people are a criminal biker gang, Daddy."

Julia grinned. "Do you know how Cole got involved with them?"

"No. I've only met King, Snake, Taco and a few others yesterday."

Compassion filled Julia's expression. "Cole should have told you, Shae."

I rubbed at my chest, where my heart hurled itself against my ribs. The palpitations were full of fear and adrenaline. I had a bad feeling that there was no happy ending to this story.

"How did he get mixed up with the bikers?" My voice cracked, betraying my vulnerability.

Julia stared at the floor for a moment, then at me. The seconds ticked by as I waited for her to answer.

Chapter Fourteen

"Shae, King is my brother," Julia said.

I gaped at her, then slammed my jaw shut. "Holy shit, are you kidding me?" I slapped my palm over my mouth. Although Daddy and Julia knew I swore like a sailor, I tried to watch my language around them out of respect.

Daddy gently placed his warm palm against my back. "Why don't we sit down? I'll bring your coffee over, Princess."

I nodded, my brain scrambling to understand how Julia and Cole had ended up in our home with MC ties. Daddy obviously knew, which meant Julia had been honest with him. It was a good thing because she would have had to deal with me if she'd hurt Daddy.

Julia and I sat at the table, then Daddy joined us with our drinks.

"The MC has been in our lives for a while," Julia explained. "I had the opportunity to join that way of life, but it wasn't for me."

Daddy grabbed Julia's hand and squeezed it. "I'm glad she didn't."

He gave her a sweet smile, and for the first time, I pulled my head out of my ass and realized how perfect they were for each other. It had been difficult to see Daddy move on from Mom. I'd spent hours crying in my bedroom, angry with him for forgetting her. I couldn't see around my grief, and somewhere along the line, I'd made a promise that although I would tolerate Julia, I would never allow her to get close to me. Hell, I'd screwed myself over and had chosen agonizing loneliness when I could have had an amazing woman on my side. I had to change that and realize how lucky I was that Daddy had married a kind and caring person instead of a money whore and complete bitch.

"How long has King been with the MC?" Suddenly, I was eager to learn everything I could about Julia and Cole—even King.

"Since he was nineteen. For a while, I refused to have anything to do with him. I understood these men weren't law abiding citizens. But King and I lost our parents early, so the bikers filled a void in him. They're very loyal to each other. Most of the time, their bond is stronger than a biological family."

Daddy took a sip of his coffee before he spoke. "They also do some good. I certainly don't agree with their methods of making money, but King has treated Julia and Cole very well."

"Cole was really comfortable around them," I said. "More comfortable than I've ever seen him."

"When Cole was thirteen, King showed up and took him under his wing." Julia offered me a sad smile. Daddy rubbed her back as she spoke, but I wasn't listening to what she'd said. I was paying attention to what she hadn't said. Something awful had happened to her and Cole. Although I mentally pleaded with her to say more, I didn't expect her to share. Even under the circumstances, I understood that it was Cole's story to tell.

A phone buzzed, tugging my focus away from the situation. I glanced around and realized my cell was on the counter near the espresso machine.

I rose from my seat. "Sorry. I need to check the message."

"It's fine. I think we've shared as much as we can anyway." Daddy pursed his lips. He only did that if he was super stressed about something.

"I love you, Daddy." I kissed his forehead, then smiled at Julia. "Thank you for sharing what you were comfortable with. It means a lot to me."

"I hope it helped, Shae," Julia said.

Curiosity pulled me over to my phone. I tapped the screen, hoping to see Cole's name. Even if he was rude, it would be better than complete silence, especially after last night.

My eyes popped open wide as I stared at a text from Ibrahim.

I need to see you.

Replying quickly, I typed out my response. *I don't think it's a good idea, but are you okay? Are you in the hospital?*

His reply was almost immediate.

The doctor needs to operate on my eye. I need money. If you don't help, I'll report Cole to the cops. I told them it happened so fast I didn't see who beat me.

As pissed as I was at Cole, I didn't want him to get arrested. I assumed there were plenty of people who'd witnessed what happened, but no one had talked to Cole about it yet. I had to fix this. It was my fault Ibrahim had been fired in the first place. It was only fair to help him with the bill.

I peeked over my shoulder at Daddy and Julia, but they were talking quietly. They didn't need to know I was going to help Ibrahim.

A frown creased my forehead as my fingers flew across the keyboard. *When and where?*

Meet me where I used to park the limo on our afternoons.

I shoved my cell into the back pocket of my shorts, then turned to Daddy and Julia. "Do you two care if I go to Zoe's for a while?"

Daddy cleared his throat and glanced at his watch. "Go straight there, Shae. If anyone looks suspicious, you call me immediately. I was going to ask that you stay here until our new bodyguard arrives today, but if it's only Zoe's house, I think you'll be fine."

Normally, I wouldn't ask when I needed to be back, but I suspected Daddy would want me to meet the new security. I wondered if I had to take them everywhere I went. Ugh. That would suck. "What time will he be here?"

"Around six. You don't have to be here when he arrives. I can introduce you after you're home. But seriously, Shae. Don't go anywhere else other than Zoe's." Daddy lifted his brow, and his tone was stern. He was serious.

Shit. Daddy would kill me if he knew I was going to talk to Ibrahim, then go to Zoe's. I would text her on my way to meet Ibrahim so she could cover for me. I would fill her in when I arrived at her house. I had to make sure Ibrahim was all right, and Cole hadn't caused permanent damage. Anger pulsed through me as I recalled Ibrahim, balled up on the sidewalk, covered in blood. Cole had taken it too far.

"Thanks. I'll see you guys later." I gave them a little wave before I hightailed it to my bedroom. Pausing before I entered, I spun around on my heel and walked across the hall to Cole's room. I placed my hand on the doorknob and turned it, then swung the door open. The hard truth smacked me in the face. I understood that Julia said he'd moved out, but seeing the bare space made it real. He'd removed the books off the shelves, the television, and his dresser drawers were open, revealing that they were empty.

Cole preferred his door closed, but I refused to shut it. Regardless of what Julia and Daddy had shared with me today, Cole had left without saying goodbye. He'd made his decision about me already. My chest tightened, and I placed my palm against it, the fragile beat of my heart reminding me that even though his actions had hurt me, I would move on. I hoped.

Backing out of his room, I focused on Ibrahim. Maybe this was a chance to make things right with him once and for all. I'd caused him nothing but pain and trouble.

After I texted Zoe that I was meeting Ibrahim, then I would meet her at her place, I grabbed my purse off the floor next to my bed. Dropping my phone into the front pocket, I double-checked that I had my emergency cash and driver's license before heading out.

Our meeting spot was only five minutes away from my house. That in itself had been a stupid choice, but Ibrahim had to be available at a moment's notice for Julia or Daddy. If I was honest about it, we also liked the danger of getting caught. I barked out a laugh as I pulled out of the driveway. I'd been so dumb. All I needed was to make things right, then sneaking off would be over.

I parked behind a black limo that I didn't recognize, picked up my handbag, and climbed out of my BMW. The bright summer sun warmed my skin as I approached the car. I assumed it belonged to the new family Ibrahim was working for. Ibrahim waited for me, then motioned for me to climb into the back. I slid in, set my bag next to me, then he joined me and closed the door. I glanced around, noting the privacy glass was raised and the space was spotless. The scent of the leather cleaner tickled my nose, and I ran my fingers along the soft seat.

A cry escaped me as I noted Ibrahim's black and purple eye and busted lower lip. For once, he wore jeans and a blue polo shirt instead of his typical suit and tie.

He flashed me a weary smile. "It's not as bad as it looks."

"Ibrahim, I'm so sorry." I moved to the seat next to him. "I had no idea Cole was even around."

"I know you didn't. I was more concerned about you." His dark eyes softened as they landed on me. "When he forced you to go with him, I was worried you were in danger."

"No. Cole was just being ... Cole." I sighed and placed my hand on top of his. "I'm glad you didn't have to stay in the hospital, and I'll pay for the surgery, but leave Cole out of this. I feel horrible about everything."

"I gave you my word that if you took care of the cost, I would keep my mouth shut. Honestly, I needed to see that you were all right. I don't trust Cole, Shae."

"He's more bark than bite." I fiddled with the hem of my T-shirt, knowing full well I was lying my ass off. Cole was capable of so much, and I had a feeling I had only experienced the tip of the iceberg.

The sound of the doors locking caught my attention. *Shit.* Ibrahim was hoping we would play around, but I didn't want to. Not only could I not let Daddy down, but this time, I didn't want to let myself down, either.

"Ibrahim, I don't think sleeping together is a good idea anymore. This should be goodbye. I can't risk you getting hurt again."

The limo lurched forward and began to move. An unsettling feeling curled into a tight ball in my stomach as I tried to understand what was happening.

"Ibrahim? Who is driving?"

"A friend." His low chuckle filled the car as he reached behind him, revealing a pistol.

I scrambled backward, dazed and confused. "What are you doing?"

He grabbed my arm, jerking me to him. "Be still." Ibrahim trained the gun on me, his finger on the trigger. I wasn't sure if the safety was on or off.

Trembling, I did as he asked, and before I realized it, his heavy hand slapped my face. Hard.

"You stupid little bitch." He sneered as he hit me again, knocking me senseless as I collapsed in the seat. "Not once did you ever realize what was going on around you. All you cared about was what you wanted. When you got caught, then I was important to you, but only then."

"Ibrahim, I'm so sorry. I never meant for any of this to happen."

He jerked on my shorts, and I scrambled to fight him.

"Ibrahim, stop!" I cried. "No! Get off me." I slapped and kicked him, trying to resist, but he was too strong. The click of the gun stilled me.

Ibrahim placed the pistol against my temple. "Scream or cry for help, and I won't hesitate to pull the trigger. Are we clear?" Laughing, he pinned me against the seat and tugged my G-string down.

With his free hand, he freed his dick, then wedged his body between my legs and slammed into me. He grunted as he fucked me, but the gun never moved away from my temple.

"Please stop, Ibrahim. You're better than raping someone."

"What did I tell you?" He said, jabbing the weapon into my chin. "Not a sound."

Tears of distress slid down my cheeks as he thrust into me, then pulled out and repositioned himself. A scream tore from my throat as he shoved his cock into my ass. Unbearable pain ripped through me as he continued. Black dots danced before my vision, and a part of me hoped I would pass out.

"Have you ever been fucked with the barrel of a gun, Princess?"

I whimpered, afraid of what he was implying. The weapon left my forehead, then he sat up, an evil grin easing across his face. The cold metal pushed against my entrance, and I trembled so hard I thought I would throw up as he assaulted me with the pistol. Horror twisted my insides as I realized he had his finger on the trigger. Too terrified to move, I slammed my eyes closed and silently pleaded with him to stop and the pain to end.

"I don't want you to ever forget me, Shae. After all, I was your first. Your first fuck, your first teacher, and now your worst nightmare."

Once he was finished using me, he raised the butt of the gun and smacked me on the side of my head. Stars appeared all around me, then I slipped away into darkness.

Sharp pains shot through my body. My ass and core hurt almost as bad as my throbbing skull. I peeled my eyelids open and blinked several times against the bright light. Trying to move my arms, I finally understood that they were tied behind my back. My heart jackhammered against my chest as I realized I was gagged and in a chair.

"Did you have a nice nap?" Ibrahim asked. He took a drink from his bottled water, then crossed an ankle over one knee, not betraying a single hint of emotion.

I glared at him as I tried to take in the details of the room—dark and musty. The dirty cement floor was cracked, and I wondered if we were in a basement somewhere.

Oh, God. Daddy thought I was with Zoe. He wouldn't know anything was wrong until I didn't show up at home later. *Shit. How could I have been so fucking stupid?*

"I'll give you a minute to recover your senses, then I'll give you a drink. I'm supposed to keep you alive for a while longer." His gaze narrowed on me. "You fucked with the wrong people, Shae. I almost felt bad for you for a second." He raised his hand, holding his thumb and first finger apart by a centimeter. "Almost."

Ibrahim shifted on his seat and blew out a sigh. "While we're waiting for my friends ..." He grabbed his crotch and laughed. "For such a rich spoiled bitch, your ass and pussy sure are good. I'll give you that."

I shook my head, terrified he was about to rape me again. Struggling against the gag, I grimaced.

"I guess I could let you talk for a bit. I'm assuming you have a few questions. I'll answer them. I have nothing to lose anymore. You already took care of that." Ibrahim stood, then crossed the room and jerked the gag from my mouth. "Drink." He placed the plastic bottle against my lips and tipped it up. Water ran down my neck, but I managed to swallow a little as well.

"Thank you." My voice was scratchy, and my throat was raw from the tears and screams in the limo.

Ibrahim sat down again, set the bottle on the floor, and stared at me with cold, emotionless eyes.

"Why are you doing this?"

"At first it wasn't about you, Shae. Then, after the video went live, I lost everything, and it became personal."

"I don't understand. You said you were working for a good family, and that you were okay." I tugged against the restraints around my wrists, but they were so tight I didn't have any wiggle room.

"Don't be stupid, Shae. It wasn't even close to all right. No one would speak to me, much less hire me. Even though you're almost nineteen, I had still fucked a sixteen-year-old girl. What makes you think any parent in their sane mind would want me around their children?" He paused briefly, then continued.

"Fortunately for me, about three months ago, a man approached me and offered me cash to spy on your family and report anything and everything to him. He handed me a very thick envelope filled with hundreds. I've worked for him ever since." Ibrahim shrugged nonchalantly. "Who was I to refuse that kind of offer? After a few weeks, I met with him again, and he shared a little more, then a little more, until I had a good understanding of what he was after. Your stepbrother pissed someone off pretty fucking bad. It wasn't planned this way at first, but you ended up bait to get to Cole."

"Cole doesn't give a shit about me Ibrahim. He doesn't even know I left the house today." I locked eyes with him, imploring. "He moved out last night. He didn't even bother saying goodbye. I had no fucking clue until this morning when his mom told me. So, whoever you're working for is wrong. Cole couldn't care less about me."

Ibrahim bolted upright in his seat. "You're lying in hopes I'll let you go."

"I'm not." From the corner of my eye, I caught sight of my purse on the floor behind his chair. My only chance was to overpower Ibrahim and grab my phone or ... holy crap. Zoe, Dani, Sibyl, Isabel, and I had loaded the life360 app on our phones, so we could track each other's whereabouts if there were ever an emergency. It would only be a matter of time before someone found me.

As soon as the thought had formed, dread replaced it. The only way they would find me is if there were any internet. From the looks of it, I was in the basement of an old house. I doubted I had a signal. My hope dwindled into almost nothing. If I wanted to live, I had to figure out a plan, and fast. If Cole was gone and Ibrahim's boss couldn't get to him, then they wouldn't have any use for me. I was disposable.

A thin ray of light peeked through the crack around a door that led outside. It was apparently still daylight outside. Somehow, I had to figure out how to get the fuck out of here in one piece. I only had seconds to hurt Ibrahim before he shot me.

Tilting my head to the side, I stretched my neck, releasing a kink in my muscles. I needed a clear my mind in order to think this through. It would only take one mistake before I died.

Ibrahim paced the room with his hands behind his back, clearly stressed. Cole had really fucked up this time, and even though I didn't know who Ibrahim's boss was, if I could get out of here, I could at least turn Ibrahim in.

I stretched my legs in front of me, finally realizing they weren't tied to the chair like my wrists were. I flexed and pointed my toes, hoping to encourage more blood flow.

Ibrahim turned to me. "I'll wait for my boss to decide, but I think your luck just ran out today, Shae." He smirked, then approached me and began to undo his pants. Bile churned in my gut, then swam up to my throat. Ibrahim pulled his dick out and laughed. "One more for old times' sake, shall we?"

A loud crack sounded, and I jumped as the door flung open. *Oh, shit. My time was officially up. I was about to die.* I mentally sent my love to Daddy, Julia, and my friends, but Cole could rot in hell. My pulse pounded in my ears as I held my breath and waited for Ibrahim's boss to stroll into the room.

Chapter Fifteen

I flinched and screamed as flashes of light and loud pops echoed through the room. The next several seconds played out in slow motion. Ibrahim jumped away from me, but before he could dive for his gun on the floor, he flew through the air, his head exploding. Blood and brain matter splattered all over me, and I shrieked on repeat until my stomach revolted. Vomit shot out of my mouth, landing noisily at my feet. Muffled voices filled the area, and I looked up, trying to understand the events that had just changed my life.

Bleary-eyed, I struggled to hear what everyone was saying. The shots had been so loud my ears were ringing. Strong hands cupped my face while another set tugged on the ropes that bound me to the chair.

Masculine arms scooped me out of the seat and carried me to the door bridal style. Several men stared at me as we passed them. My head lolled to the side, and my arm hung down, swinging with every step the person took. The noise blocking my hearing began to settle down, and familiar voices started to break through the fog in my brain. I was placed on the bed of a truck, the black liner warming the back of my legs. Glancing around, I focused on the abundance of trees, then on an old beat-up house. From what I could tell, I was in the middle of nowhere.

"Shae! Shae! Goddammit, what did he do to you?"

A mixture of confusion and relief flooded me as my vision blurred in and out, pinpointing the man in front of me. "Cole?" I wasn't sure I'd spoken his name, nor was I convinced that I wasn't hallucinating. At this point, anything was possible.

"Shae," Cole gently squeezed my shoulders, helping me focus on his blue eyes and blonde hair. "Baby, talk to me."

I'd never seen Cole Parker scared about anything in the four years I'd known him. But at this moment, fear twisted his handsome features as he looked at me, his chest heaving.

"She might not be able to hear you very well, man." King gripped Cole's shoulder. "The shots were loud in there."

Cole glanced up at his uncle, refusing to let me go. "Let's get her home."

"Daddy," I finally managed to whisper.

"Baby, can you understand me? It's Cole."

I nodded, placing my hand on his. "You came back." Tears of gratitude slipped down my cheeks. I'd never been happier in my life to see him.

"I shouldn't have ever fucking left you. Let's get out of here. After I help you clean up, I'll call Samuel. He doesn't know that Ibrahim kidnapped you." Cole lifted me off the truck bed and carried me to the front seat. He gently set me down and buckled me in. When he started to shut the door, my arm shot out, visibly trembling. "Don't leave me." My chin wobbled.

Cole rubbed the back of his neck, perplexed. "I'm not going anywhere. I just need to drive, Shae."

Words failed me as I shook my head, my body shaking so hard I was worried I would be sick again.

"Hey, it's okay." Cole unbuckled my seatbelt and helped me out of the vehicle. "Take a few deep breaths. I'm right here. I'll have one of the guys drive so I can hold you. Would that be better?" He smoothed my hair. "Shae, Ibrahim is dead. I had a wide-open shot, and I took that fucker out. He can't ever hurt you again."

I stared at him, the brain splatter still on my skin and clothes. Cole also had remnants of Ibrahim on his shirt and arms from carrying me. Apparently, blood and brains didn't bother him much. Maybe that should upset me, but I couldn't have cared less. If it weren't for Cole, I would most likely be the dead one.

Realizing that I needed to tell Cole some important information, I swallowed, my throat raw from screaming. "He has a boss. Ibrahim was hired to spy on our family and eventually get to you. I don't know any more, though. We're not out of danger, Cole. Daddy and Julia need to know right now. I'm not sure the bodyguard is there yet." How I was able to relay all of that to him, I wasn't sure, but I was scared shitless that if Ibrahim got to me, Daddy and Julia might be next. Whoever was after Cole was using the people he loved to break him. Somehow, I had to be stronger than his enemy.

"Taco!" Cole yelled.

I jumped and scrambled backward, stumbling over a rock that jutted up from the ground. Cole grabbed my arm and stabilized me before I landed on my ass.

"Shit, Shae. I didn't mean to scare you. Are you all right?" He waved at Taco with his free hand.

I squeezed his fingers. "It's okay. I know you didn't."

"Yeah, Cole?" Taco eyed me, then he ground his molars together, anger evident in his gaze.

"Tell King to call my mom and make sure the bodyguard is there. Whoever is fucking with me is going after my family."

Taco patted Cole on the back. "Anything you need, man."

"I need someone to get us out of here, too. Shae needs me close, and I can't help her while I'm driving."

"I got you. Let me talk to King first. We'll need to hide my bike somewhere safe, then I'll get it later."

Cole nodded, then focused on me again. "Samuel and Mom will be all right, Shae."

The next several minutes were a flurry of activity as the men took care of business. Once Taco joined us, Cole loaded me back into the truck, but this time I sat between both men. Cole held my hand even though I was covered in death.

All I could think about was a hot shower. I would be able to scrub the filth off my skin, but I wasn't sure I would ever feel clean again. Rape wasn't the kind of dirty that washed down the drain. It was the kind that buried its claws into my fractured soul.

A few hours later, Cole helped me to the master bathroom of his house. The bikers were on high alert and pissed as hell that Ibrahim had kidnapped me. Some of them offered to keep an eye on the situation and had remained outside, keeping watch. King had talked to Julia and updated her and Daddy. I knew I would have to speak to them soon, but I had to clean up first.

I watched as Cole turned on the shower, his blue eyes weary as he looked at me. "Shae?" He tipped my chin up, bringing my attention to him. "I need to know what happened."

I jerked away from his touch. "It doesn't matter anymore. You killed him."

He placed a gentle hand on my shoulder. "It does matter. Tell me."

I barked out a laugh. "You *need* to know?" Tugging on my blood-splattered T-shirt, I pulled it over my head and tossed it in the trash. My bra and shorts were next. I wasn't sure what had happened to my G-string, but I wasn't wearing it anymore. It wouldn't have made a difference. Ibrahim's come would have ruined my underwear. I stood in front of Cole, naked. "What do you see?" My voice hitched, and my throat grew tight. Deep inside myself, I realized that Cole wouldn't see me the same as before Ibrahim had assaulted me.

"The beautiful woman that I would do anything for," he whispered, keeping eye contact.

"I'm going to give you an opportunity to retract your statement, Cole." I tore my gaze away, tears streaming down my cheeks. "He raped me." I dared a glance at him, expecting to see pity on his face. "He fucked my pussy, then my ass, then ..." I choked on the brutality of my words. "He fucked me with the barrel of the gun while he had his finger on the trigger, Cole." My shoulders shook from my sobs, but I refused to turn away.

I braced myself for his cruel words. Cole had never held his tongue, so why would he now? But also, I had to know once and for all. I needed Cole to tell me that he wasn't interested in my weak, abused, and discarded shell because I was no longer the girl he used to know. I wasn't sure his rejection could make my bruised and broken heart any worse, but once he confirmed what I suspected I could at least walk away from him for good after today.

Cole's fist shot forward, busting a hole in the wall. "It's a good thing I killed that fucker, or I'd go after him right now." He scrubbed his face with his palms, then he placed his hands on his hips and looked at the floor. When he looked at me again, tears welled in his eyes. "I'll say it again and again. I see the beautiful woman that I would do anything for. I was a fucking idiot for leaving. I'll make it up to you somehow, Shae. Just give me another chance to set it right."

I wasn't sure I was hearing him correctly. "You can't save me, so stop staring at me like you can." I moved around him, opened the glass door of the shower, and stepped under the hot spray. I was sick and tired of wearing Ibrahim. His blood was caked on my arms, making me itch. I started to scrub my skin when Cole strode in behind me and closed the door. Naked. I gulped as I looked over every hard plane of his chest, biceps, abs, his prominent V, and toned legs. His long cock was soft, which told me where his mood was. He wasn't trying to fuck me. For a moment, I was trapped in the twisted knots of his stare, unable to speak.

"Let me help. You have blood and white chunks in your hair."

Briefly, Cole seemed awkward and vulnerable concerning the situation, then the mask of anger I knew too well slipped into place.

"I can't have sex with you, Cole. As much as I want to ..."

A flicker of surprise flashed in his eyes. "I would never ask. That's not why I'm in the shower with you, Shae. Honestly, I was afraid you might freak out, and I can't leave you alone. If anything else happens ... I have to protect you. One of my pistols is on the bathroom counter, so don't flip your shit when you see it."

I nodded. "Can you teach me to use one?" I was surprised to hear myself ask that question when Ibrahim had just raped me with the barrel of a gun. But if I'd carried, I might have had a chance to defend myself and stop Ibrahim before he hurt me.

"Yeah. King taught me, so when you're ready I'll have him help, too."

"Okay." I returned to washing my arms and face, then rinsed the soap from my skin.

Cole grabbed the bottle of shampoo and squeezed the yellow liquid into his palm. I made sure my hair was completely wet, then turned my back to him. His fingers gently worked through my long strands as he picked chunks of white matter out and dropped them onto the tan tiled floor.

Afraid that I would break down again, I realized I needed to talk. "Why did you leave last night without saying goodbye?" I placed my palm against the wall for balance as he continued.

"I ... I was a coward. At the same time, I was trying to protect you."

My eyes widened, and I never, ever in a million years expected Cole to admit anything even close to being scared.

"After being with you, I couldn't deny my feelings any longer. It fucked with my head. You're my stepsister, and for a while I was able to lie to myself about how I felt. Then the video happened. I was so furious when I saw you with Ibrahim and Matt, I thought I was going to lose my fucking mind. I hated them both, but I hated you for not understanding that ... I've ... it doesn't matter. You're here now." He ran his hands under the hot spray, rinsing them. "I think I got it all. You can rinse your hair."

"Cole," I whispered. "Thank you. Thank you for finding me and ..." I swallowed, sifting through what I was attempting to say. "And for telling me." I turned, allowing the water to run over me, washing the last of the physical evidence away. I suspected shock was written all over my face. My heart thumped erratically, beating against my rib cage.

Cole glanced at me, then stepped out of the shower. "Sure. I'll be here until you finish."

"Okay." Even though he was still in the bathroom, I was grateful for a few minutes to myself. I gently washed every crevice of my body. Normally women would have a rape kit and exam, but Ibrahim was dead. It wasn't like the police could charge him with a crime. *Cole had killed him. For me.*

"Cole?"

"Yeah?"

"How did you know where I was?" I turned the handle, shutting the shower off. Opening the door, I stepped onto the cushy grey floor mat.

Cole had already dressed in a basic black T-shirt and dark wash jeans. He gave me a towel. I dried my hair, then he passed me another one for my body. I soaked up the droplets of water, then wrapped the soft material around me. "I don't have any clothes."

"I'll give you one of my shirts. Not sure what to do about some pants, though." Cole rubbed his chin.

"I can wear some of your boxer briefs. They're probably soft and will at least cover me."

Cole grinned like an idiot. "I might like that idea."

I smiled, suddenly shy in front of him.

"To answer your question, it was Zoe. She said she couldn't reach you and that you were meeting Ibrahim. Zoe used some app to track you before you dropped off the grid. It was enough for us to get close and search the area. Hell, I wasn't even a hundred percent sure you were in the house, but the guys and I heard voices, so I had to take the chance."

My mouth gaped. "What? Did you know he was a piece of shit when you saw the video?" My legs trembled as images of Ibrahim raping me took front and center in my brain.

Cole's cheeks paled. "I wasn't sure. We were looking into any and all possibilities. At the time, other than the two of you ..." He ran his fingers through his hair, clearly uncomfortable. "There weren't any red flags. He did a good job at covering his tracks."

Anger replaced my fear and rolled to a full-on boil inside me. I gripped the edge of the counter so I wouldn't lose my shit. One second, I was terrified and the next ready to hurt someone. Stability wasn't on my radar at the moment. "I was in danger, and you never told me?"

"No. I wasn't sure, Shae. I didn't want to scare you. Think about it, if I'd warned you away from Ibrahim would you have listened?"

"Shit." I rubbed my face with my hands, regretting the day I'd ever met that fucker. "You have a point." I stared at the floor, desperately needing to change the conversation. "Can I get dressed?"

"Yeah. Come on." He led us into the same bedroom he'd handcuffed me in. I sat on the edge of the bed, my temple and body still pounding and throbbing from the abuse. "Do you have any Advil?"

Cole knelt in front of me, his blue eyes finding mine. "If you're up for it, I'll feed you and grab you some pain reliever. You've got a nasty bruise and lump close to your eye. Shae, you need to be checked out. You might have a concussion."

I shook my head, then winced. "No. I can't have anyone touch me other than you, Cole. Please." My lip trembled as sorrow sucked me in like a whirlpool in the middle of the ocean.

Cole stood, then opened his dresser drawers and removed some clothes for me. "The MC has a doctor on call. She's good and it's all confidential. If you want, we can reach out to her, and she'll come here." Cole's face was full of compassion and understanding. "I need to know that you're okay."

"I'll never be okay again." I looked out the window, the green tree leaves moving in the summer breeze.

"Shae, I'll make sure you're all right." Cole gave me a pair of his boxer briefs.

"I don't want Daddy to know I was raped. I'm too ashamed, so if your doctor will keep that secret and you'll stay, I'll let her examine me."

"There's nothing for you to be ashamed about, Shae. Ibrahim was fucking unhinged. Let's get you fed, and I'll have King make the call." Cole placed a kiss on the side of my head. "Meet me in the kitchen when you're ready."

I watched him stroll out of the room, his shoulders were squared and stiff with tension. Whoever was fucking with him would be lucky if they walked away from the shit show they'd started. Oddly enough, I felt safer with Cole and the MC. Protected. But I sure as hell wouldn't ignore their warnings anymore. Even though Ibrahim was dead, I knew the danger wasn't over. Not for me, and not for Cole.

Chapter Sixteen

All eyes were on me as I walked into the kitchen. King patted the barstool beside him, and I slid onto the brown leather seat. Snake, Taco, and a few other bikers were watching television in the living room. At least I thought they were, since the TV was on.

"Hungry, kiddo?" His concerned gaze searched me, and I assumed he was assessing where I was at mentally and emotionally after the assault and kidnapping.

"She's eating," Cole stated, then placed a plate in front of me with a peanut butter and jelly sandwich, apple wedges, and a glass of milk. Four Advil were on a napkin next to my drink.

I couldn't help but smile, feeling touched by the sweet gesture. "You remembered."

When Julia and Cole moved in with us, I would grab an apple or peanut butter and jelly sandwich for dinner if Daddy wasn't home. As hard as Julia tried, I refused to eat what she'd cooked or sit at the table with them. Finally, Daddy put his foot down and demanded that I join the family. To him, it was simple. If I protested, I didn't eat. Cole had given me shit about it until I explained that my mom made that same meal the evening before she died. He must have realized it was soothing for me because he left me alone about it. The pit of my stomach twisted into painful knots. I wished Mom were here. If anyone could make me feel better, it would have been her. Mom would immediately have slipped socks on my feet. To her, socks made everything okay.

Cole brushed off his hands as if he'd just cooked me a gourmet meal. "I remember a lot of things." His attention traveled over his orange and black Harley Davidson T-shirt that hung off my petite frame. If it hadn't been for comfort, I wouldn't have needed any underwear because the shirt reached my knees.

"Samuel and Julia will be here later with some clothes for you. You're staying here with me." Cole folded his arms over his chest, his expression daring me to challenge him. "Also, Zoe knows you're here and safe. I told her you were shaken up, but that you were all right. I wasn't sure what to say to her. I figured you would tell her when you were ready."

Even though I'd lived through a major trauma only hours ago, Cole shouldn't be making decisions without me, and my temper flared.

"Don't you think we should have talked about this before you decided what was best for me? It's my choice where I live."

King and a few of the other guys snickered. I reached for my milk and took a sip of the creamy goodness, willing myself not to pick a fight with Cole.

"Eat." Cole pointed at my untouched sandwich.

"Cole, I'm not a child. Stop treating me like one." I kept my voice down. I wasn't trying to embarrass him, but he needed to knock it off. I'd been assaulted. I wasn't brain dead.

Cole turned his back to me, and I hopped out of my seat and joined him at the kitchen counter. "Hey, I'm speaking to you." I grabbed his arm. After what I'd just lived through, I should be jumpy around people, but I wasn't. At least not with Cole and King.

With a few quick steps, Cole backed me against the refrigerator, his gaze full of fire. He placed his palms on the sides of my head, boxing me in. "I'm well aware that you're not a child, but you belong to me now, and I will be involved in the decisions that keep you safe."

My chin tilted up in defiance, and amusement flickered across his features. Then, I realized what he'd said. "I belong to you?" I asked, butterflies fluttering in my stomach with the question.

He gently pulled me to him, holding me against his hard body. I wrapped my arms around his waist, allowing myself to accept that at some point, Cole had decided to stop seeing me as his stepsister. As much as I'd been trying to deny my feelings for him lately, it was a relief to no longer lie to myself.

"That's what I said. You're mine. Get used to it." He kissed the top of my head, then released me. "Now, please go eat. The doctor will arrive in thirty."

I gave him a shy smile. "Okay." My cheeks burned red as I sat back down, realizing we'd given his friends a show. At least Cole hadn't banged on his chest, howled, and slapped me on the ass. As much as I liked that I belonged to him, he also needed to understand that he belonged to me, too. It was a partnership. I didn't care who he'd killed for my benefit. I would never fully submit to him.

After taking a few bites of my sandwich, I toyed with an apple slice. "Thanks for calling Julia," I said to King, who was polishing off a beer.

He swept his bangs out of his eyes and nodded. "I told her you'd had a hell of an afternoon, but you're strong and doing pretty good under the circumstances. I didn't say a word about the ... uh ... that you had some fucker's brains all over you. Thought I would leave out those details. You can tell her what you want." He gave me a sheepish smile. "Cole's a hell of a shot, though." Pride flickered in his gaze as he glanced at Cole.

"I'll tell Julia and Daddy only what they need to know." I peeked at Cole from the corner of my eye. Hopefully, he would keep his mouth shut about the rape. That was for his ears only, and I wasn't even sure why I'd told him, except that I'd still been in shock.

The doorbell rang, and I nearly jumped off the barstool.

"I got it." Cole walked with purpose to the door, peeked through the wooden blind on the window, then answered it. "Hey, doc. Thanks for coming."

"Hey, Cole. It's good to see you."

I cautiously analyzed the woman. She appeared to be in her early thirties and her brown hair grazed her shoulders. Her light green eyes sparkled as she greeted him. She was pretty and seemed comfortable with my stepbrother ... boyfriend? What the hell was he?

"King." The doc kissed him on the cheek, then extended her hand to me. "I'm Natalie. You must be Shae. I've heard a lot about you. All good, of course." She gave me a warm smile, and I shook her hand. Natalie gripped the strap of her brown leather bag, which looked more like a satchel than a purse.

"We can use my room," Cole said as he took my arm and helped me off the barstool.

King ran his fingers through his hair as he shot Cole a concerned look. Regardless of what King suspected had happened to me, I wouldn't ever confirm it. I didn't need everyone in the club to know my business. Plus, it would be weird as hell if they all tried to take care of me. One bossy badass was enough. I wanted people to act as normal as possible around me.

Cole closed his bedroom door behind us, flipped on the overhead light, then leaned against his dresser. I sat on the edge of his bed, hating what was about to happen.

"King didn't give me a lot of detail, Shae, only that a young lady needed my help." Her tone was gentle and kind.

I tucked my hair behind my ear and took a deep breath. "I was kidnapped. Cole is concerned that I might have a concussion." I turned so she could see the big lump and bruise. When she'd first arrived, she'd been on the wrong side of me to notice it.

Natalie reached into her bag and pulled out a baggie with a few pairs of medical gloves inside. She slipped them on, then grabbed a penlight from the front pocket of her shorts. "I'm going to be really gentle, but I need to touch your wound."

"Okay." I winced as she pressed against the swollen area.

After she shined the light in my eyes, and I was able to follow her finger, she turned the flashlight off. "It's hard to know if you have a concussion, but your pupils seem to be slightly dilated so you shouldn't sleep for the rest of the day. Can someone wake you every few hours tonight?"

"I will," Cole said without hesitation. "She'll be with me."

The corner of Natalie's mouth twitched, and a slight grin briefly appeared. "Cole is a great nurse."

Cole cleared his throat and looked away, a hint of pink dusting his cheeks. Wait. Had Cole and Natalie had a thing? A sudden dislike for her sucker punched me in the gut.

"Were you hurt anywhere else?" Natalie stepped back in order not to crowd me. I didn't like the thought of her and Cole being ... whatever they'd been, but I was relieved she was a woman.

"I was raped," I whispered, refusing to look at Cole. Those words sat in my stomach like sour milk, then shame crashed over me like a tidal wave. My head hung down, my hair masking the tears streaming down my face. If I'd only stayed away from Ibrahim, none of this would have happened.

Natalie knelt at my feet and took my hand. "Shae, I'm so sorry. What can you tell me? Did you know him?"

"The fucker is dead," Cole said, his words clipped and dripping with hate.

"Good," Natalie said.

Frowning, I wiped my cheeks while giving her a wide-eyed stare. Didn't doctors think that every person deserved treatment no matter what horrible things they'd done?

"I knew him. I'd had sex with him before, but he'd never forced himself on me. He ..." I couldn't speak over the lump in my throat. A bubble of self-loathing burst open, and a sharp ache pierced my chest. Daddy had told me to go straight to Zoe's. If I'd listened to him, none of this would have happened. I slammed my eyes closed, recalling Ibrahim's deceptive text message. The cycle of anger, fear, and questioning my instincts kicked into gear all over again.

Natalie stood. "Cole, can you give us a few minutes?"

I peeked at him and nodded.

"I'll be on the other side of the door." He left quietly, allowing us some privacy.

Natalie sat down, facing me. "I was raped a few years ago ... more than once. Cole and Taco found me in an alley, bloody and beaten. I would have died if they hadn't taken me to the emergency room. What was worse was all the questions and the exam. The humiliation just kept coming."

"I understand that I need to be tested for any diseases," I muttered. "But at least he can't hurt me or anyone else again."

Natalie squeezed my hand. "I hope you can heal sooner knowing that justice was served."

"That's an odd thing for a doctor to say." I suddenly viewed her in a new light. Maybe I could like her after all. She seemed strong and resilient. Natalie didn't have a hard time stating her views, either.

"My job is to treat the patients that are put in front of me. No one said I couldn't have an opinion about it." She grinned, then her expression grew serious. "Are you okay if we do a quick exam?"

I swallowed while the memory of the gun jabbed inside me gripped me with a paralyzing fear. "He raped me ... he ... he raped me in the ass after he fucked me ... then." A soft wail escaped me. "He shoved a gun into me and used it while he had his finger on the trigger." I gritted my teeth and hissed, "I'm glad that son of a bitch is dead."

To my surprise, Natalie hugged me. "I want you to understand that most victims know their rapists. In no way did you do anything wrong. This wasn't your fault. No one should ever be hurt like this."

I clung to her as the sobs flowed freely. I wasn't sure if it was because she'd lived through an assault or because she genuinely understood the magnitude and wide array of emotions coursing through me—humiliation, blame, anger, and fear that someday a guy would hurt me again.

After a few minutes, I pulled away and wiped the moisture from my skin. "Let's get this over with."

Natalie riffled through her bag and produced a kit. "King didn't tell me you'd been raped, but when he said you were female, I figured I should bring this with me just in case."

"King doesn't know, but I think he suspects. When Cole and the guys broke through the door I was tied to a chair in a basement. It doesn't take much to assume I'd been hurt. Cole is the only one that knows for sure though ... and you."

Natalie's features softened. "He's a good guy. I'm glad you have him."

Natalie continued to chat as I ditched Cole's underwear and prepared for the exam. I figured since she was face-to-face with my lady bits, no questions were off-limits. "Did you and Cole ever date?"

"Date or sleep together?"

A bitter laugh escaped me, then I flinched from her touch on my bruised and battered core. Gripping the comforter between my fingers, pain radiated over my body, stealing my breath.

Silent tears slipped down my cheeks. Finally, I answered between clenched teeth. "Either."

Natalie finished the tests and offered her hand to help me sit up. "I know you're sore, and there is some vaginal and anal tearing, which is to be expected. I have some Proctofoam that will stop the bleeding. Physically, you'll feel better in a few days. If you ever need to talk, I'm always happy to get together for a drink. It helps when someone else has been through it and has resumed a normal life. Everything you share is confidential, of course."

She removed her gloves, tossed them into a separate baggie, then dropped them into her purse. "As for your other question if I'd slept with Cole. I tried." She grinned at me. "After Cole and Taco found me, and I had time to heal, I reached out to him. At first, I wanted to thank him for helping me, then it turned into something else. He's smart, gorgeous, and funny." She gave me a half-shrug. "I know I'm older, but hey, why not?"

I sank my teeth into my bottom lip, a lash of insecurity whipping my ass for a second. I'd certainly not seen the funny side of Cole—ever.

"Eventually, I asked him out. He shot me down, which hurt my pride a little, but I suspected there was someone else." She picked her bag off the floor and hefted it onto her shoulder.

"Was there?" Secretly, I was relieved that she hadn't slept with Cole. I couldn't help but like Natalie, and it would have made me super uncomfortable when I saw her. I would have constantly questioned what Cole had done to her in bed and compared myself to her.

"When I asked him, he said the only girl for him was on his bike. We were having drinks at a bar, so I looked out the window and spotted his motorcycle. There wasn't anyone on it. I just figured he was trying to let me down easy." She gave me a slight shrug.

My heart skipped a beat. The face in the flames ... He'd never answered me the other day. Standing, I grabbed Cole's boxer briefs and stepped into them again. "I had blood and brain matter all over my clothes." I wasn't sure I should have mentioned those details, but she'd said everything was confidential.

"I assume from that statement he was shot in the head while you were nearby." Natalie pulled her hair into a ponytail and wrapped it with a black band.

"Yeah."

"That's pretty traumatic, Shae. Maybe consider some counseling to help you deal with this. I realize the assault just happened, but think about it." Natalie surprised me again and gave me a kind hug.

"Okay. Thank you."

She stepped away. "I'll contact you in a few days with the test results."

"I really appreciate you coming here." I nibbled on my thumbnail.

"You bet. If you want to hang, give me a call. Otherwise, I'll see you the next time one of these guys is hurt." She softly laughed, then opened the door.

Cole was at the end of the hall, staring at the bedroom when we finished. Worry lines creased his forehead as he hurried over to me. He didn't ask any questions, just pressed a kiss to my temple.

"Thanks, doc. See you soon, I'm sure," Cole said.

"Later."

The men told her goodbye, then Taco watched her leave from the driveway. I guess the shitty day with Ibrahim had shaken everyone up, and they wanted to make sure we were safe from the bastard that was after Cole.

"Since I don't have any shoes ... I suspect they're in whatever limo Ibrahim used." I could feel the blood drain from my cheeks, the events punching me in the chest until I could barely breathe.

"Hey, it's all good. The guys searched the limo and found them. I'm not sure who was driving, but no one else was around, so the car got wiped clean. It's as if you were never there."

Holy shit. I had my own crime cleaning crew. "Thank you. If you hadn't shown up when you did ..."

Cole cupped my chin and pinned me with an intense stare. "Stop. We did get to you in time. You're safe." He rubbed his thumb along my bottom lip, his gaze darkening with need. He dropped his hands, then placed one protectively against my lower back. Cole's touch warmed me as he guided me down the hall and into the living room.

"Can we go outside?" I asked, searching him for any resistance.

"Sure. Let me get your shoes." He scanned the area around him. "Taco, where are Shae's shoes?"

Taco shoved his fingers through his hair and pointed at the front door where my tennis shoes were waiting for me. After I put them on, Cole and I walked outside. Crickets chirped, filling the early evening air with their song. Otherwise, it was peaceful and quiet. I took a deep, slow breath, overwhelmed with gratitude that I was alive.

Cole cleared his throat, and his attention swept over part of the property. I assumed he was checking to see if anything was out of place.

I lifted my face to the glow of the setting sun and closed my eyes for a moment. "We heard a noise right before you busted down the door. I thought it was Ibrahim's boss. I'd told Ibrahim that you'd moved out last night and had no clue that I wasn't home. His play to get to you through me wouldn't work because I wasn't sure when I would even see you again. He said since you'd left, I was disposable, but he would wait for his boss to arrive, then take care of me." I shuddered and rubbed my arms, realizing I'd barely escaped death.

Cole slipped his arm around my waist and pulled me to him. I placed my palm against his stomach, feeling safe and secure in his touch. I glanced up, losing myself in his gaze for a moment. "If I'd died, Cole, what would you have regretted not telling me?" *Shit. I just went there.* I hadn't meant to. Hell, I wasn't even sure he would answer my question, but apparently, my brain was seeking answers without my mouth's consent.

Cole smoothed my hair, then bent down and pressed his lips to mine. Soft. Sweet. So gentle and a complete contrast to the savage that I was used to seeing. He stepped away and stroked my cheek with the pad of his thumb. "So many things, Shae. So many things." His chest heaved with his words. "Soon."

Disappointment tugged at me. "I understand, but will you answer one thing?"

"I'll try." His voice was husky and gruff. His emotions danced across his face, revealing how tough and vulnerable he was at the same time.

I took his hand and led him down the driveway to his bike. I pointed to the artwork. "Who is she?"

Cole massaged the back of his neck, staring at the woman on his motorcycle. Guilt shadowed his expression, and a conflicted look painted his features.

Chapter Seventeen

T he beat of my pulse ticked off the seconds as Cole and I stood there, hand in hand while I waited for him to answer me.

He ran his fingers through his hair and released a soft sigh. "It's you, Shae."

"Me? But why? I don't understand." I suspected I understood. I just needed to hear him say it. Plus, I might be wrong. "When was I airbrushed on your bike?"

"Two years ago," he admitted.

My mouth gaped. "Seriously?"

"It was right after I graduated high school. I was packing for college, and you and Dani had been swimming and getting some sun. You were tan and still a little bit wet. The two of you were walking down the hall to your room, and you tossed your head back and laughed. Anyway, I peeked out of my room, expecting to tell you to shut the fuck-up, but ... You were so beautiful in that moment, smiling and happy. I hadn't seen you smile very often, and all I knew after that was ... I wanted to be the one who made you happy."

I frowned. Confused wasn't even the right word. "Then why

were you such a fucking dick, Cole? What the hell?" I stepped away from him, furious all over again with how he'd treated me.

He massaged the back of his neck, then his crystal-blue eyes bore right into my soul. "Because I'm. Not. Good. For. You." His tone was firm, yet full of pain. "I know who I am, Shae. I know that I can kill someone without even blinking. I've done some bad shit. Eventually, I might join the MC. That's no life for you. You deserve better." He blew out a big sigh. "I can't seem to walk away from you, though. When you went missing, it fucking gutted me. All this time, I'd tried to convince myself I didn't have feelings for you, then something would happen to make me crazy ... like Ibrahim. I almost lost you today. I can't lose you again, Shae. I fucking can't. So whatever this is ... whatever we are ... I know I need to leave you alone because of who I am, but I don't think I'm capable of it, which makes me a selfish son of a bitch."

His confession speared right through my heart.

Cole blew out a sigh and stared at the ground. "I figured if I was an asshole to you, then you would leave me alone."

I threw my hands up in the air, on emotional overload. Why I just had to know about the girl on the bike right this minute was beyond me. But I was a glutton for punishment. "Well that obviously didn't happen."

"I put you in danger, Shae. What happened today is on me. My past ..." He shook his head and offered me a sad smile. "I keep bouncing between sending you away or keeping you next to me, so I can make sure nothing bad ever happens to you again."

"Don't you think I have a say in all of this? What happened today ... I don't know why I became a target, but someone knew you cared about me. But Cole, even if you didn't care, Ibrahim could have still taken me. I was your stepsister, and a way to get to you. Don't you get it? I was in your life because our parents fell in love. Your feelings about me wouldn't have changed that."

I shifted my weight, mentally weighing my next words. "You humiliated me, Cole. Embarrassed me at Harrison's party, and were a fucking asshole, but ... when you saw the video and I got in your face. You pinned me against the wall and wrapped your fingers around my neck ..." *Oh Jesus, what was I about to admit?* "I liked it. I couldn't stop thinking about you."

The corner of Cole's mouth lifted into a slight grin. "I would never hurt you. I do like rough sex, but I would never hurt you."

"And that's the thing. I instinctively understood that. You might have a monster inside of you, but I see all the good, too. You love your mom more than your own life, and whatever dude romance you and my daddy have ..." I lifted a brow and smirked. "He trusts you with my life or I wouldn't be here. He and Julia would have been here minutes after we arrived."

Cole chuckled. "Your dad is fucking fierce sometimes. I've got a lot of respect for him."

"Me, too. Cole, I don't know how things will play out between us, but you're not responsible for what happened to me. And someday, I hope you can trust me enough to tell me what happened and why you're in a mess now."

The crunch of gravel interrupted our conversation. Cole quickly pulled me behind him, and a few of the bikers appeared next to us, guns at their sides. The one shitty thing about Cole's driveway was that you could hear a car coming before you could see it. I had no idea if it was a friend or an enemy behind the wheel.

"Get her in the house," Snake said.

Cole scooped me into his arms and ran inside. He didn't stop until he'd deposited me on the bed. I trembled and my stomach rolled with fear. "Stay." Before I could reply, he hurried out of the room, closing the door behind him.

"Fuck!" I heard him yell.

Completely disobeying him, I cracked the door open and peeked down the hall.

"Sorry, son. We didn't mean to scare you. I should have called and let you know that we were almost here."

I sagged with relief as Julia's voice carried down the hall.

"Where's Shae?" Daddy asked, his words thick with worry.

"I'm here." I said, hurrying toward him. "Daddy." I flew into his arms like I had when I was a little girl, wrapping my arms around his neck. Sobs wracked my shoulders as Daddy's love wrapped me in a warm cocoon. For the first moments since the assault, I felt completely safe. Daddy had always taken care of me.

"Princess, are you okay?" He released me, his fearful gaze examining me and immediately fixating on the lump on the side of my head. He wiped my cheeks, then kissed me on the tip of my nose.

"I'm all right." I gave him a sad smile. It was then that I spotted a guy with light brown hair and emerald green eyes. An ex-military vibe rolled off him, filling the space in the room. His black Westbrook Security polo stretched across his broad chest and conformed around his massive biceps.

Cole slipped his arm around my waist, glowering at the poor guy.

"Shae, this is Zayne, our bodyguard." Dad motioned to him.

"Hi," I said, a little too breathlessly.

Cole's hold tightened on me as Zayne shook our hands, then continued to stand silently near the front door.

"We should sit down. The guys will hang outside." Cole nodded to the men on the couch and chairs in the living room.

"Let us know if you need anything, man." Brute patted Cole on the back before the men went outside and left us alone with our parents.

Cole and I sat on the couch while Julia and Daddy sat in the chairs across from us. Daddy's nerves were showing as he sat on the edge of his seat, his attention bouncing between us. "What happened?"

I glanced at Cole. He nodded his encouragement, slipping his cool, calm mask into place. "Before I left the house this morning, I got a text message from Ibrahim. He wanted to see me. After Cole beat the shit out of him the other day, I wanted to see if he might need help with the hospital bill. It was the least I could do since I'd already gotten him fired." I shifted in my seat, uncomfortable. The

Advil was wearing off, and the exam had hurt, making the pain worse.

"Shae." Daddy frowned hard, disappointment registering in his features.

I peeked at Julia, but she remained quiet and unreadable. I wondered if Cole's ability to conceal his emotions came from his mom.

"I'm sorry I lied. I was trying to make things right without throwing shade at Cole."

"What happened? Why do you have a big lump on the side of your head?" Daddy demanded.

I shot a questioning look at Cole. Why had I thought he'd explained part of what happened? Granted, I'd been pretty out of it all day, but ... *dammit.* I rubbed my forehead and groaned. Suddenly a sharp desire to tell them everything rushed up inside of me. "I'm just going to say it. I don't know any other way." I looked my daddy directly in the eyes. "Ibrahim attacked me. He hit me on the side of the head with his pistol, then he raped me. Cole and the guys found me tied to a chair in a basement. Ibrahim didn't make it out alive."

Julia's gasp filled the room, and horror coasted over Daddy's features.

"Needless to say, I regret not listening to you."

Tears filled Daddy's eyes, then he shot out of his chair and paced, practically wearing a hole in Cole's floor. "That son of a bitch deserves to rot in fucking Hell. If he were alive, I would kill him myself. Whoever took him out deserves a medal." Daddy scrubbed his face with his palms, then pulled me into a hug. "I'm so sorry, Princess." He smoothed my hair and held me. "Have you seen a doctor?" His voice cracked with grief, intertwined with anger. I knew Daddy well enough that after he processed what I'd shared, he would be hot-pissed. Not at me, but that I was assaulted.

"I had Natalie, the MC's doc, visit. She talked with Shae, and I assume checked her out. I was waiting for her in the hall while it happened. I wanted to give Shae some privacy," Cole explained.

Tears slid down my cheeks. "Just to be on the safe side, she's testing me for any diseases. She also suggested I talk to someone to help me process what I lived through." My knee bounced uncontrollably.

The grim set of Daddy's jaw told me he was thinking. Hard. "Cole, keep her here. Julia packed a bag for you, Shae. You should have enough clothes for …" Daddy looked at Julia.

"Four days, hon. You know how I like to pack for the worst-case scenario." She gave me a sheepish smile. "I'll bring you more, though."

"So, that's it? I'm going to stay here with Cole? I can't come home?" I turned and pointed to Zayne. "Can't Zayne keep me safe?"

"No," Cole barked out before anyone else had an opportunity to speak. His gaze narrowed briefly before he folded his arms across his chest, standing firm.

I hid my face in my hands, inhaling deeply before I punched Cole.

"Shae, you'll be safer here. Not many people know about Cole's house. Plus, King will be around, I'm sure."

I understood everyone's concern, but it felt more like jail. "Julia, can you talk any sense into them?"

She smiled for a second, then grew serious. "Just because Ibrahim is dead doesn't mean you're not a target. I know that's not what you want to hear, but we're all trying to keep you safe."

I shifted in my seat. "Cole, can Zoe at least come over and keep me company? If so, then I won't argue about being held captive … *again*."

Cole scowled at me. "You're not a prisoner, Shae. Stop being dramatic."

"You're giving me whiplash," I mumbled quietly. "If you all would like to continue to decide my future, then I'll excuse myself." I rose. "Is my bag in here or the car?" I asked, not seeing it.

"I'll get it," Zayne's deep voice rumbled through the room.

"Thanks." I crossed my arms, feeling like absolute shit. "I'm sorry.

I'm not trying to be difficult. Summer break hasn't started off well, and I don't want to have to hide from the world for the next few months."

Daddy stood, a stern expression on his handsome face. "In no way is this your fault, Shae, but if you learned anything today ... the danger is real. Whoever is screwing with Cole has no problem coming after his family. I can't risk losing you, Princess."

My heart twisted into painful knots. "I know. I'm just struggling with how to deal with everything. I'm angry one second and crying the next."

The door opening pulled my attention away from our conversation.

Zayne handed the bag to me, but Cole took it instead.

"Thank you, Zayne."

"I'm going to go change into my own clothes. I'll be back in a few." I left the living room, my mind spinning with chaotic thoughts. Once I closed the door and changed into my own clothes, I tossed Cole's into the hamper, then located my phone.

My fingers danced across the keyboard as I texted Zoe.

I'll be at Cole's for a while.

Only seconds passed before my cell vibrated with her message.

Wait. As in Cole's house? He has his own place?

I sighed. I hadn't had time to tell her all of the important details.

Yeah, but it's kind of a secret. I'll explain when you come over.

The little black dots bounced as she typed.

Girl, I think Cole is full of secrets.

Agreed. I'll talk to Cole and see when you can come over. I'll let you know.

Sounds good.

I tossed my phone on the bed. A ball of anger, confusion, and a chest-squeezing depression began to unravel inside me. The longer I was around Cole, the more I learned about him and his family. His earlier confession that he'd killed people without blinking should have terrified me, but it hadn't. I wondered if it was possible to still be a good person with blood on your hands. Even though I hadn't realized it at first, Cole shooting Ibrahim saved my life. I certainly wasn't going to hold that against him.

Flopping back on the bed, a heavy exhaustion pulled at me. Zoe's comment returned to my thoughts. There were some secrets I couldn't share with her, but I suspected Cole had a lot more. It would only be a matter of time before I saw the darkness firsthand. I hoped I was ready.

Chapter Eighteen

The following days passed agonizingly slowly, and my moods bounced around like a four-square ball on bumpy asphalt. One minute I was ready to take on the world, and the next, I questioned my judgment of character. How had I not seen who Ibrahim really was? After plenty of time to allow the assault to sink in, I'd decided he was right. I hadn't bothered to pay attention to the people around me. As long as I had money and did what I wanted, then I didn't give a shit about anyone except my friends and Daddy. The rape had been a big wake-up call, and at times I wasn't sure if the fear and pain would ever subside. I'd spent an increasing amount of time in bed, too.

The darkness I'd been battling was too heavy to fight alone, and I finally picked up the phone and reached out to Natalie. She'd become my saving grace, calling me every day, listening to me cry, hate the world, hate men, and hate myself. Just when I thought I was feeling better, another tidal wave of depression and fear, accompanied by nightmares, crushed me again. The first week was hell, but my tests had come back clean, which was a huge relief.

By day eight, Natalie showed up at the door, dragged me out of bed, and ordered me to shower. She sat on the toilet and talked to me while I cleaned up. She suggested some mental exercises to practice when the flashbacks were bad. Before she took me home, she handed me a list of things to do each day—shower, take a walk on the property with Cole, call her even if it was only for a few minutes, and reach out to Zoe.

Natalie shared about her harrowing assault, what she felt afterward, and the steps she took in order to move forward again. She visited at least once a week, and Cole made himself scarce when she was there. It was probably a good break for him. Babysitting me probably sucked ass, but he never made me feel like shit about it.

The fifth week after the assault, I was feeling stronger. I was experiencing some good days again.

Even though I was doing better, I was confused about Cole. Since he'd admitted his feelings for me, he'd barely touched me. Most days, I would get a sweet kiss on the forehead and long hugs, but nothing else. I didn't understand, except that his feelings had changed and were more from a place of pity and guilt than caring about me as a girlfriend. Maybe in his opinion, I was damaged goods. Broken and tarnished.

I slept next to Cole in his bed at night, but he stayed on his side with his hands resting on his chest or stomach. Regardless of whether he realized it or not, he was crushing my heart. I thought things between us were going to be different. They were different, all right, but not how I'd expected.

Plus, I couldn't get away from him here. I was barely allowed to use the bathroom without him following me, worry in his attentive watch. The house was small, but he also followed me when I went outside for fresh air. His hovering was driving me insane.

The soft creak of the bedroom door opening pulled me from my thoughts, and I threw the blankets over my head, hoping Cole would understand and leave me alone.

"You need to get up, Shae. Zoe is messaging me, worried about you. Have you not talked to her recently? I'm not sure you two have ever gone a week without talking." Cole sat on the edge of the bed, the mattress dipping beneath his weight.

"I don't want to speak to anyone."

I heard Cole sigh. "Talk to me, Shae."

Confused, I tossed the comforter off and sat up. His gaze flashed darkly, and I pinned him with an accusing scowl as a swell of anger and hurt swallowed me.

"Talk to you?" I snorted. "You mean about how I'm frustrated that you don't want me anymore? One minute you say I'm yours, and now that I'm damaged goods, you're no longer interested in me?"

His head snapped my way, his eyes wide and filled with caution. "You've got it all wrong." He rose and tugged on the collar of his T-shirt.

"Don't you dare walk away from me. You wanted me to tell you what was up, so let's do this." I stood on the bed, my pale pink tank and pajama short set slightly twisted around my waist. "Say something to me, dammit!" Rage sizzled beneath the surface, battling with sorrow and disappointment, and my fists clenched into tight balls.

Cole walked to the bedroom door, then glanced over his shoulder at me. "You'll never be damaged goods to me, Shae. Never." Pain slashed across his face, and a muscle clenched in his jaw.

My pulse spiked. "What does that mean? You do realize people talk to each other, and not in half-assed riddles. Like adult conversation." I jumped off the bed, hauling ass down the hall after him. Apparently, I'd reached my limit with the guessing game Cole was playing, and I was about to end it. He could tell me what in the hell was going on, or I was out of here. I would stay with Daddy, and if he said no, I would hide out at Zoe's.

Cole walked into the kitchen, opened the fridge, and produced a beer. He twisted the top off, then tossed it on the counter. The lid bounced and pinged off the granite, finally wobbling on one side before it stopped. Taking a long drink, he sat down on a barstool at the island, his lips pursing.

"Great, you can't even talk to me unless you have alcohol." Frustration and hurt coursed through my veins. I'd been through too much to risk being damaged by him any longer. "I'm done. You can take me home, or I'll walk, but either way ..." I glared at him. "I'm finished." I stomped off toward the hall.

Before making it very far, Cole grabbed my arm and whirled me around. "You're not fucking going anywhere, and you're definitely not done." His blue eyes were full of fire and determination.

My breath hitched with the depth of his stare. For the first time in weeks, I felt as though he was seeing me again, not just the shell of a girl I'd become lately.

"Then you better start talking," I hissed.

He placed his palm on the wall over my head, never taking his gaze from mine. "You have no idea how bad I want you, but I'll hurt you, and I can't."

My brows knitted in confusion. "What do you mean?"

He looked away, then back to me. "What kind of man asks to be with you after you've lived through an assault and trauma?" He skimmed his knuckles down my cheeks. "It fucking kills me not to touch you, but I'm afraid I won't stop until my cock is buried inside you. Then I lay awake at night, watching you sleep, and wondering if you're having nightmares about what that sick bastard did to you. All I want is to put a smile on your beautiful face again, but I ..."

"What is it?" I placed my palm on his chest, feeling his heart thump against my palm. "Cole, don't shut me out."

His head hung down, and he pressed his forehead against mine. "Dammit." He dropped his hand and backed away. "Maybe you staying here isn't a good idea ... for either of us." His shoulders slumped, then he stalked off.

A frustrated and fury-driven scream tore from my throat as I shoved him. He stumbled forward, and I took advantage of the moment and punched him in the back. Cole whirled around, shock registering in his features. I hit him in the chin, then in the stomach. My fists flew faster than they ever had as I wailed on him.

"Shae, calm down."

Ignoring him, I brought my fist back and aimed for his face. His hand shot in front of mine, blocking me before I made contact with his mouth.

"Goddammit, Shae! Stop!"

"I hate you, Cole. I fucking hate you." My hot, anger-fueled tears fell, and I swiped at them.

Cole crouched down and picked me up, catching me completely off-guard. He sat me down on the top of the island, then grabbed my wrists. My stomach dropped, my breathing became labored, and butterflies scattered in my chest as his gaze rested on my lips.

A crackle of electricity connected the space between us, and my pulse pounded against my wrist with anticipation. This next moment had the power to make or break me ... us. The longer he stared at me, the more I wanted to throw caution to the wind.

He groaned from the base of his throat before his lips crashed down on mine. He bit my lip and swept his tongue deep into my mouth, tasting me, sharing his need as if kissing and touching me were the only things he lived for.

My cheeks flushed as a newfound heat coursed through my body. I tugged at his shirt, practically ripping it off him. My pajamas and panties landed on the floor as Cole and I touched and kissed as if we might never see each other again. If this was goodbye ... goodbye had never felt so right.

He leaned me back on the counter and paused as his gaze raked over my naked body. Somehow, he was still mostly dressed. He gave me a tortured smile, then reached into his pocket, retrieved his wallet, and removed a condom. Cole released the button on his jeans, lowered the zipper, then freed himself.

My tongue darted over my lower lip, his length and girth sending shudders through me. Once he rolled on the rubber, he hopped up on the counter and hovered over me as his cock twitched.

As much as I tried to focus on Cole, Ibrahim's devilish smile flickered to life and my blood chilled. A multitude of thoughts scrambled and collided inside my jumbled brain—Ibrahim shoving the barrel of the gun into me as he held his finger on the trigger, the pain that ripped through me as he violated me. Anxiety pulled and tugged at my insides, my pulse kicking into high gear.

Cole's clean, woodsy scent invaded my space, grounding me in the present. Ibrahim was dead. Cole had defended my life, and I was safe. Sweeping my attention over Cole's handsome features, I settled on his focused eyes that hadn't left mine.

"Shae?" His worried gaze peered straight into me. "Do you need to stop? You're pale."

I breathed in as deep as my lungs would allow, and I swallowed my fear. Fuck Ibrahim. That bastard was rotting in Hell, and I refused to allow him to steal any more from me. He'd taken enough. I wouldn't allow him to control me when he didn't even walk this planet any longer.

"I'm good now."

Unconvinced, Cole searched me for any signs that I was lying.

I grabbed his hips and dug my nails into his flesh as I parted my legs and made room for him. He pushed at my entrance, then eased into me, his eyes full of concern but dark with desire.

A moan escaped me as he moved slowly, torturing me and setting me on fire. Everything about Cole felt different—how he moved inside me, touched me—healing yet possessive.

"You're mine, Shae." He pumped into me, thrusting a little harder. His tongue flicked across my nipple, then tugged on it with his teeth.

I ran my fingers through his hair, arching into his mouth as he worshipped my breast. "Cole," I whispered. Wrapping my legs around his waist, I lifted my hips, rocking with him. My fingertips traced the muscles and valleys of his back down to his ass. Cole rolled his hips, massaging my clit with the movement.

"Jesus, you feel so good." Cole closed his eyes as he picked up the pace.

Sex had always just been sex to me. I'd never truly cared about anyone the way I did Cole. In a few short weeks, he'd turned me inside out. As he continued to touch me, the walls around my heart began to crumble, and I let go of the idea that I lost the people I loved. Losing mom had shattered me more than I had ever admitted. I'd refused to bond with anyone on a deep level other than Zoe. Loneliness had become my best friend, and I'd welcomed it, all in an attempt to protect myself.

But at this moment, as we connected, exposing our feelings and bodies to each other, something shifted inside of me. For the first time in my life, I wondered if I could honestly give myself to someone. Even through all the craziness and ups and downs, I knew Cole would do everything in his power to protect me.

Flipping Cole over on the counter, I straddled him and took him in deeper. He cupped my breasts, then slipped a finger between our bodies and massaged my sensitive bud.

Cole's eyes closed, and pure pleasure filled his expression ... all for me.

"I need to see you come, Shae. Come for me, baby."

His deep, sultry voice sent goosebumps over my skin, and heat pooled low in my belly. Cole wrapped his hands around my hips, and with strength I hadn't seen before, lifted me off his cock and placed me over his face. I scrambled to keep my balance as he licked me, then fucked me, spearing so deep, he hit my clit with his teeth, his nose buried into my flesh. His tongue dove deeper, possessing every dark part of me and fucking me faster.

My body hummed and throbbed as he brought me to the edge, then with a hard suck to my bundle of nerves, his name escaped me as desire licked every inch of my sensitive skin. My muscles clenched, and my world exploded from his skilled mouth. Before I'd had time to recover, I crawled down his torso and slid his cock into me. He sat up and wrapped his arms around my waist, burying himself deeper. In a quick move, he flipped me on my back, the cold granite startling me for a second. He placed his hands on either side of my head and plowed into me.

I whimpered my approval. "Harder, Cole. Fuck me hard."

He slowed, grabbed my right leg, and pinned it against my chest.

"Goddamn, your pussy feels so good."

I moaned as he continued, another sweet orgasm swirling and building inside me.

"Tell me you're mine, Shae. Say it," Cole growled possessively.

"I'm yours, Cole."

A moan traveled through him as he jerked and tightened. Knowing that I was the one he just came for, my release ripped through me, and I shuddered beneath him. His lips pressed against mine, a small smile lifting the corner of his mouth.

His nose nuzzled my ear. "I like it rough, but I didn't want to hurt you ... not this time."

My pussy clenched around his thick cock with his words. He already knew what I liked after watching the video. The bastard had a head start on me. Somehow, I would have to even the playing field.

Cole held onto the base of his dick, then pulled out of me and removed the condom. He hopped off the counter, then strolled across the kitchen to the trashcan in the cabinet beneath the sink. I rolled over on my side, my gaze taking a slow, sensual hike up and down his toned and muscled back, ass, and legs.

He turned, a smile on his face. "Are you staring at me like a piece of meat?" A low chuckle filled the air. "I feel so used." He covered his cock and fluttered his eyelashes.

I sat up, gawking at him. "Did Cole Parker just make a joke and laugh?"

He flashed me a sheepish grin. "I do that sometimes."

"Huh. I had no idea." I softly giggled, basking in the realization that Cole and I had finally crossed the line and had sex.

Cole's eyes swept over the curves of my body, appreciative and adoring. Butterflies fluttered in my belly. No one had ever looked at me like he did.

I scooted my butt to the edge of the counter, then he picked me up and lowered me to the floor. He ran his fingers through my long hair, then fisted it, tilting my head back. "You're not leaving. You're staying right here with me. If you try to go. I will deal with you." He gave me a quick peck on the lips, then released me, but not before he playfully swatted my ass.

"Guess if I try, you'll have to catch me first." I flashed him a mischievous smile before I gathered my clothes off the kitchen floor.

"I'll do a lot more than try, baby."

This playful, sexy side of Cole was what I needed. At least I understood why he'd waited to touch me, and a part of me appreciated him for caring. The other part of me was hurt and confused. I'd needed to be with him. Whether Cole realized it or not, he'd reached inside me and touched my heart, giving it strength to continue beating. When you're lost in the darkness, even a single ray of light can give you hope. Cole was my light.

I piled my pajamas on the kitchen counter and wrapped one arm around his neck while my other traced his back. Frowning, I paused. Several raised scars pulled my attention away from the fact that he was very naked and pressing against me. I hadn't even noticed them before, but I'd never touched him like this either.

Suddenly dread slithered through my veins, and reality crashed down on me. Julia's words rang in my ears. *Cole needs to tell you about his past.*

"What is it, Shae?" Cole cupped my face in his hands and pressed into me, his cock resting against my thigh.

I didn't want to deal with the real world yet—one full of dark secrets, murder, and lies. Instead, I wanted to stay in the safe cocoon with Cole, but I understood life didn't always work out that way.

"Can I see the tattoos on your back?"

A quick frown clouded Cole's features, then he turned slowly.

"They're beautiful. Whoever drew and inked them is a real artist." I traced the skull with angel wings, a sword, and the much smaller tattoo near the tail of the panther's body. Then my eyes drifted to another one. Although it was mostly hidden behind blue and white flames of fire, there was no mistaking it this time. It was me, but this one was slightly different from the artwork on his bike—

tears were on my cheeks. The tattoo covered a long, thin scar that stretched from the flames into the black knife, where droplets of blood hung off the blade.

Cole grunted, then spun around and grabbed my wrists. He swallowed hard, his Adam's apple bobbing in his throat. Vulnerability flickered in his gaze, and my chest tightened.

I peeked at him, then pushed up on my tiptoes and gently kissed him. Studying his face, I gathered my courage to ask him a question knowing full well that his answer had the ability to crush my soul.

"Cole, why do you have scars all over your back?" I whispered.

Chapter Nineteen

ole's expression quickly morphed from relaxed to grim.

A phone vibrated against the counter, and I spotted Cole's near the coffee pot. Relief flooded through him, his shoulders visibly relaxing as he backed up, then scooped up his cell. "I have to take this."

Cole answered while he gathered his jeans and T-shirt, then strolled to the bedroom. His voice was hushed as he walked away.

While he was occupied, I dressed in my pajamas again, then busied myself making some hamburgers for a late lunch. My appetite had been complete shit lately, but sex with Cole had made my world a little better. Either I was fucked in the head, or Cole's touch was so different than Ibrahim's, it didn't send me into a full-on anxiety attack. Even if I'd had a difficult time, I wouldn't have stopped. I'd struggled with depression, but I was bound and determined that the rape wouldn't stop me from having a good sex life. It was more the fact that Cole had been so weird around me after he'd shared his feelings that had confused me.

The hamburgers sizzled in the skillet, and I flipped them over. Mulling over the scars on Cole's back, I chewed on my bottom lip.

Julia had made it clear she couldn't share what her son had lived through, and I didn't want to push Cole, but I needed to know what I was getting myself into.

Fifteen minutes later, Cole's footfalls alerted me that he was returning. It was perfect timing since the hamburgers were an excellent medium pink. I flipped the gas burner off and grabbed a few paper plates from the cabinet.

"Hey." Cole slipped his arms around my waist, pressing the front of his body into my back as he nuzzled my neck.

"I made something to eat. Are you hungry? I saw some lettuce and tomatoes that I can slice up for us." I turned to him and draped my arms around his shoulders.

"I'll save mine for later. Zoe is on the way over to keep you company." He nipped at my lower lip.

Catching myself before I glared at him for making plans for me again, I decided to ask instead. We'd scowled at each other for years, and I realized that I most likely couldn't break the habit overnight, but I wanted to try and save the scowls for when I really needed them. "She called you?"

"No. I texted her after I got off the phone. I'll be out this afternoon, so I thought she could bring some junk food and you two could catch up."

Although I was excited to see Zoe and share some Ben and Jerry's with her, I couldn't help but feel disappointed that Cole and I weren't going to spend the rest of the day naked together.

"Don't look sad, babe. I'll be back as soon as I can." He stroked my cheek with the pad of his thumb, and my body immediately responded to him. "If you're a good girl while I'm gone, I'll reward you tonight." His hand slid to the back of my neck. He threaded his fingers in my hair and pulled, tilting my face to his. "Until then, on your knees." His hold tightened as I lowered, my pussy throbbing and wet again.

I held his gaze as I flipped open the button on his jeans and unzipped them. Freeing his thick cock, I gripped his shaft and licked off the precum.

"Open your mouth," he ordered.

My lips parted, and he rubbed the tip of his dick along them. I sucked his sensitive head as his hold tightened. Glancing up from beneath my eyelashes, I took his long shaft until he hit the back of my throat.

Cole moaned, and once again, my panties were soaked. He needed to bury himself inside me before he left for the day.

Cole fucked my mouth, then he slowed as he blocked my airways and watched me. I grabbed his hands, digging my fingernails into his skin. Panic washed over me, then I recalled his words that he would choke me with his dick until I cried but that he would never hurt me. Forcing myself to relax, I remembered that even if he scared me sometimes, I trusted Cole.

"You're so goddamn beautiful with my cock shoved into your mouth. Your cheeks are turning red as you wait for me to allow you to breathe. You're under my complete control, and I bet if I touched your sweet little pussy, you would be drenched." He eased his hips back, allowing me a breath. His thrusts grew faster, then he pulled out, wrapped his hand around his dick, and jacked off, his hot liquid landing on my face.

Once he was finished, I began to rise, but he pushed on my shoulders and held me down. "I want to look at you like this ... with my come marking you."

I moaned as he ran his finger through the creamy substance and smeared it on my lips. "Stand."

I did as he asked, loving this side of him.

"Bend over the counter and spread your legs."

After I was situated, he tugged my pajama shorts and panties down. I kicked them off, my bare ass tipping into the air.

He grabbed my butt, then gave it a hard pinch. I gasped, not used to the pain, but a part of me liked it, and I wanted more.

Cole ran his fingers over my wet folds, then spread me apart, and a throaty moan escaped him. I pushed against him, needing him to fuck me again. Sucking cock was one of my favorite things, and it turned me on so badly. At this point, Cole could do anything to my willing body.

"Is that cunt mine, Shae?" He massaged my clit.

"Yes," I whimpered. "Fuck me, Cole. Please."

A low chuckle rumbled through his chest as he continued to torture me with his fingers, the noise of my desire filling the room.

"Oh, God." I gripped the sides of the granite counter, the sweet sensation building inside me.

"Are you about to come for me, Shae?"

"Yeah." I squeezed my eyes shut, giving in to his touch. I sucked in a breath, ready for the delicious release that was just out of my reach.

Cole removed his hand from my core and smacked my ass. He leaned over, his mouth brushing the sensitive skin on my neck. "You can come when I say you can. Not before."

He stepped back, a mischievous grin spreading across his face.

"What? You're going to leave me hanging?" I straightened and glowered at him.

"As I said, if you're a good girl while I'm gone, then I'll reward you." He kissed the corner of my mouth.

The sound of gravel crunching beneath car tires reached my ears, and my eyes widened. I hurriedly gathered my shorts and damp panties and ran to the bedroom to clean up and change clothes.

"I'll tell Zoe you'll be out in a minute." His laugh echoed through the living room.

Before I could close the door, Cole blocked it with his body. Had he changed his mind?

"Don't touch yourself, Shae." His eyes danced with mischief. "I'll know if you do."

My gaze narrowed at him. "I doubt that."

His smirk told me otherwise. "Have fun with Zoe, and I'll see you tonight. Call or text if you need anything." He leaned in for one more kiss, then hurried down the hall to answer the knock at the door.

Sexually frustrated, I made my way to the bathroom, where I cleaned up and put on a pair of black workout shorts and a T-shirt before spending the afternoon with my best friend. The thought of Cole ordering me not to get myself off sent my hormones into full throttle again. I rubbed my neck, my throat slightly sore from his cock blocking off my airway. I'd never been with a guy that called the shots, and I secretly loved it. Demanding and possessive was a new high for me, and I craved Cole's touch already.

Running a brush through my hair, I pulled it into a ponytail. I peered into the mirror, convinced that I looked somewhat presentable for Zoe. For the first time in weeks, I was excited to spend the day with her. With anyone. I wasn't sure if I was going to tell her that Cole and I had fucked on the countertop ...

"Shit." Wide-eyed, I realized I needed to clean the granite surface. I hoped like hell she wasn't sitting on the barstool, her hands where Cole's ass print was probably visible.

Hurrying out of the bedroom, the lemon scent of cleaner reached me. I muffled a sneeze, then laughed.

"Damn cleaners," I said, spotting Zoe on the couch in the living room.

I breathed out a soft sigh of relief that she wasn't at the kitchen island. Zoe shot out of her seat and ran to me, embracing me with a huge hug. "Bitch, you're in big trouble for leaving me in the cold like you have."

"I'm sorry. I'm so glad to see you."

We released each other, and she grinned. "And how fucking hot is it to have a guy that cleans his house?"

"What do you mean?"

"When I knocked on the door, I saw Cole cleaning the kitchen island. The only request I would have during the repeat performance is that he not wear a stitch of clothing." Zoe laughed, then her smile faltered as her big brown eyes searched mine.

"Holy. Fucking. Shit. I didn't catch it at first. You're glowing. Like, just got your brains fucked out glowing. You and Cole?" Her dark brows shot up to her hairline, then she slapped her palms over her mouth, giggling.

I couldn't stop from laughing. This was the happiest I'd felt since before the kidnapping. "You can't tell anyone. We haven't had the conversation about how this relationship is going to work yet." I removed her hands from her face, then took one and led her to the couch again. "Did you bring some food over? Cole mentioned you were going to."

"He put the ice cream in the freezer. The chips and dip are on the counter next to the plate of homemade chocolate peanut butter cookies I brought over. Two are missing because Cole stole a few before he left." She offered me a sweet smile.

I strolled into the kitchen. "Is it Chubby Hubby?"

Zoe and I had a love-hate relationship with Ben and Jerry's ice cream—especially Chubby Hubby.

"Of course." She grinned at me, sank onto the couch, and tucked her foot beneath her. "I might need extra, though. I have a feeling you've got a lot to tell me."

"I do." Cole must have put the hamburgers away because the pan was empty and soaking in the sink. I opened the drawer, removed two teaspoons, then collected the ice cream. We wouldn't need bowls. Zoe and I always shared the container. The memories of Ibrahim hurting me stabbed me in the chest. I swallowed over the pain and sucked in a big breath as I joined her on the couch again. Part of this afternoon was going to suck ass because I wanted to tell Zoe what had happened with Ibrahim. I suspected that my solitude over the last five weeks would make more sense to her once I did.

"I'm sorry I've been AWOL. It had nothing to do with you, just everything with Cole and ..." I plopped onto the leather seat next to her, then opened the ice cream. I set it on the coffee table to thaw for a few minutes.

"What happened? You weren't answering my texts, so I started bugging him. Cole wouldn't tell me shit, though. I mean, he told me that you were safe and staying with him."

"You probably had a million questions about me hanging out here. In some ways, it has felt like jail." I glanced at my fingers, picking at the corner of my thumbnail.

"Well, fill me in." Eagerness flickered across Zoe's pretty face. She was waiting for the juicy stuff, but I would have to back up for her to understand it all.

Over the next half hour, I updated Zoe about Ibrahim, being kidnapped, and Cole blowing Ibrahim's brains all over me. She was speechless and spent most of the time wide-eyed with her mouth gaping.

"Shae, I'm so sorry." Zoe leaned over and hugged me, tears streaming down both our cheeks.

"I didn't know how to tell you, and I wasn't ready to talk about it yet. I'm sorry I shut you out."

"Bitch, please. I get it. No apologies are necessary. I've been worried sick about you, but at least you're safe and that sleazy-ass bastard is gone. I'll be sure to congratulate Cole for taking the shot. Not many people would have. Hell, I would have shot Ibrahim in both his knees, crippling him for the rest of his life." A thoughtful expression coasted over her face. "That wouldn't have been enough, though. I suspect I would have cut off his fingers, one by one, then cut out his tongue, too." She beamed at me, obviously excited about her plan to hurt a dead man.

"You're fucking scary, girl. At least I know you always have my back. Zoe, you really are the best friend I've ever had. Thank you for being there for me. I love you tons."

Zoe choked up briefly, then flashed me a smile. "Yeah, you're my fave as well, and I love ya, too."

I leaned over and hugged her before I grabbed a spoon from the coffee table and plunged it into the creamy goodness. "It's thawed enough." I handed her a utensil, then placed the container between us. I'd forgotten how much I missed Zoe and the simple things we shared. No pressure to be perfect or live up to our family names. Just us, no judgment, and complete transparency. That's what a real best friend was.

"So, do you think the mafia would pay me to torture people for them? Hell, I would probably become rich in my own right." She snickered.

"You would probably make damn good money." I laughed, relieved that we were moving away from discussing the assault. Granted, it was a strange conversation, but it didn't matter. The weight had been lifted from my shoulders, and Zoe was in the know about what had gone down.

Zoe scooped some Chubby Hubby from the container, then shoved it into her mouth. "Fuck, that's cold." She squinted and shuddered. Zoe was funny to watch when she got brain freeze.

"All right, fill me in on the good stuff." Her attentive gaze landed on me. "When did you and Cole fuck?"

I hated my fair skin. Heat traveled up my neck and fanned across my cheeks, revealing the truth to her.

Zoe nearly squealed. "Oh, hell! He's that good?"

"It's only been once, but so far ... the best I've had. He definitely knows some hip moves." I giggled, still mentally pinching myself that I'd just had sex with my step ... with Cole.

"How are you going to tell your dad?" Zoe wiggled in her seat, clearly excited about the turn of events.

"They knew Cole had feelings for me before I did." I continued to explain the conversation with Daddy and Julia, the artwork on his motorcycle, and the similar tattoo of me on his back.

"Holy shit, that's so fucking hot. So, he's been into you for at least two years, and you didn't have a clue? I mean, come on, Shae, not even an inkling?"

"Not really. I simply thought he couldn't stand me and loved making me absolutely miserable. Squashing my dating life, getting pissed when he saw me with Ibrahim and Matt, David ... I just figured he was the kind of guy that got off on other people's misery."

"Well, there are people like that, but I'm pretty sure everyone else saw more." Zoe took another bite of the ice cream.

Somehow, we'd eaten over half of the pint already. "There's something else about Cole, though." I played with the hem of my Halsey concert T-shirt Julia had packed for me.

"What is it?" Zoe stared at me, her spoon hanging in mid-air while she waited for me to answer.

Chapter Twenty

"I think something horrible happened to him when he was younger."

Zoe motioned for me to continue.

"When Julia and Daddy strongly implied that they knew how Cole felt about me, Julia said she'd urged him to tell me about his past."

"Oh, that's juicy." Zoe reached for the lid and placed it on the empty container. "Did she say anything else?"

"No. That was it, but today when we'd finished messing around, I felt some scars on his back. I'd never noticed before because of his tattoos, but I think the tats are there to cover up the marks."

Zoe's forehead creased as she tapped her finger on her chin. "It could be anything, but he's always been super tight-lipped, ya know?"

"Yeah, he has. All I know is that Julia and Cole moved here from Hayden, Idaho. She and Daddy met through mutual friends, so it's not like I was able to learn a lot about them. I mean, it's only an hour to Idaho, but I don't know anyone outside the Coeur d'Alene area. And honestly, I was so upset with Daddy for remarrying that I didn't give a fuck about Cole and Julia."

Zoe reached over and squeezed my knee. "The stepmom bit was hard to digest after you lost your mom. At least she's not a blazing bitch on wheels. She actually seems pretty cool, right?"

"I think so. She was sweet after the video got blasted." I groaned. "I was so humiliated."

Zoe tucked her hair behind her ear, a wide grin playing across her lips. "Girl, we all thought your social life was over unless a guy was only after your holes."

I snickered at her terminology and smacked her on her arm.

Her expression grew serious. "Sorry, that was probably uncalled for after what Ibrahim did to you."

"Trust me. The motherfucker enters my thoughts multiple times a day. I'm not sure when it will get better, but at least he's dead. That gives me some peace."

Zoe's shoulders slumped with relief. "Okay, I didn't want to be *that* insensitive friend."

I grinned at her. "You're fine, but I love you for caring."

"You know, you're sleeping with a man you don't have a lot of details about. That's hot." Zoe wiggled her brows at me.

I picked at an imaginary ball of lint on my shorts, pondering her words. "I know who he is. Dark and dangerous to the wrong people, but I trust him. If I didn't, I wouldn't have let him touch me."

"After what you've just lived through, I'm surprised you were up for some dick." Zoe picked at her manicured fingernail.

"Me, too, but I was aware that it was Cole touching me and not anyone else. There's no comparison to him. When I'm with him, I feel safe."

"You're tough. Even if the assault did mess with you, you're bound and determined to not let Ibrahim steal your life or your happiness. You deserve to be with someone who treats you like the queen you are." Zoe gave me a sweet smile.

"You, too. Maybe you'll meet a hot guy that's crazy about you this next year. The college campus is huge, I'm sure there's someone there for you." I wiggled my brows at her.

A wistful expression ghosted over my best friend's face. "We'll see."

Zoe and I laughed and caught up with each other over the rest of the afternoon. I was grateful that Cole had asked her to come over.

A loud thud reached my ears, and a jolt of fear shot through me. I scrambled out of my seat and crouched behind the couch. "Get down, Zoe. Hardly anyone knows about this place ..." I glanced at her, my hands trembling as my heart knocked against my chest, skipping a few beats like a car sputtering on its last leg. I wasn't even sure where to find Cole's guns if someone showed up. Fortunately, the living and dining room curtains were still closed. I tiptoed over, then sank to the floor, peeking through the crack in the panels. Relief flooded my system, and tears welled in my eyes. I steadied myself, then stood. With my hand on my hip and a stare that could kill, I flung open the door. "How long have you been here?"

Taco's shoulders sagged. "Since before Cole left."

Understanding clicked into place, and I tapped my foot against the wood floor. "I assume he wanted you to watch over us?"

His jaw tightened. The air around us thickened and closed in as I waited for him to answer. Guilt never looked so good on someone. "King offered me up."

"Hi!" Zoe said from behind me. She stuck her hand out. "I'm Zoe, Shae's best friend."

Taco looked at her, and I wondered if he remembered how to be a gentleman, or if he'd been riding with the men too long. Finally, he slipped his hand into hers and gave her a lopsided grin. "Nice to meet you." He released her, then glanced over his shoulder at Zoe's car. "Sweet ride."

She beamed at him. "Thanks. It was a graduation gift from my parents."

Taco rubbed his chin. "Well, I'll let you two catch up."

"Try not to scare the shit out of us again." I cocked my head before I closed and locked the door. Cole and I would definitely be chatting when he got home.

Zoe gripped my arms and gently squeezed. "I want to ride *him*."

I giggled. "I told you he was hot."

"With a capital yum." Zoe licked her lips, then her attention landed on something behind me.

"Since Cole didn't tell you he was keeping an eye on us, we should drink some of his liquor, have some fun before he gets back."

"I knew there was a reason I missed you so much."

Laughter filled the house as we made our drinks, then turned on Netflix and binged the first season of Georgia and Ginny again. Even through the alcohol, I realized that the sun had set a while ago, and it was nearing ten in the evening. I hadn't heard a word from Cole. An uneasy feeling nudged me in the gut. Something was off, but I had no clue what it was. Chiding myself for being paranoid, I reminded myself that Taco was outside, keeping us safe from the boogeyman. Plus, Cole disappeared while he was living with Daddy and Julia all the time. I just hadn't bothered to care ... until this evening. Ibrahim might be dead, but his boss wasn't. I don't think anyone knew for sure who was after Cole, either, which kept me in a perpetual state of anxiety. Whoever it was wanted him pretty badly, but why? And would he kill Cole?

I kicked the disturbing thought out of my mind and refocused on the show.

"Shae. Wake up, babe." Cole squeezed my knee.

My neck screamed at me as I attempted to turn my head. "Shit. I must have fallen asleep on the couch." I peeked at the other end. Zoe had curled up beneath one of the blankets I'd grabbed from the guestroom upstairs. "What time is it?"

"After two in the morning. Let Zoe sleep. Come to bed."

I stood, my legs wobbling slightly. "I think I'm still drunk." I raised my hand to my mouth, snickering behind it.

"I noticed my vodka bottle looked emptier." Cole grinned at me.

"Yeah, we got into it after Taco scared the living shit out of us. You should have told me he was here."

"He wasn't supposed to get caught." Cole slid his arm around my waist and guided me down the hall. He turned on the lamp, then kicked the bedroom door closed with his foot.

I flung myself on the bed without taking my clothes off.

Cole sat down, then removed his black combat boots and tossed them on the floor.

"You were gone for a long time." I swallowed, my mouth dry from my overindulgence of Cole's stash of alcohol.

"I had business to take care of."

I rolled over on my side and propped up on my elbow. "Another business meeting?"

"Something like that." He leaned over and kissed me. "I was a bit distracted while I was gone, though."

"Oh?"

"Yeah, I kept thinking about you on your knees with your pretty lips wrapped around my dick."

"Ah, I get it now. I'm just here to serve your cock's every whim?" I smiled, letting him know I was playing.

Cole rolled me onto my back, then placed his lips on mine, dominating my mouth. Wrapping my arms around his neck, I welcomed his touch. His tongue dove deeper, possessing every part of me.

"Were you a good girl while I was gone?" he asked, his voice a deep, throaty whisper.

Still a little buzzed from the vodka, I pondered what might happen if I said no. "I touched myself," I lied, sinking my bottom teeth into my lip and holding my breath.

"Did you come?" Cole took my arms from his neck and pinned them over my head. I peered up as he collected the handcuffs that were hanging on the slatted headboard, then secured them around my wrists.

"No." I gulped, wondering if he would leave me here while he slept in the guest room upstairs, or if he was going to finish what he'd started earlier today.

"Tell me, Shae ..." His fingertips trailed across my cheek, down my neck, and over my collarbone. "Tell me what you thought about while you fingered yourself."

I sucked in a quick breath, my core clenching at the thought of him inside me again.

Cole slipped his fingers beneath the waistband of my shorts, then tugged them over my hips. I lifted my ass off the mattress, so he could remove my clothes. He parted my legs, then brushed a knuckle over the satin fabric of my thong. He applied a bit of pressure to my clit and my eyes briefly fluttered closed.

"I thought about your tongue fucking my pussy ... and recording it. Then, we watched the video together while I sucked you off."

"Have you watched a video of yourself with anyone before?" He circled my clit and ran his finger to my soaking wet slit.

"No."

"Good girl." He slapped my pussy and a jolt of pain and excitement shot through me. "But I know you're lying."

My head shot off the bed and my eyes narrowed on him. "How?"

He slid a finger beneath the thin fabric and pressed against my entrance. "I'm the only one that's been inside you today." He smirked, then slipped a finger into me, then curled it.

I gasped, my focus on what he was doing to me rather than learning how he knew I'd lied.

"Cameras, Shae. In the bedroom and bathroom."

I should have been furious, but I should have fucking known. "You watch me?"

Cole slid another finger into me, stroking the fire. I bucked against his hand.

"Sometimes. I did when I left, so I know for a fact that unless you got off with Zoe ..."

"Bastard." I flopped back on the pillow.

Cole's thumb circled my sensitive bundle of nerves, agonizingly slow. "I am a bastard, baby, but you know that already." Cole removed his fingers, then he ripped my thong off and tossed it on the floor.

He stared at my bare pussy, then to my heated gaze. "I'm going to turn on the camera." He stood, then grabbed his phone from the nightstand and tapped the screen.

Holy shit. We're doing this.

Cole flipped open the button on his jeans and the sound of his zipper filled the room. He pushed them down his legs, his cock bobbing free. After he'd ditched all of his clothes, he crawled back on the bed, then straddled my chest. "Since you lied to me ... you don't come until I decide you can." He wrapped his fingers around his dick and stroked himself. His free hand gripped the top of the headboard for stability as he looked down at me.

I licked my lips, ready to taste him, then I ran my tongue around the tip and sucked the sensitive head of his cock.

Cole slid in and out of my mouth, watching me. My core throbbed with need, my juices running down my ass. He picked up speed as he thrust into me, and his moans of pleasure filled the room. "That's it, baby, take it all the way ..." He hit the back of my throat and my gag reflex triggered. Cole stilled as I gasped for air, my face heating from the desperate need to breathe.

With my hands cuffed, I couldn't sink my nails into his thighs, reminding him to not hurt me. He quickly pulled back, and I sucked in a breath. As nervous as I was when he did that, it was hot as hell. I glanced up at him, pleading with my eyes for him to do it again as I sucked on him and lifted my head off the pillow.

His brow rose slightly, then he shoved in, cutting off my oxygen. "You're so goddamned pretty with my dick in your mouth." He controlled my air longer than he previously had but moved halfway out as black dots started to dance across my vision.

My jaw ached like crazy. He moved down the bed, his hot mouth finding my breast. He tugged at my nipple with his teeth and pinched the other one. Heat coursed through me from his touch, my body tingling with anticipation.

Cole nipped and licked a trail down my stomach. Reaching my center, he ran his tongue over my slit, then spread me apart, allowing him full access. His breath grazed the inside of my thigh, and I whimpered.

"Please, Cole." Begging wasn't my usual style, but if he didn't get me off soon, I was going to implode.

Realizing that Cole was at an odd angle, I wondered if there was more than one camera. As my brain completed the thought, he latched onto my bundle of nerves and sucked. Hard.

"Oh, God." Wanting to pull his hair, I tugged on the cuffs. On the brink of coming already, I bucked against him. My chest heaved, and my eyes closed. The shock of his mouth leaving my core had me searching for him.

He rose and walked around the bed, his cock hard and magnificent. The muscles in his legs and ass flexed as he sat next to me. He grabbed one of his pillows. "Lift your ass."

I did as he asked, my body humming with need. He placed the pillow beneath me and turned to face the foot of the bed. He leaned over me, then devoured my pussy again. Gasping and writhing beneath him, I neared the edge of my release again.

He lifted his head and licked his lips. "I'll give you a few minutes to reconsider ever lying to me again."

I gaped at him as he stood and strolled to the bathroom as if he hadn't left me hanging for the third goddamned time today.

"Cole!" I hissed, afraid that if I made to much noise, I would wake Zoe.

He responded by closing the door.

Chapter Twenty-One

I huffed and reminded myself that just because I was sleeping with him didn't mean he wasn't an asshole.

The sound of water reached my ears, and I realized Cole was going to take a shower while he left me cuffed to his bed. I muttered profanities, swearing I would pay him back for this. A giggle erupted from me as I began to plan. I literally couldn't do much else, so I might as well plot.

Half an hour later, the bathroom door opened, and steam billowed into the bedroom. Cole's hair was damp and his cock limp.

As much as I wanted to say something, I clamped my mouth shut.

He folded his arms, his biceps bulging as he pinned me with a determined stare. "Are you going to lie to me again?" His tone was clipped and demanding.

"No." I looked away from him, still irritated, but also curious what was going to happen next.

"Good girl." His attention focused between my spread legs, his cock growing harder with each second. "Who do you belong to, Shae?"

My eyes stayed glued to his, butterflies erupting in my belly. "You."

"Good girl." He rubbed his chin, then stroked his dick. "Don't ever forget that I own every piece of you now. Your cunt, your ass, and your mouth. No one will ever touch you again. Do you understand?"

"Yeah." My voice cracked. *Jesus, this is hot as hell.* "Only you."

"Are you on birth control? I know your tests came back clean from Natalie."

Cole was the only person I'd shared the test results with. "The pill for the last three years."

"Good. I had tests run when you started living here. I'm clean. You're the only one I've been with since the end of the school year."

"Thank you for letting me know." *Now fuck me.*

Cole returned to the bed, grinning like the devil he was before he ran a finger over my pussy again. "You're still wet."

I wasn't surprised.

"Have you learned your lesson, Shae?"

Goosebumps dotted my flesh with the way he said my name. "Yes." My response was breathy.

Cole positioned himself at my entrance, rubbing his cock up and down my slick core. He slid inside of me, but not all the way before he eased out, then repeated the motions.

Raw need surged to the surface, and I moaned softly with the slow pull out and soft push back in. I needed him to fuck me hard, but I had a feeling he realized it and decided to torture me some more.

"You're so tight." He grunted, pushing all the way into me, then stilling. He growled, then slammed into me.

"Yes, baby. So good." I rocked against him, more than ready to come with him deep inside me.

His thrusts were rough and precise with hard pushes to hit my sensitive bundle of nerves.

"Come for me," he demanded, and I shivered beneath him.

Delicious desire licked every inch of my sensitive skin. He let out a harsh growl, grabbed the backs of my thighs, and began plowing into me hard and fast.

My back arched, my nipples rubbing against his hard chest as a mind-blowing orgasm ripped through me.

Before I finished, Cole's lips parted, then he jerked and released inside me. My core pulsed around him as my name left his lips. Our bodies calmed, then he kissed me. "Do you remember what I said would happen when I came inside you?" His thumb stroked my cheek as he spoke.

"That it would officially mark me as yours." I searched his serious gaze, fear welling inside me. Was he going to change his mind? There was no way my heart would recover if he played with my emotions again.

His intense, crystal-blue eyes found mine. "That's right. There's no going back. Not for you and not for me."

"I'm good with that, Cole." I gulped, waiting for his response.

He smoothed my hair. "Me, too, Shae." He gave me a quick peck on the forehead, then hopped out of bed. He opened his nightstand drawer and produced a key. Two clicks later, my arms dropped like lead onto the bed. Cole located his boxer briefs and stepped into them, then joined me again. He picked up one of my arms and began to gently rub, encouraging the blood flow.

I couldn't stop the silly grin from easing across my face as he took care of me. I loved the controlling side of Cole in the bedroom, but it was these moments that broke through my fears and reached deep inside of me. Basking in the moment as feeling returned to my limbs, I glanced at him. Questions bubbling to life inside me. Instead of going to sleep, I decided with the current mood, it might be a good time to talk.

"Cole?"

"Yeah?"

"Can I ask you something?" I shook my hands out. "Thanks. They're better."

Cole crawled beneath the blankets, yawning. "What's on your mind, baby?"

My chest warmed from his use of the word baby. I wasn't sure Cole realized it, but he was my first real relationship. I wasn't sure if I was his first or not, and I didn't really care. He was mine now, and that was all that mattered.

I slipped beneath the covers, preparing myself for him to skirt my question and not give me any answers. I fluffed up my pillow and looked at him.

Cole took my hand in his, then planted a tender kiss on my knuckles. His gaze was full of adoration and gentleness. I wanted to snuggle up to him and forget about talking, but I had to try.

"Why are you and Daddy close? I mean, it's not often you see a stepson and stepparent bond, but you two obviously have. When I told him I'd seen you kill a man, he shut me down. He said he'd already taken care of it."

Cole visibly tensed, then relaxed. "I remember Mom telling me she'd met someone ..." He fiddled with a thread on the corner of the sheet. "It freaked me out, honestly." He glanced at me, then stared at the ceiling. "Mom's track record with men wasn't so great."

I squeezed his hand, urging him to go on.

"Mom said we could meet in a public place and have a nice dinner with Samuel. She said they wanted to talk to me about something important, and I couldn't back out at the last minute." He smirked. "I have a habit of that, so she called me out before I had a chance to think about it."

"I could see you pulling a no show." I slid my leg over his and gave him a soft smile.

"Anyway, dinner went great. I think Mom probably prepped him to talk motorcycles with me because we hit it off right away. It was clear that Samuel was different than Mom's norm. Even though I liked him, I made a decision to watch his every move. Trust hasn't ever come easy for me."

His chest moved with his deep breath. Whatever he was sorting through, it was obvious that this was difficult for him. Julia had said Cole wasn't good about sharing his feelings, but this was the first time I'd seen him willing to try.

"After dessert, Samuel and Mom explained that Samuel knew my bio dad, Rick."

"What?" Shock was evident in my tone. I sat up in order to see Cole's expression better. "How? I mean, Daddy's never mentioned him to me."

Cole's eyes narrowed, and I wondered why the mention of his father would cause that reaction. "He wouldn't, unless for some reason you needed to know."

Confused, my brows knitted together.

"They met years ago. I don't know the specifics, only that they met through some mutual people." Indecision and regret coasted over Cole's features.

"Where's your dad now? You never talk about him." I held the covers up, brought my knees to my chest, and propped my chin on them. Dread twisted my nerves. Something was off, but getting Cole to talk was like pulling teeth.

Cole's regret-fueled gaze connected with mine. "He's dead."

An uneasy silence settled over us. I waited for him to continue, but he didn't. Instead, he rolled over on his side. "We should get some sleep." He peeked over his shoulder at me and lifted the covers for me to stretch out against him.

I placed a kiss against his tattooed back and slipped my arm around him. "I hope at some point you can talk to me, Cole."

He squeezed my hand, then turned off the lamp on the nightstand.

The rest of the night, I was haunted in my dreams by Ibrahim, but this time he wasn't alone. Even though I couldn't really make out who the man was, in the pit of my stomach, I knew he was Ibrahim's boss.

I woke in a cold sweat, trembling and nauseous. Glancing at the clock, I groaned when I realized that I hadn't woken up at one in the morning, it was after one in the afternoon. Remembering that Zoe had spent the night on the couch, I flung the covers off and dressed in the same shorts and shirt I'd worn yesterday. Even though Julia had dropped off more clothes during my depression, I still had to do laundry once a week.

Hurrying to the bathroom, I washed my face, as well as brushed my teeth and hair. I was in desperate need of coffee after drinking and a shitty night's sleep.

Once I was somewhat presentable, I strolled down the hall, noticing it was quiet. Not seeing Zoe, I made my way to the coffee pot and filled a cup with warm, leftover brown liquid. I sipped it and cringed.

Cole strolled through the front door. He closed it behind him, chuckling. "I ran out of the good stuff."

"It's bad, Cole. Like, really bad." I forced myself to drink a little more, desperately needing the caffeine. "Where's Zoe?" I set the cup in the sink, shuddering from the bitter taste lingering on my tongue.

"She left around eleven. Zoe looked pretty rough this morning, and apparently my coffee wasn't good enough for her, either." The corner of his mouth kicked up in a grin. "Are you hung over?" He made his way into the kitchen, analyzing me. He pressed a sweet kiss to my mouth, and I sighed with contentment. Waking up to him was so nice that I was willing to deal with shit coffee.

Placing my hands around his neck, I leaned into him. "No, I don't get hangovers often. By the way, you're sexy as hell when you smile. It's a good look on you."

The most beautiful smile I'd ever seen eased into place, stealing my breath as I stared at him, wishing I could stay here with him like this forever. It was rare that I witnessed him happy, and I wanted to be the reason he smiled every day.

He nuzzled my neck and then whispered against my ear, "I'll keep that in mind." Cole took a step back and nodded to the vodka.

"It's good you don't deal with hangovers often. From the looks of the nearly empty bottle, you and Zoe should both have one, but I think she took the hit for you."

I glanced at the vodka and barked out a laugh. "Oh, shit, that was a new bottle, and we left you a few drops." I hid my face in his chest, loving the closeness of him.

He rubbed my back and kissed the top of my head. "Shae?"

I peeked up at him. "Does this conversation involve a Starbucks run?"

His chuckle rumbled through him. "I wasn't sure you were awake yet, and I really had to see your expression get all twisted up when you tasted the shit I made this morning. I'll be right back."

My brow rose as I watched him walk to the front door, open it, then bend over to pick something up from the front walkway. "Oh. My. God. You're the best thing ever." I giggled as he carried in two large Starbucks cups and a small brown paper bag.

He strolled across the room and set them on the counter. "One white chocolate mocha and a slice of banana bread."

"My favorite." I nearly bounced around the kitchen like a little kid on too much sugar.

"Yup." He shot me a knowing look from the corner of his eye. "I figure you can wake up first, then we can talk."

I grabbed the coffee and removed the sticker that covered the drinking hole of the lid. "Hmm. It's still hot. How? I assume you drove your bike there and back."

Cole removed two slices of bread and took a bite. "I have a bag that keeps food hot or cold. It's easy to store everything on the back of my bike. I just have to be careful, so I don't dump drinks everywhere." He winked at me, clearly proud of himself.

I took several sips of my coffee, careful not to burn my tongue.

"I had some time to think this morning while you were sleeping." He finished off his food in a few bites, then rinsed the sticky goodness off his hands.

"Yeah? Is thinking a good or bad thing?" I helped myself to my breakfast, making a big production of how good it was. I wanted Cole to be crystal clear that him buying coffee and breakfast scored big with me.

He shoved his fingers through his hair. "Depends on how you look at it. I chatted with Mom, too."

"I'm glad you two can talk. Daddy and I are the same." I nibbled on my bread, waiting for him to continue while I stuffed my face.

"You asked me about my dad last night."

I froze mid-bite and stared at him. This time, I kept my mouth shut instead of asking questions.

Cole tugged on the collar of his black Harley Davidson T-shirt, his expression grim. "I told Mom that I was going to tell you everything, Shae. It might take a few conversations, but you're the one girl I've wanted a relationship with, and even though you might walk out that door and never speak to me again, I have to tell you the truth."

Chapter Twenty-Two

My muscles twitched as a feeling of restlessness consumed me. I set the last few bites of my breakfast on the brown bag and wrapped my fingers around my coffee cup. I had a feeling I was going to need something to hold onto.

"We should sit on the couch." Cole placed his hand on my lower back and guided me to the living room. I sat down, still not uttering a word. Any time I had in the past, it broke the spell, and apparently what was about to spill out of Cole was so big, it had the ability to send me running, and that scared the shit out of me. For the first time, I'd allowed someone behind the walls I'd built to protect myself. I'd given Cole my body. He'd touched my soul after Ibrahim's assault and held my heart in his hand until it beat again on its own. I sucked in a breath, realizing what I was about to admit to myself. But I couldn't. Not until I knew the truth.

"Mom told me about her and Samuel's conversation with you after I moved out." Cole sat on the edge of the cushion, steepling his fingers as he appeared deep in thought. He cleared his throat, then pinned me with his intense gaze. "So, you know she's strongly urging me to talk to you. Plus, she and Samuel were aware of how I felt about you before I was ready to admit it myself."

I nodded, willing him to get to the point, since my nerves were standing on tiptoes.

His eyes studied me as if absorbing every fiber of my being. "I'll start from the beginning." He massaged the back of his neck, clearly stressed. "You asked about the scars on my back." He gave me a pained look. "The first one was when I was ten. Dad had told me to be home for dinner by six. I was at a friend's house down the street. Like most kids, I lost track of time and arrived fifteen minutes late. Mom was working like she usually was ... and Dad was waiting for me. He was a big man. Not fat, but tall, broad shoulders, and he worked out, so he was strong. But I'll never forget the look on his face. Mean isn't the right word for it. Cruel maybe." He gulped as his fingers tightened into fists. "He was a smoker, and I razzed him about smoking in the house and stinking it up. That was a really stupid thing to do when he was already pissed, but there were times shit just shot out of my mouth before I could think it through." Cole shook his head. "I never saw his fist coming. He didn't only get my attention, he hit me so hard I flew through the kitchen. My own father broke my jaw."

His words hit me in the chest, cracking me open. "Cole," I whispered, unable to keep my mouth shut. If he thought I would leave him over an abusive father, he was wrong.

"Save your pity and apologies, Shae. I had plenty of those from Mom." Cole's lips pursed together. "I laid on the kitchen floor, moaning and crying in pain, unable to move my mouth or talk. Dad laughed, lifted my shirt, then put his cigarette out on my back."

I gasped, tears welling in my eyes.

"Then he lit it again and put it out on my back. He did it again and again and again in the same few places as I cried, unable to fight back or defend myself. Not that it would have mattered. I was ten. At some point, he got bored and left me there. I was terrified to move, afraid that he would come back. I wasn't sure when Mom got home, but she found me on the floor and called an ambulance. Dad told her I'd come home a few minutes earlier all busted up. He said he suspected I got jumped by some older kids. Since I couldn't argue with him, she bought into his bullshit."

"Once you were treated, were you able to write it down for her?" I wanted to comfort Cole and kiss his pain away.

"No. Dad never left my side. When I finally made it home, I went straight to bed. The next day, I stayed home from school and Mom left for work. He made it clear that if I ever told her the truth, he would kill me. And I believed him." Cole's head hung down and his knee bounced. "Over the years, he burned me again, cut my skin with his knife, whatever he could to inflict pain. He knew I was too young to stand up to him. But I'd had plenty of time to plan how I was going to stop him."

I dug my fingernails into my thigh, wishing I could use them to cut Cole's father's eyes out. That sick fucker. Tears slipped down my cheeks, and I sniffled and wiped them away. My heart had cracked open and bled all over his floor as he opened up to me. He'd shared his raw, vulnerable side, and I understood that he would never talk about it again. I didn't blame him.

"How did you stop him?" The one part I did know about his father was that the sick son of a bitch was dead. My hands shook as I lifted my coffee to my lips and took a drink. "I hope he died a slow, painful, agonizing death."

"I wish I'd been the one to kill the motherfucker, but I wasn't. When I was eleven, he got mad about my grades and was waiting for me when I got home. The second I saw him, I bolted to my bedroom and locked the door. I'd stolen some money and bought a handgun from a guy off the streets, then taught myself to use it enough to get me out of trouble. My aim wasn't so great, but it was good enough. I hurried to the shoe box I'd hidden in my closet beneath a pile of junk and pulled it out. I loaded the clip and released the safety. When he broke my door down, I was waiting for him. I held him at gunpoint and called my Uncle King. Luckily, he was only a few minutes away."

"Oh, shit. I can't see King being okay with the way your father treated you."

Cole nodded. "He wasn't." Cole stared at the floor, then spoke again. "King called in some favors and showed up with a few other MC guys. My uncle was a little surprised to walk into our home where I had a gun trained on Rick. King spotted the door, then one of the guys tied Rick's wrists and ankles and stuffed a gag in his mouth so I could tell them what happened. I finally spilled my guts to my uncle. He and the guys told me to leave and go to a friend's house until he called me. He gave me a cell phone, then I took off. To this day, I don't know what they said or did to Rick, but he never laid a hand on me again."

"Didn't King tell your mom?"

"All I know is that Rick begged him not to tell her, and that he loved Mom. He swore he'd never mess with me again in exchange for King's silence. King actually asked me what I wanted." He gave me a half-shrug. "He was my dad, and at the time I thought people could change. I told King that if he fucked with me again, I'd kill the motherfucker, but I agreed to let him have a second chance. The truth eventually came out and Mom was furious with me and her brother for not telling her, but it wasn't until ..." Cole held his hands up in surrender. "Another day." Cole wiped his face and blew out a heavy sigh.

I set my coffee down and jumped off the couch, nearly knocking him over as I flung my arms around him and kissed him passionately. "Why would you think that would make me leave, Cole?"

Cole pressed his head against mine and pulled me to him. "Because I am my father's son. His anger and desire to hurt people pumps through my veins, reminding me every day that I'm just as much the monster as he was." Deep concern was embedded in his expression as he assessed me.

My breath snagged in my throat as I realized that was Cole's reality. "No, baby. That's not true. If it were, we wouldn't be having this conversation. I know you've hurt people, you told me, but it was to protect your family from whoever is after you. That's self-defense."

Cole looked away, then back to me. "There's more, Shae. I just can't ..."

I silenced him with a kiss. "We can talk another time. I can't imagine how hard this was." I kissed him again. Glancing up, I gulped when my pulse skipped a beat, and the words I wanted to say danced across my tongue.

He lifted my chin, his beautiful blue-eyed gaze piercing my soul. "Understand one thing, I will never hurt you, and I *will* protect you no matter the cost, Shae. You have my word." He wrapped his arms around me, pulling me tight against his warm body. "One more thing."

"Yeah?"

"I love you, baby. I have for a long time. You don't need to say it back. All I need is you by my side."

Shocked, I stared at him speechless before I found my voice again. My heart did a happy dance as I soaked his words in. "I love you, too."

Cole bent down, and grabbed my thighs, lifting me. I wrapped my legs around him as he carried me to the kitchen island. He sat me down, then his mouth crashed down on mine, dominating me. I moaned while our tongues tangled, and our hands roamed over every inch of each other's bodies. A cell phone rang, and we reluctantly released each other.

"I need to check to see who it is. Don't move." He kissed the tip of my nose, then walked over to the coffee table. He answered, turned to me, and mouthed "King." The color drained from Cole's cheeks.

"You sure, man? Are you fucking sure?" He stilled as he listened, a million different emotions crashing over his expression. Fear and disbelief were quickly replaced with anger.

His anxiety infiltrated my veins and slithered into every part of me. Tension filled the air around us, and I placed my palm against my chest.

"I'll take Shae over and meet you after that. Don't do anything until I get there." Cole disconnected the call. "Get whatever you need. I'm taking you home." Cole took off down the hall, muttering under his breath.

"What? Why?" I hopped off the counter and followed him. Once I reached the bedroom, he was removing my duffle bag out of the closet. "What are you doing? I don't understand!"

"I told you, I will always protect you, even from me. You're going home."

"Cole, please!" Tears streamed down my face, frantic to understand how we'd gone from "I love you" to this in a few short minutes.

Cole tossed my bag on the bed, then whirled around and grabbed my shoulders. "Please, don't argue. This isn't easy for me."

"I don't want to leave you, Cole. Whatever that phone call was about, I know it's not good." A prickle of fear weaved through me.

"Shae, look at me. I need you to trust me." He smoothed strands of hair from my damp cheek. "Do you trust me?"

I looked into his pale blue eyes, the pain in them wrenching my heart. I wanted to trust him. I needed to trust him. Waves of fear rolled through me, and I gripped his wrists, staring into his heated gaze. My tongue darted over my lower lip. "I trust you. "

His mouth crashed down on mine, dominating and sweet all at the same time.

Cole pulled away and hurried to his dresser. "Pack your stuff. As soon as I can I'll come get you. I swear."

I shoved my belongings into my bag, then collected my toiletries. "That's all. I didn't have a lot here."

Cole closed my bag, zipped it, and took my hand. "We have to go. Do you have your phone?"

Spotting it on the nightstand, I gathered it along with my charger that was plugged into the wall. I held it up, then we hurried to the living room where Cole packed my cell and cords in my bag. Cole spun on his heel and stared at me with an intensity I'd never seen. My pulse stuttered against my wrist.

"Remember, Shae. I love you." He tipped my chin up and pressed his lips to mine. A sickening combination of fear and dread nudged me in the gut. I couldn't help but think that Cole had just kissed me goodbye. For good.

Chapter Twenty-Three

Cole leaned his motorcycle into the curve, and I clung to his waist, terrified to let go. I'd never seen him drive this fast, and the wind whipped through my blonde hair as he sped up a hill at a breakneck speed. I needed to adjust my helmet, but I couldn't take the chance. A part of me loved dancing on the edge of danger, but I also realized that whatever King had said to him, he was willing to risk our lives for it.

Forcing myself to relax, I focused on the feel of Cole's muscled abs and the strength of his body as he guided the bike. For a moment, I refused to think about anything else except being next to him. I had no idea when I would see him again ... or if I ever would. I knew that King, Taco, Snake, and the other guys would do their best to keep him safe, but none of them were bulletproof, and I couldn't pretend they were.

Minutes later, Cole pulled into the driveway at Daddy's. He cut the engine, and I crawled off, my legs wobbly from the thrill of the ride.

Cole hopped off the bike, removed his helmet, placed it on his seat, and then grabbed my duffle bag. "Keep your helmet, Shae. You'll need it when I get back."

He ran his knuckles down my cheek, and I leaned into his touch. "Promise that you'll return to me." Salty tears spilled from my eyes and down my face, stinging my wind-chapped lips.

"I'm not leaving yet. I'm going to take you inside and tell Mom and Samuel bye." He kissed me, then dried the moisture from my skin with the pad of his thumb. "This is what held me back from admitting my feelings for you. My life isn't what you're used to. If I need to take off and help King or handle some business, I know that I would have to leave you behind for a while. The idea of you upset and worried fucks me up."

I gave him a weak smile. "I understand. At least I have the girls, Daddy, and Julia. I'll try to stay busy and out of trouble while you're gone."

He pressed his lips to mine again, then threaded his fingers through mine and led me inside the house. Cole halted mid-step, and his attention landed on Zayne, who was standing in the foyer. I squeezed his hand, reassuring him.

"Cole. Shae," Zayne said, his deep voice as smooth as freshly churned butter. He ran his large palm down the front of his suit and nodded. His white shirt and jacket showcased his broad shoulders and rounded biceps. At first, I hadn't noticed how big this guy was, but I'd just been assaulted when we were introduced. My brain was anything but attentive.

"Zayne." To my surprise, Cole reached out and shook his hand. "Please take care of my family while I'm gone."

Zayne's green eyes landed on Cole's. "It's what I'm trained and paid to do. Rest assured, I'm damn good at my job."

The front door opened, catching me off guard. A guy with short blonde hair stepped into the foyer, his clothes matching Zayne's.

"This is Vaughn Reddington. Samuel decided that two body-guards were needed." Zayne nodded at his teammate.

"Shae. Cole. It's nice to meet you." He shook our hands, his palms warm and smooth.

I stood staring at him, my mouth slightly open. I'd never met anyone with one brown and one blue eye. Not only was he as good-looking as Zayne, but his mismatched gaze was so intense, I forgot my manners and hadn't realized that I was holding another man's hand.

Cole pulled me closer to him, snapping me out of my trance. My cheeks flushed as I slipped my arm around Cole's waist and leaned into him.

"Glad Samuel hired two of you," Cole mumbled, his tone sour.

I pursed my lips, realizing that Cole was jealous. Not to mention, I would be around the bodyguards until he returned for me. I placed my palm on Cole's chest, his heart pounding beneath my touch.

"Let's find Samuel and Mom." He tugged on my arm a little harder than usual, scowling.

I was sure that Zayne and Vaughn were used to being glared at. If shit weren't so serious, I would have laughed, then made it up to Cole later.

We found Daddy and Julia in the living room, sitting on the couch next to each other. My adrenaline kicked in and I vibrated with excitement. It had been too long.

"Hey, Daddy. I've missed you." I released Cole's hand and hugged my dad. He looked as handsome as ever in a burgundy polo shirt and khaki shorts. I turned my attention to Cole's mom, smiling. "Julia." I gave her a warm hug.

Cole embraced them as well.

I placed my bike helmet on the floor near my feet, and Cole set my bag down next to it. I settled onto my favorite black leather loveseat, and Cole sat next to me, our thighs touching. He threaded his fingers through mine, and I could feel the flush travel up my neck. This was the first time we'd shown any affection to each other in front of our family.

"I see you two are figuring things out," Julia said, beaming at us. Dark circles shadowed her eyes, and it was clear that she was worried about her son. Her light-yellow top and white shorts looked nice against her tanned arms and legs.

Cole rubbed his chin and sighed heavily. "Yeah. We are. I'm not sure when I'll come home. You most likely won't hear from me until I'm on my way back."

My head jerked toward him. Shit, it hadn't occurred to me that I wouldn't talk to him at all. "Not even a text?" Fear lodged itself in my throat, and my chest suddenly ached. There wasn't a single thing that I liked about this situation.

His eyes filled with sadness as they searched mine. "I can't, baby. I can't risk pulling you into my mess more than I already have."

I clenched my teeth, willing myself to stay calm and focus on the fact that he was doing everything in his power to protect me. Realizing Cole had called me baby in front of Daddy, I risked a quick peek in his direction. Daddy's expression was twisted with worry, but I wasn't sure if it was for me, Cole, or both of us. Unsure of how many days I would stay with our parents, I made a mental note to sit down and talk to my dad some more. Although I was torn up about Cole leaving, I was happy to spend time with Daddy again. Funny how a few weeks ago, I thought money was the most important thing in my life. It wasn't. Not even close. My family was, and as long as I had them and my friends, I would make it no matter what. After all, I was a Wessex.

"Please let us know the second you can, son." Julia wrung her fingers together, and I wondered if she had more information than I did.

Daddy rubbed Julia's back. "We'll worry until we hear from you. Take care of this once and for all." Daddy wasn't asking. He was telling Cole not to return until the shit show was over. It didn't seem to faze Cole, though. I had a feeling a lot of their conversations were similar.

"I will, sir. Then, I'm coming home for your daughter." Cole looked at me, then to my father. "Please keep everyone safe while I'm gone."

"You have my word," Daddy said, his shoulders tense and his voice on edge.

This conversation certainly wasn't helping me feel any better. Cole rose from his seat, and his attention swept the room. "I need to go. I'll be in touch as soon as I can. Hopefully, this won't take longer than a week or so."

Inwardly, I cringed. I used to dance with excitement when I got rid of him for a week, but not this time.

After Cole hugged Daddy and his mom goodbye, he took my hand again. "Walk me out?"

I stood, choking down the tears that threatened to flow, but I couldn't do that to Cole. I wouldn't be the sobbing girlfriend he left behind when he had to handle business. "Yeah." I gave him a wistful smile. I looked at Daddy and Julia. "I'll be right back."

"If you go outside, then take Vaughn or Zayne," Daddy ordered.

"I will." And this time, I would do what he asked me to.

Cole and I strolled through the kitchen, a heavy silence enveloping us. He opened the door that led into the garage, then closed it behind us.

"Samuel's right. You shouldn't be standing around outside. This is safer." He placed his soft palms against my cheeks and kissed me tenderly. "Promise you'll wait for me, Shae."

Our gazes locked. "You don't have to ask me that, Cole. I've waited a long time already. I'm not going anywhere."

"Swear to me, Shae. I need you to say it."

"I promise. But you have to make me a promise as well." I stared at the floor, regaining control of my emotions before I looked at him again.

"Anything, baby."

"Come home to me ... alive. I'm not sure what's happening, but I have a horrible feeling in my gut. This can't be our goodbye, Cole. We're just beginning. I can't lose you now."

Cole wrapped me in his arms and held me against him. "I would do anything to take your fear away, Shae. I would. But I can't deceive you, either. Things might get rough."

Finally, I burst into tears as I clung to him. "Thank you for not lying to me."

"Baby, I'll never lie. Not to you." He kissed the top of my head, then released me. "I need to go." He kissed me gently, his mouth parting and his tongue finding mine. He growled and deepened the possessive kiss that sent tingles to my toes.

Leaving me panting, he stepped away, his gaze on mine. "I love you, Shae. I'll be back as soon as I can."

"I love you, too, Cole. I'll be waiting, so please be careful." I touched my swollen lips as he pushed the button on the garage door opener, then slipped out. Unwilling to walk away, I watched him put on his helmet, climb onto his bike, and start it. The rumble of the engine bounced off the house. He nodded, then turned around and drove down the driveway, taking my heart with him.

I sucked in a shaky breath and closed the garage door, ensuring that it lowered all the way before I walked back into the house. Dark thoughts swirled in my mind, and I shut them down fast. I'd willingly fallen for Cole, committed to him, and as much as I ached for him, I would have to find new ways of dealing with the stress when he was gone.

Walking through the kitchen, I realized that Julia's brother had been part of an MC for a long time. Maybe she could help me cope with the anxiety. Joining them in the living room, I sat down, my attention bouncing between them.

"Cole and I met Vaughn. It was a good idea to have an additional bodyguard," I said to Daddy. It wasn't that my father needed my input, but I wanted him to know that I supported him.

"They both come highly recommended from an old friend of mine. I haven't spoken with Franklin Harrington in a while, but he was my first call when I needed to protect my family."

I wracked my brain, not recognizing the name. "I don't think you've ever talked about him." It was nice to chat about something other than what we were all afraid to say out loud ... that we'd spent our final minutes with Cole alive. Tiny sweat beads formed on the nape of my neck, and my pulse throbbed wildly. I couldn't handle thinking I'd just kissed him for the last time. My lips pursed, and I locked those awful thoughts in a deep, dark hole and threw away the key.

"We go way back. He and his family are in Canada for a while. His son and daughter-in-law are the lead singers for August Clover. Not sure if you listen to them or not."

I grinned. "No kidding? You're friends with Hendrix and Gemma's dad? Why have you been holding out on me? I need concert tickets when they tour again. Oh, and VIP passes."

Daddy chuckled. "I'll let him know. I think Hendrix and Gemma are close to your age, maybe a few years older."

"Honestly, it would be really cool to meet them. I'm not sure they're Cole's type of music, but Zoe, Isabel, Sibyl, and Dani would definitely go with me."

As grateful as I was for the distraction, it had passed too quickly. "Julia, how do you do it? Weren't you worried about King when he first joined the MC? I mean, I know Cole isn't in the club, but he kind of is at the moment."

"Honestly, I never stop worrying about King. I don't agree with everything he does ... or what I suspect he does, but he's my brother and I love him. I think I learned to stay busy and focus on what needed my attention. Most of the time, that was Cole." She reached over and placed a palm on Daddy's knee. "Until I met your dad. I feel like when he became a part of my life was when I really started living."

My hand flew to my chest, touched by her words. "I had no idea."

"You were pretty mad at me for moving on, which is normal, Princess. But Julia was exactly what I needed. You reach an age where goals and relationships shift. You decide what's important, and often live for experiences instead of chasing a career. It's different for each person, but after losing your mother ... I realized life is too short to not be happy." His expression saddened. "I miss her every day, but I feel like your mom sent Julia to me."

My brows shot up. That was a lot to take in, but maybe he had a point. Mom loved Daddy so much. I couldn't imagine she would want him to sit around miserable for the rest of his life.

"I met Samuel at the perfect time." Julia gave him a sweet smile. "Anyway, to answer your question. I realize that Cole leaving right now is going to be hard for you but try not to let your imagination drive you insane. My son can take care of himself."

I realized it was a long shot, but I had to ask. "Do you know what's going on? Cole just said he had to leave for a while. I suspect it has to do with whoever has been after him."

"I'm in the dark as much as you are. Women aren't privy to club business. If Cole joins, it's something you'll have to get used to. The only reason I have any knowledge of what's happening is because Cole has told me. King explained that Cole could share anything he wanted, but that since the MC was taking care of us, any conversations with them was off-limits." She gave me a half-shrug. "It's how it is. I'm used to it. Well, I thought I was until King offered to help Cole figure this nightmare out."

"Seems pretty chauvinistic." I huffed, folding my arms over my chest. "Do you think Cole will want to patch in?" I wasn't sure I was cut out to live that kind of life, but Cole hadn't mentioned joining either, so I couldn't jump to conclusions.

"I hope that he doesn't. I hope he can settle down, finish college, and start a new life for himself. You're good for him, Shae. I've never seen him care about someone as deeply as he does you. You have no problem calling him on his shit, either." She grinned at me.

I laughed. "I definitely let him know what I think."

Daddy cleared his throat, then leaned forward slightly. "Shae, if he does join the MC, then I'm going to ask that you reconsider dating him. If I have to, I'll force your hand. I don't want you in that lifestyle. Having King around is one thing but planning a life with a member is another."

My eyes widened. "Are you forbidding me from seeing Cole if he joins?"

Chapter Twenty-Four

I grabbed the small, oblong chair pillow and hugged it to my belly, pulling at a thread from the corner of the soft material.

Daddy rubbed his jaw, worry lines creasing his forehead. "I'm sorry, Princess, but that's exactly what I'm saying."

Julia tucked a dark strand of hair behind her ear. "We're in agreement about this, Shae. I realize that I don't have any authority over you, but I support your father's decision. I love my son with all my heart, and I think you're perfect together, but the life you would have with him if he patched in ... you deserve better."

I blinked at them stupidly. Cole was out God knew where, risking his life to take care of his family, and our parents were stabbing him in the back. I shot out of my seat, scooped up my helmet and duffle, and glared at them. "You'll feel like shit saying that to me if Cole comes home in a casket."

"Shae," Daddy said, his tone harsh and reprimanding.

Ignoring him, I spun on my heel and left. Angry tears blurred my vision as I hurried up the stairs and toward my bedroom. Exhaustion suddenly crushed my shoulders while my mind recalled the day that

I'd caught Cole watching the video of Ibrahim, Matt, and me. So much had changed since then. It was weird how life stayed the same for years, then in a blink of an eye everything flipped. Slowing my pace as I neared Cole's bedroom, I leaned on the door frame. He should be here giving me shit and being a bossy asshole instead of whatever the hell he was doing.

I walked in slowly, his woodsy, outdoor scent evading my senses. My body was thick with tension, and my chest ached for him. Daddy should have kept his mouth shut. Cole hadn't even mentioned joining the MC. Why did they have to talk to me about him when I wasn't sure Cole would return?

Setting my bag and helmet down, I ran my fingertips over Cole's dark comforter, then lifted it to my nose. His scent lingered in the fibers. Without a second thought, I crawled into his bed and buried my face in his pillow, inhaling the familiar scent I already missed so much. Finally giving in to the barrage of emotions, I allowed myself to fall apart. Once I did, it would be time to suck it up and make a plan. One that included Cole coming home.

Three hours later, I peeled my swollen eyelids open. It took a minute for me to realize where I was and that after I'd cried, I'd fallen asleep in Cole's bed. I pondered sleeping here until he returned. Being surrounded by Cole's things gave me some comfort. So I decided it was a good idea. For now, I needed a shower and some fresh clothes.

I slid off the edge of the king-sized mattress. My legs felt heavy as I dragged them across the hall and to my room. I snorted when I saw my doorknob. I hadn't ever replaced it. If I had, Cole would have never snuck in while I was mostly naked. My core throbbed, missing his touch already.

My stomach sank to my toes as I replayed the memories with him over the last several weeks. I hoped like hell he could take care of whoever it was that was fucking with him, then we could move on. Until he was home safe and sound, I wasn't even going to entertain Daddy and Julia's threat to cut me off if I stayed with Cole and the MC. Granted, those weren't Daddy's words, but his meaning was crystal clear.

Closing and locking my door behind me, I made my way to my closet and dumped my dirty clothes into the hamper, my phone and charger tumbling out as well. I'd forgotten Cole had packed my cell since my workout shorts didn't have any pockets. I tapped the screen, realizing I'd missed a message. Surprised to see a text from Cole, my pulse double-timed while I opened it up.

I wanted you to have a message from me while I was gone. I love you, and I promise I'll make my way back to you as fast as I can. Check your voicemail, baby.

With shaky hands, I located the message and tapped play. His deep, sexy tone filled the speaker.

"If you were the one gone, I would want to be able to hear your voice. So know this, Shae. I miss you already, and once I come home, I hope we can talk about our future together. I love you."

I clutched the phone to my chest, my heart in my throat. He wanted a future with me. I grinned like a schoolgirl after her first kiss, then played the message three more times.

His voice and text were exactly what I needed. Strength pumped through my veins as I kicked the sadness to the curb. It was time to take charge of my life again, regardless of what Daddy and Julia thought.

I gathered a pair of True Religion shorts and a white crop top, then strolled to my bathroom. I'd definitely missed the space, but I would give it up in a split second for Cole. For now, I wanted to take a long, hot shower, then check with the parents to see if it was safe for the girls to come over. I needed my best friends.

Daddy and Julia agreed the group of girls could stay the night, and Zoe was the first to arrive. But, once we were in the house, unless we used the pool the next day, we were to stay put. Daddy also spoke with each girl's parents to explain the bodyguards and ensure they were comfortable with their daughters being here. Although I thought it was a little much, I realized it was the right thing to do. If anything had happened to my friends, I would have blamed myself for the rest of my life.

The second Zoe was in the house and we were upstairs, she flung herself on my bed, the back of her hand on her forehead. "I need a threesome with those bodyguards." She rolled on her side, giggling. "Girl, I had no idea they made men like that. I thought my tongue was going to fall out of my mouth, and I would have to scoop it off the floor."

I giggled and sat down with her. "Vaughn's eyes are amazing, right? You should have seen Cole when we got here and met Vaughn."

Zoe's lips rounded into an O. "What happened?"

I grinned, realizing it felt good to talk about him. "He pulled me next to him and practically growled at the guys."

Zoe snickered. "He just claimed his booty."

"Marked me with a big X," I laughed. Our giggles settled down, and I glanced at my friend. "I liked it. I love that he's possessive and hot and ..." I bit my lower lip. "And that he loves me."

"What?" Zoe nearly screeched as she hopped off the bed and paced the floor. "When did this happen and why haven't you told me before now?" She narrowed her gaze, waiting for me to respond.

"It only happened this morning, so I'm telling you as soon as I can." I couldn't hide my silly smile. "I said that I loved him, too."

"Damn, I'm really happy that you both got your heads out of your asses and realized what everyone else could already see." She plopped down on the mattress, facing me. "I doubt you know the answer, but his sudden trip ... is it because of what you told me? That someone is after him?"

The good feeling bubble popped, and my mood rapidly deflated. Before I could reply, my bedroom door flung open, and Dani, Isabel, and Sibyl strolled in with massive grins on their faces.

"Bitches!" Isabel said, dropping her overnight bag on my floor and running to us.

Relief flooded me as my friends arrived, and we all exchanged hugs. I hadn't realized how much I'd missed them. I'd gone from seeing them at college every day to only a few times this summer.

Sibyl's emerald-green eyes danced as she kissed me on the cheek, then set her duffle and handbag next to Isabel's. "Girl, what in the hell is going on? You've been MIA since after Harrison's party. If Zoe hadn't given us a few updates, I would have filed a missing person's report."

"I'm so sorry. I'll explain everything later, but first I want to know what's going on with all of you."

Dani hugged me, stuck her bag near the others, then sank onto the bed, crossing her tanned legs and dropping her purse on the floor. It seemed like the girls were moving forward without me, and a sharp pang of sadness stabbed me in the chest. Life hadn't slowed down long enough for me to realize how much everything had changed.

Isabel joined us on the bed, bouncing. "Okay, I have news."

"What are you waiting for? Spill!" I grinned, happy they were finally here.

"Remington asked me out." Her smile was infectious.

"What?" Dani grabbed Isabel's arm and playfully shook it. "Cole's friend, Remington?"

"Oh, this is juicy," Sibyl added. "He's damn fine. I mean, Cole is hotter, but I'd ride both of them."

Zoe shot me a subtle look. In the past, I would get hot-pissed when the girls discussed Cole and what they wanted to do to him, but this time was different. There was no doubt in my mind who Cole belonged to.

"What did you say?" Zoe shifted and tucked her feet beneath her butt.

"I told him I would have to think about it." Isabel giggled. "I do not have to think about it, but this bitch can't come across as too eager." She pointed to herself for emphasis.

"I don't see him as often now that we're in college. Even sharing a campus, it's easy to not see a person for weeks at a time." I flipped my blonde hair over my shoulder. "Out of the group of friends Cole has, he seems the nicest." I narrowed my eyes, pondering my statement. "I think."

"He either got in less trouble than Cole, Anderson, and Sterling, or he was better at hiding it." Dani rummaged around in her handbag, then produced a ponytail holder.

"When do you plan on answering him?" I asked, wondering if we could double date sometime. Even though Cole had been busy taking care of his problem and spending time with King, he and the guys were tight. If he were here, I would pin him down on his bed, kissing his face repeatedly, and demanding his opinion on Remington and Isabel. The thought of being with him again sent little shivers through me.

"He asked a few days ago, so I figured I would wait to respond, but now that I'm here ... I think I should tonight." She beamed at us.

"Yes! Plus, we won't have to group text, we'll get all the deets live," Sibyl said.

Over the next hour, we chatted about who wanted to date who, how fast the summer was blowing by, and what styles were going to be in for the fall. I loved chatting about clothes and fashion with them. Sadness churned in my belly as I wondered what it would be like if Cole did join the MC. My life would look drastically different. I'm not even sure my friends would be interested in hanging around me anymore, except for Zoe. If Taco were nearby, she would be happy drooling over him, I'm sure.

Parched from the chit-chat, I picked up my bottled water from my nightstand.

"What about you, Shae? I mean, David is starting Eastview

University in the fall." Isabel wiggled her brows at me. "He's hot as hell. You should tap that."

I choked on my water and wiped off my chin. "What?"

"Yeah, full football scholarship," Dani added. "How did you not know this?"

My cheeks heated. "I, uh ... A lot has been going on. I was going to fill you all in this evening."

Zoe rubbed my back, giving me some support. "First, the good stuff."

Four pairs of attentive eyes stared at me, waiting in anticipation. I couldn't stop the silly smile from spreading across my face. "Cole and I are together."

Mouths dropped, then squeals filled the air. Seconds later, I was bombarded by their questions of when, how, and was he good in bed? For a while, my heart was lighter as I updated them with the details.

"There's more. I know Daddy talked to your parents, I'm just not sure what he told them about the bodyguards. I can't go into detail because I don't have a lot, but something is going on with Cole and it's seriously not good." I picked at my comforter, searching for the courage to tell them about the assault. I swallowed hard, forcing the lingering images of that fateful night away. "Whoever is pissed at him ... had Ibrahim kidnap me."

A heavy hush descended over the room. "Ibrahim raped me, then I was tied and gagged in someone's basement. Obviously, I was found, but that's why I disappeared for a while."

Tears clouded my vision as I glanced at them.

"Fuck, Shae. I'm so sorry." Isabel was the first to break the silence. She wiped away her tears. "Is Ibrahim in jail?"

I gulped. "No. He's dead. I can't say anything else. I can't force myself to share the horrible details. It was awful."

Dani pulled me over for a hug. "Girl, love your ass so much. I'm here if you need anything."

"Same," Sibyl said, wiping her runny nose from her emotional response.

Dani's serious gaze landed on me. "Shae, I know that we don't talk about it much, but therapy ... this is some serious shit. Have you considered talking to someone?"

Dani was right. It was frowned upon and wasn't acceptable to have a therapist to tell your dark secrets to, and whoever thought it wasn't cool could suck it. "I'm talking to someone and it's helping a lot. She also went through ... she was gangraped, and she's regained her life again."

Zoe hopped off the mattress, located a box of tissues in the bathroom, then set it in the middle of the bed.

"Thanks," we said in unison as we all grabbed one.

Once we had all collected ourselves, Zoe piped up. "Cole is different with Shae. He's super sweet to her. I'm happy they finally got together."

I appreciated Zoe shifting the conversation to one I could handle talking about. The rest of the evening, although more subdued than usual, was also filled with giggles, snacks, and lots of alcohol. Daddy didn't care if we drank as long as we were safe at home. Although it helped to have my friends here, anxiety reared its head often. When it got to be too much, I would slip into my bathroom and listen to Cole's voicemail. I wasn't the type of person to pray, but I whispered one for Cole. I wasn't sure I believed in it, but I figured at this point, it wasn't going to hurt anything.

It was almost four in the morning when I finally drifted off to sleep, only to be awakened three hours later to Julia frantically banging on my bedroom door, then barging in.

"Shae, honey, wake up."

I rubbed my bleary eyes, attempting to clear them. "What?" I groaned, trying to understand.

Zoe sat up in the bed next to me, her hair sticking up in every direction. "What's wrong?" One by one, Isabel, Sibyl, and Dani popped up. They'd all crashed in sleeping bags on the floor.

"The girls need to go home. Vaughn will take them."

"I don't understand." I pulled myself up to a sitting position, then my foggy brain cleared enough for me to realize that Julia would only be here for a few reasons. All of them included someone in our family being hurt.

"Cole?" I whispered, my hand flying over my mouth.

"King called me. They're at Sacred Heart." Julia gently squeezed my shoulder. "We need to hurry, Shae. Cole's been shot."

Chapter Twenty-Five

I flung the blankets off me so fast I accidentally smacked Zoe in the nose.

"Is he okay? Is he even alive?" I choked on the sob that had lodged in my throat as I scrambled to piece it all together. "Shit, where's my shoes and shorts?"

"King didn't tell me anything else. Just to get our asses to the hospital." Julia stood, moving out of my way. "As I said, Vaughn will take the girls home. I need to make sure they arrive safely since their drivers brought them over."

Fearful eyes watched my every move as I located my clothes, dressed, then ran to the bathroom before I peed myself. I brushed my hair and teeth while I used the toilet.

The girls were dressed and packing when I returned. Zoe handed me my phone and hugged me. "Go. Keep us posted, and I love you."

"Love you guys, too." My heart slammed itself against my chest, and I darted out of the room, leaving them behind.

Nearly falling down the stairs, I frantically searched for Julia and Daddy, who were filling coffee cups and packing a few snacks while they waited for me.

"I'm ready. Let's go." I hurried to the garage door, then realized I wasn't sure who was driving.

"Zayne will drive us, Shae. The Mercedes is waiting out front. You and Julia go, and I'll lock up after the girls leave. I'll meet you there." Daddy kissed my forehead, his gaze full of pain and worry.

Julia grabbed her purse, gave me a large coffee, and we rushed outside. Zayne opened the back door for us, and we settled in quickly. Within seconds, Zayne was speeding down the driveway toward Division Street.

"Thank you, Zayne," Julia said, taking my hand.

"Of course. If the family needs any food or drinks, I'm happy to make a run. Whatever any of you need, let me know."

"That's very kind of you and much appreciated." Julia looked out the window, squeezing my fingers harder as the minutes passed.

I held my phone tightly, praying that I would hear Cole's voice again. It was pure torture not to know how badly he was hurt.

Once Zayne parked in the garage, he escorted us to the main section of the hospital. An older lady at the front desk gave us directions to the surgery waiting room.

"I never knew this place was so big," Julia said, hurrying as fast as she could to reach the elevator.

"Me, either." It was the first time I'd ever been inside Sacred Heart, and I realized it would be easy to get lost. The idea of Cole not making it through surgery sent my pulse racing, and my breathing became erratic.

Zayne stepped into the elevator and pushed the third-floor button. He seemed to know his way around, which sucked for him.

The doors whooshed open, and Zayne stepped out, searching the area before we followed. Spotting King in the waiting area, I took off at full speed.

"King!"

He turned in time for me to throw my arms around his neck. "Is he going to be okay?" I sniffled. I stepped away, allowing his sister to hug him as well.

I stared at him expectantly.

"What happened?" Julia asked, adjusting her purse strap on her shoulder. "And no goddamn MC bullshit. I want to know what in God's name happened to my son."

Damn, Julia showed up ready to deal with her brother. I respected the hell out of her for that. We needed answers.

King's blue eyes flashed with understanding. "He was shot in the gut. He's in surgery now, but we don't know how bad it is."

I masked my tears with my hands. "Is he going to die?" I asked, my voice muffled. I was afraid to look at King when he answered.

"Shae, I don't know, there's nothing else to tell you. When he went down, we had to move fast, and we got him airlifted. The tough little bastard was awake most of the way here. They've been working on him for the last two hours, so hopefully, we will know more soon."

I frowned. "A few hours? You waited that long to call your sister?" My voice hiked up a notch, anger coursing through me at full throttle.

"Shae." Julia gently grabbed my shoulder. "Cole was airlifted, but King still had to ride in. Plus, it took an hour for us to get dressed and arrive." She rubbed my back, then pinned her brother with a furious gaze. "Do you know who hurt him?" Her voice quivered with her question.

"Julia," Daddy said as he rushed over to us. He wrapped one arm around his wife and the other around me.

"King, what can you tell me?" Daddy's tone left no room for negotiation.

"Samuel, Sam, why don't we step into the hall where we can talk." King raised his hand, motioning for them to walk ahead.

"Wait, I can't be a part of this conversation? Cole is my boyfriend. I have a right to know what's going on."

"Let me talk to the folks, then they can figure out what to tell you." King gave me a clipped nod, then turned away.

I opened my mouth to object, then thought better of it. I watched them leave, my blood boiling. I should be included in the conversation. After counting to ten, I stepped to the side of the room and followed them. The hallway was empty except for Daddy, Julia, and King. Lucky for me, King's voice carried even when he was trying to speak in a hushed tone.

I pressed myself against the wall near the door and slowed my breathing in order to hear better.

King rubbed his chin. "I don't know how to tell you this, but ..."

"Say it already, King," Julia demanded.

"Rick is alive, Sam."

Julia gasped in horror, shaking her head as the color drained from her cheeks. "No. That's not possible."

"This has to be a mistake. He's dead. Do you have proof?" Daddy asked with a stunned expression.

"Yeah. When Cole came to me about someone fucking with him, I called in a favor with a private investigator. I had him dig into every possibility, including Rick. After what Cole did to him ... It wouldn't surprise me if someone that was close to Rick wanted revenge. Then shit blew wide open. But my guy didn't find someone trying to settle a score for your dead husband. What he found was your ex ... alive and well. He tracked him for a few weeks, making sure it was Rick before he let me know. Rick had some surgery and dyed his hair and he's been living overseas. Luckily, the motherfucker messed up and used his debit card for groceries instead of cash, which made him traceable. Not sure where he's been all this time, but he made the buy in Canada, a few hours from here."

Shock wasn't the right word to describe my reaction. *Cole's dad is alive? That piece of shit shot his son?*

"Has he been reported to the police?" Daddy ran his hand through his hair, clearly stressed.

"No pigs, Samuel. Not if you want this taken care of the right way. For good," King said, folding his arms over his chest. "No one fucks with my family and lives to talk about it."

Good. Take the motherfucker down! My pulse quickened, blood crashing through my ears. My palms slickened with sweat, and I wiped them on my shorts as I continued to listen.

"Samuel, it's time to lay low. Get the family out of the country while the MC takes care of the problem."

Daddy stood tall, his shoulders tense. "I won't leave without Cole. If he survives, then we stay until he's healthy enough to move." Daddy rubbed his chin, then blew out a heavy sigh. "How did Rick live? The son of a bitch had a death certificate."

Before King could respond, Julia's phone rang, and she looked at the screen, then answered.

"This is she." She gripped Daddy's hand and looked at her feet, her hair hiding her face. "Yes, we're all here. Okay, thank you."

My body trembled violently, and I slapped my palm against the wall in a shitty attempt to steady myself. Had the call been from a doctor with news about Cole? Fear, grief, and anxiety drowned out my thoughts as I waited for someone to tell me what in the hell was going on.

Chapter Twenty-Six

Realizing I shouldn't get caught eavesdropping, I hurried to a chair and sat down. Zayne pretended that he hadn't witnessed me pressed against the wall listening, which I greatly appreciated. It was one thing to be a bodyguard, another to tattle like a little kid. I stared at the floor, picking at my fingernail as my parents entered the waiting area.

"Shae, one of Cole's nurses called. He's still in surgery." She wearily sank into the seat next to mine while Daddy and King continued to chat quietly at the other end of the room.

"Do they know if he's going to be okay?" I demanded, chewing on my bottom lip. "Why won't they tell us anything?"

Julia took a slow breath. "He's getting the best medical care available. He was shot in the stomach, but since King acted so quickly, his chances of making it are a lot better." Julia flashed me a sad smile. "Try not to worry Shae, we both know that Cole is a fighter."

I nodded. "He's a tough guy, for sure. He told me about Rick hurting him when he was younger." I glanced at her from the corner of my eye, trying to catch her off guard. Although Cole had spoken to his mom before he talked to me about the abuse, I couldn't let her know I'd been listening to their conversation.

"I wasn't aware of what Rick had done to Cole until it was over." Julia hung her head, her dark hair hiding her face for a moment. "We had a beautiful house in a nice area. I worked a corporate job as a vice-president for a technology company. I traveled a lot. Rick and I had agreed he would take on side-work or a part-time job so he could be there for Cole." She covered her mouth with her fingertips, a tear escaping. "Wanting to provide a good life for my son cost me dearly."

I took her hand in mine. "It's not your fault, Julia. You didn't make Rick do those awful things to Cole."

"I know, but if you ever have babies of your own, you'll realize the guilt you might carry outweighs anything else. If I hadn't married Rick, Cole wouldn't have been hurt."

I sat up straight and squared my shoulders. "Julia, if you hadn't married Rick, we wouldn't have Cole at all."

She smiled through her tears. "He's what has kept me going all these years. Now he's grown, and all I want is for him to be happy and healthy." She gently patted my cheek. "You're good for him, honey, but I don't know what path Cole will take. I don't want to see you hurt like I was."

We fell into an anxious silence as the minutes ticked by without a word about Cole. My brain spun a million different scenarios, including what casket he would be buried in, or what our wedding might look like. My emotions were on overdrive, dipping and cresting from one second to the next.

Time refused to appease me and dragged its feet like a child refusing to walk while the parent was using every trick possible to get them to stand. I'd used it on my mom several times.

I relentlessly paced the hall near the waiting room, stopping to stare out of the window that overlooked Spokane. The sun had shifted and began its afternoon trajectory. We'd been here for five hours, and I was about to lose my mind. Since I'd never had surgery and neither had Daddy, I had no idea what was taking so long.

Lightly banging my forehead against the pane, I considered texting Zoe, but I'd already blown up her phone earlier. There was nothing else to say until we had news.

"Shae," Daddy's voice reached me, and I spun around, hopeful. He waved me over. "Princess, we have news."

Chapter Twenty-Seven

I thought I'd hauled ass this morning when Julia woke me, but I'd just broken my record. Daddy wore a solemn expression, and as much as I needed answers, I was terrified to hear them.

"What is it? Is he out of surgery?" Something similar to fear scraped its ugly nails down my spine. I rubbed at my chest, where my heart hurled itself against my ribs. The palpitations were full of dread and adrenaline.

Daddy wrapped me in a hug and kissed the top of my head. "Yeah," he whispered.

I clutched his shirt between my fingers, recalling the conversation he'd had with me about mom. That she was gone, and the doctors couldn't help her. I was old enough to realize she was dead the moment I found her, but I guess he needed to make sure I was clear about the situation.

"Shae, he's going to be okay. The bullet hit his large intestine, but they were able to remove part of his colon. Cole will make a full recovery."

I rubbed my stiff neck, trying to collect my scattered thoughts while his words registered in slow motion. I stepped away, giving myself over to the galloping beats of my pulse. I bent over, wrapping my arms around myself as I fell apart. My knees met the hard, tiled floor as the sobs ripped through me.

"It's all right, Princess." Daddy sat down and pulled me against him.

"I love him, Daddy," I confessed as the emotional whiplash finally began to calm.

"I know, honey. Let's talk about this later. We should go see Cole."

Daddy helped me stand, and I spotted a bathroom. "Give me a minute." I was a mess, and if Cole was awake, I didn't want to let him know that the thought of losing him almost broke me.

After blowing my nose, rinsing my face with cold water, and taking some deep breaths, I felt a little more presentable.

I messaged Zoe to pass along the good news and let her know I would update her as soon as I learned more.

Shoving my phone in my back pocket, I then removed it again. I would need something to hold onto when I saw Cole.

Surprisingly, we were all allowed into the ICU. Cole gave us a lopsided grin, clearly on some serious pain medication.

"My favorite people," he said groggily. "I'm glad to see everyone."

Cole was in bed, wires everywhere, but the relief I felt when I looked in his beautiful blue eyes nearly crippled me as I thanked God that he was alive.

"Son, don't ever do that to me again," Julia chided him, tears slipping down her cheeks.

"I'm sorry, Mom. Shit went sideways so fast." Cole's head rolled to me. "Hey, baby." He reached for my hand, and I took it.

"Hey, are you in a lot of pain?" There wasn't anything I could do if he were, but I could still ask.

"Not too much. I'm sure I won't be saying that in a few days.

They pump so many drugs into your system for surgery ..." Cole frowned, his tongue darting across his lower lip. "I'm thirsty and my throat is sore."

Julia reached for some ice chips and put a few in a cup, then gave them to him. "Here, honey." He raised his arm, careful not to disturb his IV. The soft beep of the machines was the only sound as he placed one chip in his mouth and closed his eyes.

Suddenly he frowned, then stared at his mom. "Rick." He swallowed. "He's alive. Not sure how. He's the fucker after me."

"What?" I pretended to be horrified before I bowed my head, hiding my face in order not to reveal my true reaction. I wasn't supposed to know that Rick was still walking around on this earth, but I didn't want to mention that I'd listened to King and Julia's conversation at the hospital.

Cole nudged me with a finger, and I looked up at him. "I'll explain this to you later," he said.

I frowned and nodded. He had a lot to update me on.

Julia smoothed his hair from his forehead. "I know, King told me. We'll figure this out, Cole, just focus on healing."

"King has it under control." Daddy gently patted his leg.

"I don't understand how, though." He shook his head, then winced. "Fucking headache."

"Get some rest, honey." Julia glanced around for a chair, then Dad brought her one from the other side of the room.

"Yeah," Cole mumbled, sounding as though he was falling asleep already. "First." He swallowed. "Shae?"

I rose and squeezed his hand. "Yeah?"

"I love you. When I got shot, all I could see was your face and remember how it felt to kiss you."

Tears pricked my eyes. I probably should have been embarrassed at his drug-induced confession in front of Daddy and Julia, but I couldn't have cared less.

"Kiss me," he whispered.

I leaned over, careful not to touch his torso, then I pressed my lips gently to his. Heaven couldn't have been sweeter than Cole's mouth against mine. Everything around me slipped away as we shared our hearts and soul. I straightened and ran my knuckles down his cheek. "I love you, Cole Parker."

He flashed me a sweet smile before his eyes fluttered closed, and he fell asleep. I refused to look at our parents because, even if they had disapproval written all over their expressions, I didn't give a fuck. The only thing that mattered was that Cole was alive.

Chapter Twenty-Eight

I remained by Cole's hospital bedside over the next week-and-a-half. By the time he was discharged, I wasn't sure who was more excited to go home—him or me. He'd grown restless and grumpy with the staff and wore a sour expression often, but I guess that was to be expected after surgery. After riding his motorcycle anytime he wanted, being cooped up was difficult on him.

Daddy helped Cole to his bed, and I made several trips to the kitchen to gather drinks and snacks. Julia fussed over him and expressed how relieved she was that he was home. We all were. She propped up several pillows and helped Cole get as comfortable as possible before she and Daddy cleared the room, leaving us alone for the first time since he'd left with the MC.

Once I closed and locked the door, he smiled and patted the space beside him. My stomach plummeted as I realized we needed to have some serious conversations about what had happened. Cole had lived through a trauma, and I was well aware that he couldn't rush the healing process, but we had plenty of time to talk.

"I've missed you in my bed. Get your sweet little ass over here." His deep voice sent shivers all over my body.

I climbed in next to him, smiling and happy that he was alive and home. "No sexual activity, Cole," I said, mimicking the doctor. "Two more weeks of healing before you even consider it."

Cole chuckled and placed his hand on my knee. "Who said anything about having sex? I've had days to think about all the ways I can get you off without fucking you."

His response stunned me, and I stammered, but my body was fully alert and eager to hear what he had in mind.

"Cole, you'll get worked up, and I can't even suck you off. You're not allowed to tighten your abdominal muscles. That's not fair. As much as I would love to play around, I'll wait with you." I leaned over and nipped his bottom lip, then pressed my lips to his. "I missed you so bad."

"I'm here, baby." He carefully smoothed my hair. "And I need to see you come."

"Cole, I'm not sure what to do with you. Do the pain meds make you horny? If the parents catch wind of us messing around, they'll ship me off to college early and you'll be bingeing Netflix by yourself."

His forehead creased in a frown, then he grabbed my chin, his hold tightening. "A week. No longer. I highly recommend you not argue with me, or there will be consequences. Do you understand?"

Was it wrong that my pussy quivered from his demands, and that I couldn't wait until he was healed to dominate me?

"Yeah," I whispered.

"Until then, under no circumstances are you to touch yourself or use the vibrators in your nightstand." He smirked before his hand slowly fell away.

I snorted and shot him a horrified look. "First, snooping is not cool. Second, that's taking it too far. I'm not the one laid up in bed, so I should be allowed to have a little fun while you heal." I tilted my head and quirked my brow, challenging him.

"Then reconsider and let me lick your cunt now." His expression grew serious.

I shook my head. "You would have to lay on your belly, and that's a no, babe."

"I'll lay flat, you straddle my face. Simple." He quirked a dark brow. "Let's try it. Just one taste, baby. If I move a muscle in my stomach, we'll stop."

I stared at him, wondering if he was crazy, but I also understood that he was relentless until he got what he wanted.

"Take your shorts and panties off," he ordered. "Then help me lay back without the pillows."

I hopped off the bed, ensuring the door was locked before I stripped down.

"That's my girl." His greedy gaze raked over me.

After we gently situated him flat on his back, I crawled over him and propped up on my elbows with my face near his hard cock that was pressing against his basketball shorts. It took everything inside me not to suck on him, but he would clench his tummy muscles if I did.

"You haven't left me since the accident. Relax, and let me give you this." He dug his fingers into my sides, and I hovered over him. His tongue swiped my wet slit, and I moaned.

"Jesus, you taste so damned good. I've missed my pussy." His hold tightened as he teased and touched me in the best way possible.

My attention was glued to his stomach until the pleasure was too much, and I could no longer focus. Somehow, he kept true to his word and hadn't moved except for his mouth. I gasped and moaned, trying to be still. If I jostled him, I would feel horrible. I was already surprised I'd given into him.

He shoved his tongue inside while he massaged my bundle of nerves with his thumb. Apparently, he had figured out how to make this work without hurting himself. It didn't take long before I quivered, my release hitting me hard. I bit my lip in order not to yell his name. All the tension and fear from the last several weeks slipped away as the pleasure took over.

Cole slapped my ass, and I yelped.

"Told you I could do it." He smacked me again, then I lifted a leg over him and carefully hopped off the bed. It had been a while since I'd seen his bathroom, but it was as large as mine, with a huge walk-in closet. The light turned on as soon as I entered, then I searched for a couple of washcloths. I cleaned myself, then located a fresh, damp cloth for him along with his tube of toothpaste from his counter and took it to him.

"Here." I offered him a smile as he wiped his mouth and chin.

He squirted a little toothpaste on his finger, then licked it off like it was candy. "Probably shouldn't talk to mom smelling like your pussy."

"Ya think?" I snorted, then returned the items, and repositioned his pillows before I climbed into bed. I looked at him briefly, noting the way his hair covered his forehead, the sharp nose I'd learned to love, and the angular, well-defined line of his jaw. I took his hand in mine, overwhelmed with gratitude that he was alive and next to me.

"Cole, are you up for a talk?"

He grinned. "A postcoital conversation, huh?"

I rolled my eyes at him. "We didn't have sex, but something like that."

Cole kissed my knuckles. "Before we start, I love you. I can tell by the look on your beautiful face this is important."

I nodded. "Are you too tired? If so, this can wait."

"All I've been doing is sleeping, I'm ready to stay awake for a while. What happened while I was gone, baby?" His thumb traced small circles on the back of my hand.

"You got shot," I whispered through the heartache. "I almost lost you. We all did." I swallowed, glancing away and collecting my thoughts before I looked at him again.

"I'm going to be okay, though. That's the important thing." He carefully shifted on the mattress, then relaxed.

Pulling my knees up, I propped my chin on them. "Are you planning on joining the MC?"

A thick, heavy, dream-crushing silence blanketed the room.

His gaze remained on me. "I haven't decided, yet."

Tears pricked my eyes, and I stared at our joined fingers before I continued. "Daddy and Julia are fine with us dating. We have their support."

Cole nodded, giving me the space I needed to continue.

I toyed with the hem of my T-shirt. "But ..."

"If I prospect, and I'm voted into the MC," he continued for me, putting the pieces into place.

"If you join and we're together, then Daddy will cut me out of the will and Julia will support his choice. Those aren't his exact words, but I've known my daddy for nineteen years, and I'm very capable of reading between the lines."

"I don't disagree with them, Shae. It's no life for you. You need someone who will be there for you and doesn't have a thirst for destruction. A motorcycle club isn't for everyone, especially not a one percenter club."

This wasn't where I'd anticipated the conversation to go. I wasn't sure what I'd expected, actually, but it wasn't this. "Couldn't I be your old lady?"

Cole chuckled. "Baby, I can't see you putting up with being treated less than the beautiful, intelligent woman you are. Women aren't respected by most of the guys. King, Taco, Snake, and the others understand what you mean to me, so they're good to you."

My stomach dropped as I thought about what Cole was telling me. "I guess I thought, since you were hurt and almost died, that you might have made a decision. If you pledge, I'm sure you'll be patched in." My soul was breaking right in front of him, and I wasn't sure he even realized it. In my mind, he would see King and the other men occasionally, and we would plan our future. It was what he'd said in his voicemail. Unless he'd planned on me going with him. But he was right. I wasn't sure I was cut out for that lifestyle.

"I won't lie, Shae, I'm on the fence. King is my family, and those guys are my people, but there's another side of me, and what my heart and head want are completely opposite. I should have thought this through before I dragged you into hell with me." He scrubbed his face with his free palm and blew out a heavy sigh.

"Yeah, you really should have." I released his hand. "I'll be across the hall if you need anything."

"Shae, don't." He tried to grab my wrist, but I ducked out of reach.

I left him alone in his room to think about what he wanted. Anger simmered beneath my calm exterior. I'd fallen in love with him, not understanding all of the moving pieces. But there was one thing I knew how to do and do well ... protect my heart, and I'd just built brick walls around it.

Chapter Twenty-Nine

I'd left Cole alone for the rest of the day and occasionally checked on him. Instead of hanging out, I spent some time meditating in my bedroom, then called Natalie when I realized I was spiraling. I flopped on my bed and stared at the ceiling as we chatted.

"I'm glad he's home, but he sounds as hardheaded as he was before he was shot," Natalie said.

I could imagine her grinning. "I'm not sure what to do. What I want is to force his hand and make him choose, but Cole would dig his heels in. I wish I'd known about the stakes before I fell in love with him." I slapped my palm against my forehead. "Fuck. Natalie, I'm in love with my stepbrother, who might join a one percenter MC. What is *wrong* with me?"

Her soft laugh filtered through the line. "Not a damn thing, but I have a question."

"Yeah?" I chewed on my bottom lip.

"What do *you* want, Shae? What would make you happy?"

My breath caught in my throat. No one had ever asked me that before. "I want to be happy with Cole and keep my relationship with our parents intact. I want to finish school and plan our future together. I want *him*, Natalie. And a part of me hates Cole for it." My chest heaved with relief. "Holy shit, it felt good to say that." I sat up. "I'm really pissed at him for going out there, thinking he's fucking Superman and getting his ass shot. I'm pissed that even though he almost died, he's still not clear about what he wants in life." I propped my knees beneath me and bounced on the mattress, my anger and anxiety driving my need to move.

"It's okay to be mad at him. Hell, I am," Natalie admitted. "He's got his shit, but he's also a great guy, and he's at this huge fork in the road. I want him to make the right choice. He might think the MC is for him, but I think walking away from you would cripple him. I've never seen him so happy, and that's saying a lot."

Her words thawed my heart a bit. "I want him to choose me, but I have to offer him the opportunity to walk away. If I force his hand, I'll always wonder if he chose me because of an ultimatum, or if he really wanted to be with me."

"Then you know what to do. Keep your chin up, try to give him a little time. He's got nothing better to do than figure this out while he's stuck in bed. And until it's safe for you to get out of the house, I'm happy to come over and hangout. Plus, you have your other friends. You have the support you need, Shae. Take a breath and find something to keep you mentally occupied. When does school begin?"

I glanced at the kitten calendar on my wall. Since I had one on my phone, I didn't need one in my room, but I adored all the cute baby cats. "Mid-September, so in about four weeks. Right after Cole is healed enough to start living again." I dramatically flopped on the mattress.

"Then make plans with the girls, go shopping, do whatever helps."

Shit! With all of the chaos, I'd forgotten that Daddy had put a hold on my credit card. I knew it hadn't been that long ago, and maybe he would change his mind under the circumstances. If nothing else, I would have an allowance for clothes. I made a mental note to talk to him.

"I will, and thanks for listening. I'm not sure I would make it through this shit without you. When I first met you, I thought I had competition, so I'm grateful we're friends instead." I giggled with the confession.

Natalie laughed. "Nope. As I said before, Cole turned me down for the girl on the motorcycle ... Hmm, now that he's with you, I wonder who he was talking about."

My heart lit up as I remembered the conversation with Cole about the airbrush art on his bike and the tattoo near the shoulder blade on his back. "It's me," I shyly admitted.

"That would make sense, but how do you know?" Curiosity weaved through her words.

"Because there's an airbrushed image on his motorcycle and a tattoo on his back. It's my face with blue and white flames over it." I shifted to my stomach and propped my elbows on the mattress.

"Shae, that's intense. Guys don't paint their bike or ink their skin unless they're head over heels in love. Listen, I don't want to speak out of turn. Give Cole some time, but honestly, I think he'll make the right decision."

"I hope so." Although I loved her vote of confidence, I understood that she couldn't be certain. The only thing I knew was that I wasn't sure about anything.

"I need to get back to work, Shae, but thanks for making my dinner break interesting. It's always good to chat with a friend."

"I'll keep you posted. Hopefully Daddy and Julia will learn more about who is after Cole, and it will be resolved soon." *Or kill Rick once and for all.* "I'm ready to get out of the house. At least it's big." I laughed. "Thanks, Natalie. Have a good night."

"You, too, Shae."

I disconnected the call. It was time to check on Cole again. Maybe he was sleeping or watching something good on Netflix.

Climbing off the mattress, I strolled out of my room and across the hall. I knocked before I opened the door and poked my head in. "Cole?" Frowning, I entered, not seeing him in bed. "Cole?" I ran to the bathroom, but he wasn't there. I searched the space in case he'd fallen and knocked himself out in the process. At this point, I was pretty sure that anything could happen. Pulling his cell number up, I called him. My pulse broke into jumping jacks while it rang.

"Hey, baby," he answered.

"Where are you? I've been scared to death." My hand fluttered to my chest.

"Downstairs in the living room. Come on down."

Frustrated that he hadn't bothered to tell me he'd moved, I snapped at him. "Why are you there?"

"I didn't mean to worry you, but we have company."

The blood in my veins chilled with his words, and I swallowed over the ball of emotions that had lodged itself in my throat. "What's wrong?" I whispered, closing my eyes, wishing the nightmare would fucking end.

Chapter Thirty

Scrambling down the stairs so fast I almost bit it, I heard unfamiliar voices carry through the foyer. As I approached the living room, my gaze swept over the people gathered. I quickly assessed the expressions of my family and the beautiful blonde standing near a tall, dark-haired guy. I didn't recognize either of them.

"Shae," Daddy motioned for me to join everyone. I spotted Cole stretched out on the couch, and I carefully sat next to his feet.

I chanced a quick peek at Cole, his eyes full of apology. Maybe our earlier conversation had hurt him, too.

"Shae, this is Pierce and Sutton Westbrook from Westbrook Security. They're Vaughn's and Zayne's bosses, and also own the business."

That would explain Pierce's military-style posture. Intense and badass. His white polo shirt sported the gold company logo, and his biceps strained the sleeves when he rubbed the back of his neck. He was several inches taller than his wife, even with her heels on.

"Hi, it's nice to meet you." I stood and extended my hand, greeting each of them.

"It's nice to put a face to the name," Sutton said, smiling. She smoothed her green silk blouse, then tucked her hair behind her ear.

I nodded, unsure what to say.

The door opened, and I leaned forward to see who had arrived. King stepped inside and removed his black boots, leaving them near the entrance. He quickly walked toward us, and my pulse skipped a beat. This shit was serious if King was here. Butterflies flew around in my belly, igniting a windstorm of anxiety that reached down to the tips of my toes.

King introduced himself to Pierce and Sutton, then stood next to Julia and Daddy, who were sitting in the chairs. Julia wrung her fingers and plastered on a smile, pretending that she was doing better than she actually was.

"Now that everyone has arrived, I'll explain why the Westbrooks are here," Daddy began. "After Cole was shot and King identified Rick as the shooter, we needed to find out how he was alive. Zayne recommended that I reach out to his bosses and explained that Sutton could dig up anyone's secrets given the time. I made the call that day. I thought it would be easier to have a family meeting instead of having to repeat the details to each person and not being able to recall all of them accurately."

Now it made sense why Daddy hadn't called me downstairs, yet. We were waiting on King as well.

Pierce shoved a hand into his slacks pocket. "I would just like to say that you have our condolences for what the family has been through. Cole, I'm glad that you're on the mend. I think what Sutton and I have found will explain a lot."

At times, I hated polite conversation. It was fucking killing me at the moment, and I clenched my jaw to control any obnoxious outburst to tell Pierce to hurry the hell up. Daddy would be horrified if that happened.

"As we all know, Rick MacBride is alive. From what everyone understood, there was an attack about nine months after he was sentenced to prison. The public was told that he died there. Julia, I'm sure you saw the death certificate to verify the information," Pierce said.

I desperately wanted to ask why he was in jail, but I didn't want to interrupt. The way the conversation was unfolding, I would find out soon enough. I already understood that Rick was a well-connected and extremely dangerous man.

"Unfortunately, Rick's death was faked, and he escaped," Sutton explained. She reached for a manilla envelope on the end table near Cole's head. "I've collected everything for you to review later." She confidently strolled across the room and gave it to Julia.

Pierce rubbed his jawline, his intense gaze landing on Julia. "After further investigation, Sutton was able to find the medical examiner, Mr. Petrov, who had signed the death certificate as well as performed the autopsy." Pierce indicated air quotes as he mentioned the autopsy. "Mr. Petrov is older and dying of cancer, so he answered our questions without hesitation."

"A dirty cop, and a guard along with Dr. Petrov helped stage Rick's death, then he was smuggled out of the prison. Mr. Petrov was paid half a million dollars to make this happen. Rick's reach was wide," Sutton said.

"Son of a bitch," Julia muttered, looking away from everyone. "He was always crafty."

"He's been living overseas, but recently made his way to Canada, only a few hours from here. We suspect that Rick was waiting until Cole wasn't a minor any longer before he closed in. We also know that he hired Ibrahim to report on his son, including when he was home, where he went when he left, and who he spent time with," Pierce explained. "Fortunately for us, Rick made a few mistakes with a debit card. Well, honestly, I'm not sure he messed up. He's been smart about hiding over the last several years. I think he wanted to make his presence known."

King fisted his hands and rocked back and forth on his heels. "The second Cole showed up and told me he was getting threats, I put a man on the situation. After shit went down with Ibrahim snatching Shae, I knew things were getting hot. Then, we got a tip from my guy that Rick was not only alive but had crossed the border from Canada to Washington. So yeah, he wanted us to know. Unfortunately, we went to meet the sorry piece of shit and got blindsided." King's features twisted with regret as he glanced at Cole.

A million questions spun around in my mind. Why had Rick spent time in prison and faked his death, but more importantly, why the hell was Rick trying to kill his son? I fidgeted in my seat, a tension headache building behind my temples.

"Before anyone says anything else, I need to have a conversation with Shae," Cole said.

Baffled, I turned toward him, careful not to jostle his abdomen. "I don't understand."

"Mom, do you need me here any longer?" Cole asked.

Pity flickered in Julia's gaze. "Go ahead, I'll update you later."

My eyes locked with Cole's, and fear seeped into my bones, weighing me down. Daddy helped Cole off the couch and up the stairs as I followed. My legs grew heavier and heavier with each step. Cole had said that he would tell me about the rest of his past, and now I wasn't sure if I wanted to know. His previous words whispered in my head, and I clutched my chest.

I am my father's son. His anger and desire to hurt people pumps through my veins, reminding me every day that I'm just as much the monster as he was.

Cole's body relaxed, clearly relieved that he was in bed again and stretched out. "Sitting on the couch hurt like a bitch."

I closed and locked the door, then settled in next to him. "I'm sorry. Do you need anything?"

"Just to tell you the rest of my past, Shae. You seem to think that it's my decision whether we stay together, and that's not the case." His face twisted, conflicted, and he gently squeezed my forearm.

I sucked in a deep breath, reminding myself to breathe no matter what Cole was about to say. "I'm listening," I whispered. In those moments that I waited for him to speak, I wondered if his secrets would send me running out the door. I steeled myself, reaching into the core of my being for every ounce of courage to listen with an open mind. Little did I understand that, as the events continued to unfold, the truth would devastate me, leaving only a shell of my former self in its wake.

Chapter Thirty-One

"After King dealt with Rick, he left me alone. He and Mom seemed happy, so I kept my mouth shut and hid the truth from her. She worked her ass off for the house we lived in, and I couldn't rip her life away." Cole leaned his head back on the pillows and licked his lips. "Mom continued to work and travel, but Rick stayed true to his word and didn't hurt me."

"That's a good thing." I placed my hand on top of his, the warmth of his skin soothing my nerves a little.

"Things were decent for a few years. Not great, but it seemed we were making progress. Rick even talked to me like a human being and spent some time with me. As far as I could tell, our relationship was getting better. I had hope that he'd really changed."

My pulse hammered against my wrist as I listened.

"Days after my thirteenth birthday, Mom left for a ten-day business trip. That morning, when I got ready for school, I had a shitty feeling something was off. I figured some TV show or shit had triggered me. Plus, Mom hadn't been gone that long before, so I assumed I was simply overreacting. I went to school and forgot about it ... until

I got home." Cole turned away from me, but I hadn't missed the pain that coasted over his face.

Panic seized my chest and impatience jetted through me as I waited for an answer. "Take your time, Cole." The second the words left my mouth, I wanted to scream. I hadn't meant one word. I needed him to hurry up before I died on his bed of a goddamned heart attack.

He looked at me again. "Promise me something, baby."

"What?" I should be comforting him, but I was rooted in place.

"Remember that I love you no matter what." Moisture pooled over his eyes, and tears welled in mine. His thumb gently stroked my thigh, attempting to soothe me before the darkness arrived.

"I will." My voice cracked with my words.

"It was nearly seven in the evening by the time I got home from school. I'd had football practice and we'd run late. I strolled into the house and dropped my pads and helmet in the entryway. Rick normally had dinner made, but that night I didn't smell anything. I searched the living area and kitchen but didn't see him. After calling out his name and not getting a response, I went upstairs. A sound came from his and mom's room, so I walked that way. The door was partially open, so I walked in ..." He rubbed the back of his neck, his gaze full of so many emotions I couldn't grasp what he was feeling.

"Rick was sitting at the end of the bed with my gun beside him. I should have fucking run, but what I saw next paralyzed me."

I sunk my teeth into my bottom lip so hard I tasted blood.

"He had a tiny baby in his arms ... feeding her." He shook his head as if to clear his mind from the agonizing memory. "I was so stunned I just stood there. Mom sure as hell hadn't been pregnant. And the sight of a man that had beaten me holding a baby so gently ... It fucked me up." Cole placed his free hand on his stomach and winced.

"What do you need?" I asked, leaning forward. "Advil? Tylenol? Prescription pills? What can I do?" I realized my barrage of questions wasn't aimed at his physical pain as much as it was meant for his emotional turmoil. Seeing him destroyed like that nearly gutted me.

"I'll take something after we're done," he gritted out.

"Okay." I should have forced the issue, but I needed to know what had happened.

"Anyway, Rick nodded to the chair in his bedroom. It was then that I realized one of Mom's dresser drawers was open, and her soft sweaters covered the bottom. Finally finding my voice, I asked whose baby it was. Rick explained that it was a friend's daughter, and he was helping out for a few days. That should have been my second clue that something was wrong. The gun had been my first. Once Rick had finished feeding and burping the baby, he placed it in Mom's drawer. She was so tiny, there was plenty of room. The dresser was sturdy, so I wasn't afraid she would fall. Rick picked up the pistol and slipped it into the waistband of his jeans. He ushered me downstairs where he locked the doors and closed all the blinds and curtains. The rest of the evening, he pretended like everything was normal. He watched television and took care of the baby." Cole released a sarcastic laugh, then winced.

"He carried the gun for the two days he took care of her, and I wasn't allowed to leave the house. Rick never touched me, but he made sure I saw the pistol during those forty-eight hours. The mental games were torture. I was terrified I might do something wrong, and the fucker would shoot me. I locked my bedroom door at night and slept with one eye open. The baby crying also kept me awake, which was okay since I was waiting for him to kill me in my sleep. I wanted to check on her, but Rick never left her unattended unless I was with him. After the weekend was over, I went to school like I always did, but Rick made it really clear that if I breathed a word about the baby, he would end me."

"Why is this fucker still alive?" I spat, seething with anger about how Rick had physically and mentally tortured Cole, then escaped prison.

A growing sense of apprehension hung in the air.

"I'm still trying to figure that out." He shoved his fingers through his hair and continued. "During English class, the teacher asked me to make some copies of a worksheet she needed to hand out. Happily, I made my way to the office. When I got there, the teacher's lounge door was open, and several teachers were watching the TV. The copier was slower than shit, so I started the machine, then moved closer to find out what was worth everyone's attention. The entire world came to a halt as I stared at the television banner scrolling across the bottom of the screen. The guy from the news was explaining the situation, too. My brain began to register the words kidnapped, missing, dangerous. Then, they showed a picture of the baby. It was her."

Unable to stop myself, a horrified gasp escaped me. "Oh, Cole."

"Rick had stolen the baby from the hospital, Shae. The cops didn't know it was him, but all the pieces tumbled into place. I'd never been so terrified in my thirteen years. I knew I had to turn him in, and if I was wrong ... if I was wrong, I understood that my life was over. He would bury me alive and dance on my grave as I struggled to breathe."

"He's sick. Why would anyone steal a baby?" I wiped the moisture from my cheek, not realizing I'd been crying.

"After the cops questioned me and Rick was arrested, I learned my father was an integral part of an organized crime syndicate. He stole babies and sold them on the black market."

A waterfall of emotions washed over me as I stared at him without blinking. There was no way I could have understood what Cole had told me. "Sold babies?" I sucked in a breath, my shoulders shaking. Rick MacBride's blood ran through Cole's veins. And now, the monster in the closet had revealed itself. Rick was a psychotic sociopath. Cole had warned me all along, and I hadn't listened. My stomach churned with the revelation.

"Mom was sick when she saw the news of Rick's arrest and took the first flight she could schedule. My best friend at the time had let me crash with him until she got there. It was then that I told her everything—how Rick had broken my jaw, cut me, burned me, and terrorized me for years." Cole ground his molars, and he briefly looked away. "I've never experienced so much pain in my life. I was powerless to help Mom as I ripped her world apart. She'd done everything humanly possible to take care of me, love me ... and she came home to ... Hell." Cole glanced at me, tears in his eyes. "I love my mom, and I'll fucking never hurt her like that again."

It was then that it hit me. Cole might have Rick as a biological donor, but he was not his father. Cole had a mean side, but he felt the emotion deeply if he loved someone. I suspected that any time he allowed someone close to him, Cole was afraid he would hurt them like he had his mom, and it stabbed him in the heart all over again.

"Cole, you were a kid, and in no way responsible for your father's actions. None of it was your fault."

Cole's chest rose and fell with his slow, careful breath. "The only good part of this story was that I put that son of a bitch in prison. I testified on the stand in front of him and an overflowing court room full of reporters. Every seat was filled, and people were standing against the wall. No one told me for sure, but there were a few guys there that glared at me the entire trial. I think they were members of the black market and were trying to intimidate me. Mom received death threats, and she had to pull me out of school for a while. The teachers were cool and let me get shit done at home, so I didn't fall behind. As soon as it was over, Mom packed us up and changed our last name. She didn't want my father to overshadow any opportunities we had to move on. But the bastard is back and wants to end me for putting him away. Clearly putting him in prison hasn't stopped him," Cole ground out through gritted teeth.

"You did the right thing. I can't imagine how hard it was for you to start over." My soul ached for what he and Julia had lived through. All this time, I'd thought Julia had a perfect life, yet she'd lost her marriage to a monster and probably carried a horrible amount of guilt for what Rick had done to her son.

"Now that you know where and who I come from, I'll ask once more. Are you sure you want to be with me?"

Fear clung to his words, his expression revealing his vulnerability briefly before the stoic mask slipped into place. My emotions shifted through the different flavors of confusion, hurt, then anger at the injustice of our situation until there was nothing else left to express.

And I was well aware that this was it. The following words I spoke would set the rest of our relationship into motion one way or the other. We either moved forward, or we said goodbye.

Chapter Thirty-Two

"Before I can answer you honestly, I need to know one thing. Have you made a decision about the MC?" I had to have the final piece of information before I made my choice.

"If you stay with me, and we plan a future together like I want to, I won't patch in, Shae. I've had time to think about it, and it's been on my mind since I got shot. King and the guys will still be in my life, though. If you can deal with that, then I choose you."

"Really?" My chest swelled with love, but I still had to ask the difficult question. I had to know if he was sure. "Are you going to be happy walking away from that life? You can't choose me, then be miserable. It's no way to live our lives, Cole."

"If you're okay with me taking off with them a few times a year to ride and hang, then yeah. King is my uncle, so I'll always be connected to him and the MC. I'm all in with you. But are you?"

"You're such an asshole." I licked my lips, tasting the salt from my tears. I swiped my damp skin and blew out a heavy sigh. My attention bounced around the room, recalling how our story had started only a few months ago. Now, he was asking if I wanted to be with him on every level.

"Yeah, but you've known that about me." He stared at his lap, waiting for me to commit or leave.

"Yeah, well you're an asshole who owns my heart, and I can't walk away from you, Cole. I want you. I want a future with you. I know someone's past can shape who they are, and you have some doubts, but I see who you are—brave, strong, protective—everything I want in a guy. Everything that I love so much about you." I smiled at him, feeling a little shy about laying my feelings out on the table. "I really want to jump on top of you and snuggle. I need you to hold me, Cole."

"Haven't you realized by now that I will move heaven and earth to give you what you need, Shae?" He grinned. "Grab the pillows from the stack behind me but leave one."

I quickly helped him and watched as he laid down. "Come here." He moved his arm to the side, and I snuggled up to him, my head on his chest. Sometimes words weren't necessary, and we settled into a comfortable silence. Cole had shared the dark demons that haunted him, and all I wanted was to love him for trusting me and allowing me a glimpse of the moments that had defined who he was.

His steady breathing lulled me into a peace I hadn't experienced in a while. "I love you, Cole."

"You, too, baby." He rubbed my shoulder until my eyes fluttered closed, and I drifted off to sleep.

Chapter Thirty-Three

The next three days passed without a word concerning Rick. There wasn't a doubt in my mind that King would take care of the situation. I was just eager for it to be over. As Cole continued to heal, he was ready to get out of the house, but even if Zayne or Vaughn drove us, Julia said it wasn't safe. We'd certainly lived through enough Hell, but my patience was wearing extremely thin, and I was about to find Rick myself and end his sorry life.

Cole and I had watched an unhealthy amount of movies and Netflix. I texted and talked to Zoe and Natalie daily. Zoe offered to keep the girls updated for me, so my phone wasn't constantly blowing up with a group chat. I was excited to see my friends again, though. I was curious to know if Isabel had a date with Remington yet.

"I have to get out of bed, babe." Cole carefully pulled himself into a sitting position. His hair was messy in a sexy kind of way, and I couldn't wait to run my fingers through it.

With each passing day, he grew stronger and could move more. It had also been a change to see him wear basketball shorts all summer instead of jeans, but they were more comfortable, and he wasn't on his motorcycle.

"Do you want to go downstairs and see what Annabelle is making for dinner?" My stomach growled, revealing my true intentions.

Cole chuckled, then stood and straightened fully. The doctor had placed him on light activities for another week, then he could begin lifting things and walk a lot more.

The start of school was right around the corner, too, and we were both eager to start a routine that included dates, parties, and classes. I craved normal, especially since Daddy had lifted the restriction off my credit card. He said I'd handled the life changes so well that I'd proved I could be trusted again. I was way happier over earning Daddy's respect back than the money, but it would be nice to know the funds were available.

Cole used the wall and slowly descended the stairs while I followed, giving him some space.

"I know that Annabelle is cooking, but sushi sounds so good right now." I rubbed my belly as it growled again.

"It does. I'll call in an order from your favorite spot," Cole offered when he reached the bottom of the steps. He kissed me, then threaded his fingers through mine.

"Thanks." I beamed at him. "Do you want to eat in the kitchen or upstairs?"

"Kitchen. I need a change of scenery." He led the way, our bare feet smacking the cool-to-the-touch marble floors.

"Goddammit," Daddy's voice carried from his office.

I released Cole's hand and rushed down the hall. "Daddy? Are you okay?"

Daddy looked up, his eyes full of pain and his face ghostly white. Fear stabbed me in my stomach, leaving me breathless.

"Are you sick? Do I need to call 911?"

He leaned back in his chair. "No." His voice was rough, like he'd choked on sandpaper.

I glanced at the images scattered across his desk, wondering what was upsetting him.

I sank into the seat. "What's wrong?" My knee bounced, the tension in the air palpable.

With a grim expression, he said, "Cole needs to hear this, too, Princess."

Confusion clouded my thoughts, and a tight band wrapped itself around my chest. Maybe there was more news about Rick. "I'll get him." I rose and headed out of the room. I located Cole in the kitchen and asked if he could comfortably sit in one of the chairs in Daddy's office. He agreed, and when we returned, Julia had joined Daddy. She wore a solemn look on her pretty face, which set my nerves on edge even more.

I made sure that Cole was settled, then sat between him and Julia.

Daddy cleared his throat. "Shae, I just received some information from King that affects you. Rick is threatening to make my name public ... unless I turn Cole over to him, which I wouldn't do even if my life depended on it. I protect my family."

"What is it?" I tucked a strand of hair behind my ear, trying to calm my overactive imagination.

Cole grabbed my hand, bracing for the news.

Daddy leaned back in his chair, his body rigid with tension. "I've talked to Julia about my concerns. Cole also mentioned that you had some questions about how I knew Rick. Cole doesn't know the details of how I met his father, either ..."

I stared at Cole, my heart thundering in my ears.

"Shae, before you were born, Lori ... your mom and I tried to get pregnant. We tried every method possible, tests for both of us, in vitro fertilization with a clinic, but nothing worked. Your mom was a hormonal and emotional wreck. Everything she did centered around having a child, and it was tearing us apart. When I mentioned adoption to her, she said it would take years to find a newborn. She grew depressed and aloof, and I was afraid she was going to hurt herself. I became a desperate man to save the woman I loved."

The chiseled lines of Daddy's face were etched with emotions I didn't understand. Nervous silence stretched between us, my mind scrambling to fill in the blanks.

"I shared my concerns with one of my friends at the time. He offered to connect me with a guy that could help with a newborn, but it would be expensive and completely confidential. If I breathed a word of it to anyone, the deal would be off, and my life would be in danger."

Cole squeezed my hand and gave me a concerned glance while Julia focused on the floor.

"I was desperate to not lose your mom, Shae." Guilt and regret twisted his expression. "I met with Rick, and he arranged the adoption. No questions were asked. I paid him cash so there wasn't a paper trail ... other than the necessary papers, so it appeared legit." Daddy choked on his words, tears glistening in his eyes. "It's not something I'm proud of, Shae."

"Wait ..." I pursed my lips, attempting not to think the worst. Surely, I was confused. "I don't think I understand what you're saying."

"Baby, Samuel bought you off the same black market my father was a part of." Cole's tone was so soft, I wasn't sure I'd heard him correctly.

Horror pumped through my veins as I stared at Cole. The air crushed us, dense and accusing and pointing out the fact that whatever had just happened was out of our control. Our fathers had lied and betrayed us. *Father? Daddy isn't my real father.*

"You tore me away from my real family?" Like the calm before the storm, anger clouded my vision.

"I don't know anything about your birth parents, Shae. After you turned eighteen, I began to search for them, but I came up empty-handed. It's a good possibility that your biological mom could have died during childbirth and the father couldn't raise you on his own." Tears slipped down his cheeks. "I've never regretted a decision more in my life, but then I had you. A beautiful, intelligent, feisty girl."

Daddy's words screamed at my broken soul. My dark thoughts

expanded, and I was thrown into an emotional and chaotic tailspin. My jaw clenched, and I balled my fingers into fists, swallowing back the scream building in my chest.

I stood, hatred prickling my skin. "You fucking paid for me. Is that all I was? I was a means to an end, and your money could solve the problem?" My stomach squeezed tight, twisting into painful knots. "As far as you and I go, *Samuel* ... we're finished." I spun on my heel and stormed out of his office, ignoring the gut-wrenching pleas from him and Julia.

Sobs escaped me as I ran upstairs, grabbed my phone and purse, and hurried to the front door.

"Shae, wait!" Cole said.

I paused and waited for him to catch up. "I'm going with you. Let's get the fuck out of here." He kissed my cheek, then slipped a protective arm around my waist. "I'll have Zayne or Vaughn drive, you're too upset, and we need to stay safe."

I sniffled, attempting to see through the moisture in my gaze as we stepped out into the summer air. The heat slapped me in the face, but I didn't give a shit. My entire world had been ripped apart, and everything I loved and respected about Daddy was all fake. Samuel was a big fat liar.

Cole located Zayne and told him we needed to go somewhere safe and quiet. Zayne opened the door to the Mercedes parked under the covered carport, and we hopped into the back seat. Within seconds Zayne was settled and started the engine. The car purred to life, then he eased down the driveway. Zayne must have done this before with a sobbing chick in his car because he handed Cole a package of tissues he had stashed in the glove box.

I carefully collapsed against Cole, wishing we never had to return to Samuel's house.

"I'm so sorry, Shae. I had no idea." He smoothed my hair and planted sweet kisses on the top of my head as I continued to fall apart.

"How? How could he have done something so awful?" I hiccupped.

Cole sighed heavily. "I know you need some time to process, but I think Samuel was in a really shitty place and made a bad decision to protect the woman he loved." His tone was soothing, calm, and even. "If I'd been in his shoes and I was about to lose you ... Shae."

I looked him in the eye. "What?" I wiped my stuffy nose with a tissue.

"I would have done the same thing. Your dad and I are a lot alike in that way. When men like us love someone, the lines of what is right and wrong blur. We'll do things other men wouldn't ever *consider*. As horrible as the news was today, I understand because I would do anything to save you. Anything."

"Is it wrong that I love that about you?" My pulse fluttered with every blink of his lashes and the way his blonde hair shined in the sun that streamed through the back window.

He gave me a crooked grin. "As long as you love me, that's all that matters." Cole kissed my forehead and stroked my arm with his fingertips. "Take some time, baby, but don't dismiss Samuel yet. The man that raised you, fed you, supported you is still there. You're still his Princess."

"But it was all a lie, Cole. My *entire* life is a lie." I seethed, the anger inside me igniting again.

"Yeah, but I'm sure the thought of prison terrifies the shit out of him. Not only would he lose his freedom, but you, too."

"I don't know what to think, Cole. It's too much all at once, and now Rick is trying to blackmail Samuel in exchange for you." I sat up straight, my nostrils flaring. "I'm ready to kill that goddamn motherfucker myself."

I didn't miss Zayne's intense gaze in the rearview mirror, but I ignored him. So far, he'd never betrayed my trust. At least not that I knew of.

"King's on it. He's not sharing details because he can't. It's too risky. Hopefully, this shit will be over soon." Cole shifted on the black leather seat.

"Are you in pain?" I placed my hand on his knee, grateful that he'd left with me but still concerned about him.

"I'm feeling pretty good."

I glared at him, wondering if he was telling me the truth. "Are you just saying that after the shit show to pacify me?"

The corner of his mouth kicked up. "Nope. I would tell you."

I fell back against the seat and stared out of the window as the trees passed by. I wasn't sure what to do with the information I'd learned, but it felt good to get out of the house. Zayne turned down a backroad and dodged the potholes as he drove us out of town. My stomach growled, and I rubbed my belly.

"Can you eat?" Cole asked.

"Strangely enough, yeah."

Before we left Spokane, Zayne stopped at a diner, and we all ordered a burger and fries. Cole bought me a chocolate shake as well. Zayne said it was okay to eat in the car while he drove since he wasn't comfortable with us sitting at the restaurant in plain sight.

Nibbling on my fries, I tried to sift through what Samuel and Cole had said. If Samuel had found out who my biological parents were, would he have told me if he hadn't been forced?

An hour later, Zayne parked in a shaded area at the lake. I couldn't wait to get some fresh air. The majority of the shoreline was thick with trees, allowing us some privacy.

"You both should be safe here. Not many people know this spot exists. Just don't go too far." He slipped on his sunglasses, climbed out of the car, and opened the back door for us.

I hopped out, then hurried to Cole's side, but he'd already gotten out on his own.

He held his hand out to me. "Shall we take a walk?"

"I would love that." We strolled to the water's edge, and I squatted down and dipped my fingers into the calm water. "It feels nice." I toed off my shoes and walked in up to my knees, my toes digging into the soft sand.

"Remember when Samuel bought the ski boat?" Cole toed his shoes off, then waded in up to his calves with me.

"Yeah, it was the year you and Julia moved in." I smirked. "I was *not* happy to have you there with us."

"Me, either. Even though I liked Samuel, I wasn't sure how it was going to play out."

Zayne cleared his throat, and I glanced over my shoulder my blood chilling in my veins. "Cole," I whispered. "We've got company."

Cole turned quickly, his jaw tensing as his gaze landed on a man that appeared to be in his early fifties. His dark hair was streaked with grey, and his brown eyes were menacing as he trained his gun on Zayne. It took a moment for me to realize that he had a pistol in both hands and the other was pointed at us.

"Hello, son."

With a quick step, Cole placed himself in front of me, shielding me from Rick.

"Rick," Cole spat. "What the fuck are you doing here?"

"Is that really how you should greet your old man? Seriously, Cole, can't a man visit his kid? It's been years. You're all grown up, and I just wanted to spend some time with you." Rick's words dripped with hate and sarcasm.

"You're too late for family time, asshole," Cole growled.

I peeked around Cole, my attention on Zayne who was several feet away from Rick. If Rick had been stupid enough to stand closer, I suspected Zayne could have disarmed him. The only problem was that Rick would easily get a shot off at one of us.

My heart hammered against my chest, my breathing was shallow and traveled in short bursts. "Cole, be careful."

Cole moved his arm slowly, reaching back for my hand. "What do you want, Rick?"

Rick sneered and my legs began to tremble. "To finish the job, of course. I owe you, son. We have a score to settle. I mean, don't you think it was shitty to turn your old man into the cops?"

"You can't have him!" I yelled and stepped around my boyfriend.

Rick's maniacal laugh filled the air. "Look at you. Baby Shae is all grown up and protecting her boyfriend. How sweet."

I gulped, remembering that this was the man who stole me from my family and sold me to Samuel. Bile churned in my stomach and I spat into the water. "You're a sick fuck, you know that?" I took a step forward. Cole attempted to grab my arm, but I moved out of his reach.

"Shae," Cole hissed. "What the fuck are you doing?"

"Do you know who my family is?" I stared at Rick, hoping that he would focus on me, and Zayne could move in and disarm him. There was a chance I might get shot, but at least it wouldn't be Cole. I couldn't lose him again even if it meant that I didn't survive.

A movement caught the corner of my eye, and I realized Zayne had inched closer to Rick.

"I never met your parents, Shae. I had a job to do and that was to make money. Who you belonged too was none of my concern." His brow quirked, clearly irritated with my questions.

"You're lying," I challenged. "I need to know who they are. I'll trade you Cole for that information." My heart ached with my lie. I would never give Cole up for this monster, but I was trying to shock Rick.

The air thickened with tension as Rick and I stared at each other. I wasn't sure if he were considering the offer or not. My brain scrambled for something else to say in order to keep the conversation and attention on me. Zayne had to be able to reach Rick if we wanted to walk out of this alive.

The rumble of bikes approaching caught my ears, and a slow grin eased across my face as I remembered that King and his guys had been trailing Rick. "Looks like things could get interesting in just a minute."

Rick glanced behind him, and Zayne sprang into action, kicking one of the pistols from Rick's hand. Rick dropped the weapon and staggered backward nearly tripping. He regained his balance and fear filled his blue eyes.

Cole grabbed me from behind and practically picked me up before we flew out of the water and onto land.

Desperation twisted Rick's features, then he sprinted away from us and into the trees. I assumed his car or bike was hidden there because we never heard him arrive.

"Goddammit! Is everyone all right?" King asked, breaking through the trees.

"Go! He went that way," Zayne yelled. "I'll take care of the kids."

The overpowering sound of motorcycles muffled the rest of the conversation, then King disappeared in the direction he'd come from.

"Are you two, okay?" Zayne asked, meeting us on the other side of the Mercedes.

We stood slowly, my body trembling now that Rick was gone. "Yeah," I muttered, fighting the tears forming in my eyes.

"Stay put behind the car." Zayne nodded at us, then opened the driver's side door and produced a little handheld device.

Cole pulled me into his side and looked at me. "Don't you ever put your life in danger like that again." His tone was harsh while he smoothed the hair from my face, his expression grim.

"I had to distract him, Cole. I was banking on Zayne's training and that he could disarm him if he got closer. It worked."

"King worked, and your idea was stupid." Cole grabbed my shoulders and faced me. "Dammit, I could have lost you." His Adam's apple bobbed in his throat. "Promise me, Shae. Promise me you won't play the hero again."

My chin trembled as fat tears slipped down my cheeks. "I can't. I would move heaven and earth not to lose you again."

Cole pulled me against him and wrapped me in his arms. "I love you, babe. I love your strength and courage, but you scared the shit out of me."

I dug my fingers into his shirt, thankful that no one had been hurt. "I love you, too." I sniffled. "Losing you was the hardest thing I've lived through, and all I could think of was keeping you alive."

"Son of a fucking bitch," Zayne said, reappearing and interrupting our conversation. "I checked the car for a tracker before we left the house, and the Mercedes was clean. I suspect Rick followed us from a distance. Dammit! I had my eyes on the mirrors the entire time. He clearly knows how to hide himself until he's ready to be seen." Zayne rubbed his chin, his green-eyed gaze narrowing.

"King has gone after him now, so hopefully the guys will catch him and end this once and for all." Cole rubbed my back as I swiped the moisture from my cheeks.

"Let's get you two home." Zayne opened the door, and Cole and I settled into the back seat.

Cole refused to let me go all the way to the house, and my nerves were on edge as Zayne parked the Mercedes in front of our garage. If I went inside, I would have to face Samuel. As if reading my mind, Cole climbed out of the car, took my hand, and led me to the back of the mansion. Zayne was hot on our heels and opened the gate for us. Once we were protected behind the fence, I released a huge sigh.

Cole stood near the edge of the pool and tilted his face to the sun. "School starts in a few weeks. What do you think about us renting a place together?" He peeked at me with one eye open and one closed.

I halted mid-step, my heart happily dancing. "Yeah?"

"I was actually looking for places on my phone before shit went down with Samuel. There's a three-bedroom available. I can easily afford it, and the guest rooms would be perfect for friends to crash when we've been partying. I just wasn't sure what your plans with Zoe were this year."

"Oh, shit." I slapped my palm against my forehead. "I almost forgot."

"Talk to her and see what you can work out. If worse comes to worst, I'll move in with you two." His expression turned cocky. "You're in my bed one way or the other."

"Are you threatening me, Mr. Jennings?" My chin jutted up as I folded my arms across my chest, daring him and loving every second of his heated attention.

"Careful, Princess." He closed the gap between us. He gripped my chin, forcing me to look at him. He bent slightly, his crystal-blue eyes penetrating my soul. "I'm almost well again. Don't tempt me to turn you over my knee and spank that sweet little ass of yours."

"If we have a roommate, noisy sex is off the table." I trailed the tip of my fingernail up his abdomen, his T-shirt bunching up his stomach and revealing the red, thick scar.

"Never underestimate me." His gaze flashed with mischief, then he firmly pressed his lips against mine.

The sun hid behind the trees as it made its slow descent. Pink, purple, and orange hues painted the sky as Cole and I walked along the pool, talking and planning our future. It was exactly what I needed. There was nothing else to say about Samuel or Rick. At least not that night. For now, I had to stay at the house because that's where Cole was living. Plus, I couldn't stay with Zoe or any of the girls, since it would put them in danger. My only option was to stay here and suck it up until Cole and I moved out. Finances were another hurdle. Samuel was paying for my college and housing until I graduated, and I wasn't sure how to navigate the tricky waters and still be able to attend.

A dark cloud hovered over me as I wondered about my real parents. Were they alive? Rich? Poor? Maybe I'd gotten my sass from my biological mom and my tenacity from my father, but I might never know thanks to Samuel.

One thing I wouldn't do was be dishonest with Samuel about how I felt concerning his betrayal. I might have been his Princess for all these years, but it didn't mean I had to follow in his footsteps and lie to the people who trusted me most.

Chapter Thirty-Four

The following few weeks were filled with broken hearts and awkward silences between Samuel and me. I'd asked myself if I were able to forgive him, but I couldn't. I needed time. Plus, I was considering searching for my biological parents, but I still wasn't sure I wanted to meet them. What if they were awful people? Junkies or abusive? Cole had suggested that I begin the process, then decide if any information turned up. A quick call to Sutton Westbrook put the pieces into motion, and the rest was a waiting game.

"Zoe is blowing up my phone with crying emojis." I folded Cole's T-shirts, then placed them in a box. We both had more to move this year since we'd rented a place together. Zoe had expressed her disappointment but was totally cool about it. Dani had found a house for her, Sibyl, Isabel, and Zoe. I'm not sure how she'd located a four-bedroom, but she did. From the images on the internet, it looked like a lovely home with an alarm system.

"She'll still see you every day. Tell her to suck it up." Cole shoved his fingers through his hair and glanced around. "I'm glad we bought some furniture for the rental."

I scrunched up my nose. "When you said beds were included at the new place ..." I wagged my finger. "Hell no. I'm not sleeping in a bed where some skank fucked a million guys."

Cole laughed. "There's my girl."

"What?" I put my hands on my hips, glowering at him. "Do you want me to sleep in some guy's come stain?" That did it.

Cole stepped around the boxes on the floor, his eyes dangerously flashing as he backed me against the wall and placed his palms on each side of my shoulders. He dipped his head, his minty breath fanning across my cheek before he whispered against my hair. "The only come you're going to be anywhere near is mine ... in your sweet little pussy, your tight ass, and down your throat."

I whimpered, my nipples pressing against my T-shirt. I hadn't bothered wearing a bra since we were packing and getting sweaty.

His knuckles trailed down my face, my neck, then to my breasts. I gasped as he pinched my taut bud. "I bet you're already wet for me, aren't you?" He nipped at my lower lip, then wrapped his fingers around my throat as he slipped his tongue into my mouth.

A loud knock had me smoothing my hair and making a mad dash for the chair across the room. Although Cole and I slept next to each other every night, due to the doctor's orders, we hadn't had sex. He'd kept me coming for him, though. I snickered, then busied myself with folding another shirt before Cole opened the door.

"Hey, Mom." Cole let her in.

Hopefully, she didn't notice the hard-on pressing against his jeans.

"How's it going? I can't believe you two leave tomorrow." Julia pressed her hand against her mouth. "I'm going to miss you both."

Cole wrapped her in a big hug. "We have guestrooms, or you can stay at a hotel, but you can visit any time you want." He kissed her on the forehead.

"I know, but you both will be in another state. It's not like I can zip across town to bring over dinner."

"It's only a five-hour drive. Plus, you really love Oregon. It will be a good change of scenery," Cole assured her.

"I do love how green everything is. Well, and hopefully you both will be here for the holidays." Julia glanced at me.

She didn't have to say any more. I realized Samuel wanted to patch things up and try to salvage our relationship. I just wasn't sure I was ready, and Thanksgiving was only two months away.

Footsteps echoed in the hall, and my gut clenched. The only other person in the house was Samuel. He cleared his throat before he appeared at Cole's door.

"Sorry to interrupt, but King is trying to reach you, Julia." Samuel gave her his cell, hope written all over his face.

"King, are you all right?" She stared at her feet, listening.

I hated that every time he called, we held our breath, waiting for the bad news.

"What? Are you a hundred percent sure?" She looked at Samuel, then over to us. "It's really over?" She laughed, happy tears streaming down her cheeks. "Thank you, I'll let everyone know." She turned to Samuel. "Love you too, big brother." She disconnected the call and returned the phone back to Samuel. "They got Rick. He's gone. Dead. King confirmed it all. I have no other details, but it's finally over. No more blackmail and no more death threats."

My knees nearly buckled beneath me with the news. The sorry fucker that had hurt Cole and hired Ibrahim was finally gone. Relief flooded through me, igniting a spark of hope that we could all move on.

Samuel clapped his hands, grinning as if he'd just won the lottery. In a way, he had. He wouldn't be exposed for buying his daughter on the black market and lose his company and life.

I hopped out of my seat and hugged Cole.

"We're finally safe, baby." Cole rubbed my back as he held me.

Cole embraced his mom, and so did I. I couldn't imagine how relieved she must feel to finally be rid of the son of a bitch.

Samuel and Cole hugged as well, which left me staring at Samuel after everyone was finished.

"Congratulations, your secret won't be exposed." I tucked my hair behind an ear, then I cleared my throat, selecting my words carefully. "You have my word that I'll keep it as well. You've provided for me my entire life, and for the most part it's been a good one. I just don't want you to live in fear that I'll turn you in. If I locate my birth parents, we'll come up with a story to tell them."

Relief and gratitude filled Samuel's face, and the tension visibly melted from his neck and shoulders. "Thank you, Shae."

"I can't promise you anything else at this point, but I didn't want to leave for school without telling you that at least." I looked at Cole when he placed a palm against my lower back.

"I hope that someday you can forgive me," Samuel said, his voice low and haunted. "This might not make sense to you right now, but as horrible as my actions were, I never regretted bringing you home. You gave Lori and me years of happiness. I loved your mother with every fiber of my being, but ... I hadn't ever experienced a love so deep and pure ... until I held you. Spending the rest of my life in prison would be worth the time I had with you, Shae."

Julia took his hand, smiling up at him. Even when Samuel mentioned how much he loved my mom, Julia seemed to understand that each person had the ability to hold a special place in their heart, and it wasn't a competition. And for all I knew, Samuel and she had already discussed Mom, and she'd worked through any jealousy, so it really wasn't any of my business.

Cole's words ran through my head as Samuel and I stared at each other, the air thickening around us. *When men like Samuel and I love someone, the lines of what is right and wrong blur. We will do things other men wouldn't ever consider in order to protect the people most important to us.*

"Thank you for taking care of Mom." My chin trembled. "If it makes a difference, I want to forgive you. My heart and head just need to catch up to each other."

Samuel nodded. "I understand." He looked away, then to Cole and me again. "If you kids are interested in dinner by the pool, I can grill some steaks. Maybe we can have one last evening before you two leave tomorrow."

Memories of Mom's smile and snuggles flashed through my mind. I never saw her broken the way that Samuel had described her. Maybe what Cole said was true. If Cole had gone to the same extremes to keep me safe and happy, wouldn't I love him more for it? I wasn't sure since I hadn't lived through that experience.

"Cole?" I asked softly.

"It's your call, baby."

I swallowed over the tight feeling in my throat. "That would be really nice. What time should we be down there?"

Samuel's smile lit up the entire room and reached inside my chest, cradling my heart. It felt good to see him happy, even if for just a moment.

"How about seven? That gives you two some time to finish packing."

"Sounds good," Cole said.

Julia and Samuel left, leaving the door open. I nearly rolled my eyes, but Cole and I would have our own place tomorrow.

We'd also agreed that Cole would leave his motorcycle here until summer. As much as it rained in Oregon, it didn't make sense to take it and let it sit outside.

I stretched, my back popping. "Guess we better get busy." I gave him a quick peck on the lips, then focused on preparing for the move. One thing I loved about Cole was that he never pushed me to talk. He always gave me the space to process. This was one of those times that I needed a few minutes to think.

Over the next several hours, we knocked out the packing for both our rooms.

I glanced at the alarm clock on my desk. "I should change clothes and put a bra on for dinner."

"Okay. I'll confirm with the guys that we're still on for tomorrow afternoon." Cole sighed. "Remington will help Samuel load my truck in the morning, but I'm glad Anderson and Sterling will be able to help unload when we get to Oregon."

"No shit. I think Isabel and Zoe will be there to help, too."

I was so used to Cole riding his motorcycle I'd completely forgotten that his bright blue Ford F-250 was parked in our garage.

"Excellent, then everyone can see the house, too." Cole slipped his arms around my waist and brought me to him. "You did well with Samuel today. How are you feeling about dinner?"

"I'm okay. I'm trying to work through everything, but I think some distance from him will help clear my mind. It's too easy to stay angry all the time when he's around constantly. I figure one evening won't be a big deal since we can excuse ourselves when we need to. Eight in the morning comes awfully fast." I pushed up on my tiptoes and kissed Cole.

He threaded his fingers through my hair and pulled, exposing my neck to his warm mouth. As quickly as he began, he stepped away and grinned. "Get dressed."

I shook my head. "You're so fucking bossy." I laughed as I watched him walk out of my room, appreciating the way his jeans fit his ass and legs. I couldn't wait until after dinner when we would finally be able to fuck like bunnies.

Chapter Thirty-Five

The first week of freshman year was filled with a flurry of books, schedules, and wrapping my head around studying again.

The mid-September breeze blew through green tree leaves as I walked across campus, toward my next class. The early afternoon sunshine warmed my face as I took my time, breathing in the fresh air. People were gathered on blankets, chatting and laughing, while others rushed past me in a frenzy. Some professors locked students out of the classroom if they were late, which was bothersome during the first week since everyone was learning where the classrooms were, but the teachers didn't care.

I adjusted my backpack and tugged down my navy top that kept riding up my stomach.

"Shae!" A familiar male voice called.

I spun around with the mention of my name and spotted David. He gave me a thousand-watt smile as he jogged over to me.

"Hey! I heard you were here this year. Congrats on the football scholarship. Maybe we'll finally win some games." I grinned, genuinely excited for him.

He chuckled, his brown eyes sparkling as his signature lazy smile eased across his tan features. The football team had already returned and were practicing crazy hours each day. "The guys are looking pretty good. I'm happy about that." His attention traveled over me, pausing on my legs, then back to my face. "Will you be at some games? Maybe the parties after?"

"No," Cole said from behind me. "Unless she's with me." He slipped his hand around my waist as I looked up at him. His mouth crashed down on mine, possessively. "Hey, baby."

"Hey. I was on my way to class."

Cole's threatening gaze landed on David. "Let everyone know Shae belongs to me. Anyone who wants to test that idea will wish they'd never looked at her."

David's eyes widened as his focus bounced between us. "You two are together?" He pointed at us, clearly surprised.

"Got a problem with it?" Cole asked.

David was a tall, well-built guy, not to mention in shape, but he was no match for Cole.

"Nope, just making sure I'm clear, so I could let the guys know." David massaged his neck, wincing. "See you around." Then, he hurried off.

I nearly creamed my G-string with Cole's fierce protectiveness. Not only was he making sure that everyone knew that we were together, but it was a warning that if anyone hurt me, he would personally take care of the situation. Unfortunately, rape on campus was a real thing.

"Fucker," Cole muttered before he kissed me again.

"You've always cockblocked me, Cole." I laughed, feeling bad for David. Cole was up to the same games he used to play, but I never understood why he wouldn't ever allow anyone to date me until recently.

"I'll block anyone's cock except mine." He pulled on me, and we started walking to class, teasing each other.

I hadn't missed some of the familiar students staring at us. Since

Cole was a year ahead of me, he knew a lot more people, but his reputation preceded him. I suspected before the day was over, whispers and gossip would fill the campus. After all, I *was* fucking my stepbrother. But this time, I didn't care what anyone else thought. I was madly in love with him, and he was all I needed.

"Sorry it took me a while, but I was finally able to find out who released the video of you and ..." Cole ground his molars, the muscle in his jaw flinching. "Ibrahim and Matt."

I stopped and looked at him expectantly.

"Blaire Gordon." He shoved his fingers through his hair.

"My arch nemesis?" I seethed. "That bitch. I will fucking destroy her." This time, she'd gone too far. Lucky for Blaire, she attended a different college in another state. She better hope I never saw her face again. I would fucking bury her.

"How, Cole? How did it happen?" Placing my hand on my hip I narrowed my gaze at him.

"It was an accident, I swear, babe. When we were at Harrison's party, I was sitting upstairs with the guys and a few girls and Blaire were there. When I saw you, I jumped out of the chair and my phone fell between the cushions. I'd just used it, so it was unlocked. This is on me just as much as it's on Blaire."

I took a deep breath, asking myself if it was worth being mad at him again. It was months ago and in the past. Cole had nearly died, plus he'd also just apologized to me. Not to mention, he'd found out who had released the video.

"Cole, it's over. I'll deal with her later. Thank you for sharing. You could have hid it from me, but you were honest."

Cole reached up and tucked my hair behind my ear. "I love you, Shae. I've had secrets from you long enough. You deserved to know the truth." He pressed a sweet kiss to my mouth.

It was moments like these that made it easy to forgive him. We'd come so far since that evening at Harrison's party, and it was all that I wanted to hold onto.

After a long day of classes, I unlocked the front door of our house and closed it behind me. Flipping the bolt into place, I dropped my backpack on the floor and toed my Gucci shoes off.

Strolling over to the table near the new cream leather couch, I placed my keys on the table near the door, then headed to the fridge for a snack. Cole had pretty much let me furnish the home with an understanding that we would either stay here until we both graduated or sell the furniture when we were finished. It had been fun picking out the pieces for our first place together. A few pieces of artwork along with a coffee table and matching recliner complimented the light wood floors. Brown, floor-length black-out curtains hung over the shades, providing the room with some contrast. Cole had insisted on as much privacy as possible, so we'd doubled up the window treatments.

The kitchen was small, but I couldn't have cared less as long as Cole and I had a place to ourselves. The appliances were high-end stainless steel, and the white granite counters were beautiful. Since we weren't on campus, Cole had found a nicer home for us. He wanted to make sure we were in a good area, too. I realized he could take care of himself, and the area and security alarm were for my benefit and his peace of mind. His protectiveness meant the world to me.

Samuel and Julia were so thrilled when Cole told them he wouldn't be prospecting to the MC, they paid for the house, then loaded it with food and supplies. They'd been true to their word and had been very supportive of our relationship once Cole had shared his decision.

Spotting a yellow piece of paper stuck to the refrigerator, I picked it up.

I'll be home around five. Get naked and wait for me.

Giggling, I peeked at the clock on the wall above the sink—fifteen more minutes. I hurried upstairs to the bathroom and freshened up.

While brushing my teeth, I heard the front door open and then close. *Fuck, he's home already!* I quickly rinsed and dried my mouth.

"Shae!" Cole's voice boomeranged off the walls.

Just to be ornery, I took my time strolling to the top of the stairs and looked down at him, heat pooling low in my belly. "You're home already."

"I said five o'clock," he growled. His heated gaze swept up and down the length of me. "Why aren't you ready for me?" He rubbed his chin, and I guessed he was thinking about how he would punish me.

"Because you're early," I said innocently, descending the stairs, my body craving him. I watched his every move in anticipation.

He made his way to the couch and opened the drawer in the coffee table. Cole glanced at me as he placed some items on the top. Curiosity reared its head as I joined him. *Oh. Shit.* I sank my teeth into my lower lip as my focus landed on the items. A butt plug, lube, and a purple dual vibrator. Cole wrapped my hair around his fingers and pulled until I sank to my knees. "Do you know what I want?"

I quivered with excitement. I was pretty sure I could guess from the toys in front of me.

"What?"

"I'm taking every part of you tonight. Talking to David and not being naked when I got home." He tsked. "You've been defiant, Shae."

I gawked at him. "David approached me. How is that my fault?"

"No talking."

I did as he asked, peeking up at him beneath my eyelashes.

He popped open the button on his jeans and lowered his zipper with his free hand. He freed his big cock and rubbed it against my lower lip. "Disobedient girls get spanked."

I grimaced. *Dammit.*

"Open."

I did as he commanded, and the smooth skin of his shaft glided over my tongue.

"That's it." His attention was trained on me as I sucked his dick, the otherwise quiet house filling with his grunts as he moved his hips. For whatever reason, he stepped away. "Take your clothes off. Slowly."

He watched me as I slipped off my shirt, bra, shorts, and shimmied out of my G-string. Standing in front of him, my stomach dipped to my toes as his gaze latched onto my waxed pussy. He removed his shirt, jeans, and boxer briefs, then sat on the couch, his erection bobbing against his abs. "Bend over." His voice was gruff and sexy as hell.

I settled over his lap, my butt in the air. A loud smack startled me and I yelped. Attempting to cover up my ass, he pinned my wrists behind me as he spanked me again.

"Dammit, Cole that hurts!" I cried.

He responded with silence as he spanked me a few more times. Tears stung my eyes as he rubbed my tender skin.

"Next time obey me, Shae."

"I will," I stammered, still reeling from the pain.

Cole spread me apart, then ran his finger up and down my slit, but this time, he smeared my juices up to my asshole. No one had fucked me in the ass since Ibrahim, but I was ready.

He slipped a finger inside me. "So wet."

I whimpered as he fingerfucked me. "Do you like that?"

"Yes," I responded breathlessly.

"Be a good girl and sit on the couch."

The second I settled in, he knelt and parted my thighs and lowered his head. His tongue circled my clit, and I grabbed his hair as I bucked against him. Nipping and licking, he brought me to the edge, then stopped. A mischievous smile graced his lips as he crawled on the couch and hovered over me. Then, he startled me and forced his cock into my mouth again.

His hips thrust faster as he shoved the tip to the back of my throat, and his lips parted. He growled as his hot liquid coated my mouth. I gulped it greedily, sucking every drop from him.

Cole pulled out, then stood. "You took that like a good girl." His dick began to soften, and my lip jutted out. "Don't worry, Shae. This time will be well spent. Stand up and bend over the couch."

Relaxing, I let him set the tone. I got up, then eagerly bent over.

"Spread your legs."

I gave him the access he wanted and waited for his next move. "Goddammit. Just looking at you has my dick getting hard again."

After lubing me and the vibrator, he slid it into my core, turned it so the shorter end wouldn't penetrate my ass, but didn't turn it on.

He eased it in and out of my pussy before he moved his cock to my tight hole. He pressed against me, then pushed the tip in.

"More," I pleaded.

"You're so tight, baby. That sweet little ass is all mine." He eased in some more, still fucking me with the vibrator at the same time. Impatient, Cole ditched the toy. His fingers dug into my hips as he worked his long dick inside me and began to pick up the pace.

My whimpers and moans escaped me as he reached between my legs and pinched my clit. Jolts of pleasure rippled over my flesh.

"Do you like me fucking your ass?" He rubbed my bundle of nerves.

"Yeah," I answered breathlessly. "Fuck me, Cole."

"Who do you belong to, Shae?"

"You."

"No one will ever touch you again. You're all mine. Say it."

"No one else ever again," I said.

"That's my good girl. Come for me, Shae."

My body seized as black dots danced across my vision as an intense orgasm ripped through me, peaking his release as well. He jerked, his hold on me loosening, and I sucked in a much-needed breath. Panting, I nearly collapsed on the couch, but he was still inside me.

Cole dotted a few kisses on my shoulder before he eased out, then swatted me on the ass and disappeared down the hall of the main floor. I sat down, sore from our playtime. The water running in the bathroom let me know he was cleaning up. When it turned off, his footsteps sounded against the wood floors as he joined me.

He knelt and tenderly cleaned me with a warm washcloth. He kissed the inside of each thigh, then rose, his expression full of love. "Are you hungry? I'll order dinner."

I grinned at him. "How could I refuse that offer?" I placed my hand in his, then he tugged me off the seat and into a standing position. I rested my palms against his chest and peered up at him.

Cole smoothed my hair and kissed me. "I love you, Shae Wessex."

"I love you, too."

He wrapped me in a warm embrace, and I molded into him. This must be what heaven felt like—warm, safe, and full of love. With Cole I had heaven right here on earth.

Don't Miss **Illicit Obsession, a dark, stepbrother, sports standalone is coming Oct, 2023. Preorder here! Turn the page for the Sample!**

Illicit Obsession Sample

The day my stepsister died; she took my heart with her.

Now, I'm a shell of a man, a cold-hearted monster.

Imagine my surprise when the love of my life shows up at Whitmore University alive and well.

I'm ready to make her pay for destroying me.

This isn't a fairy tale, and I'm sure as hell no knight in shining armor.

I have no problem dragging her into my dark world along with me.
But when I dig for the truth of what happened that fateful day
I can no longer deny how I feel about the only girl I've ever loved.
Others see us as an abomination and will do anything to keep us apart.
And just as I vowed to destroy her,
I vow to protect her even if it costs me my life.
She was once my target. Now she's my everything.

From the international bestselling author, J.A. Owenby, comes a ***new dark, forbidden stepbrother, sports, secret society, second chance standalone romance. Illicit Obsession*** features a hot, **possessive/jealous hero and a strong, curvy heroine** who knows how to tame her twisted and morally grey stepsibling. **No cheating, no cliffhanger**, and a **happily ever after** guaranteed!

This standalone is a **BRAND-NEW story with Jagger and Ariana from the Whitmore Elite Series. If you have read Forbidden Obsession, this book is completely different but with the same character names.

Download Illicit Obsession on Amazon or **FREE** in Kindle Unlimited! **Click Here!**

Turn the page for the Sample of Illicit Obsession.

Jagger

"What the hell is this?" I blinked rapidly, trying to clear the haze from my eyes. "Where am I?" Despite the struggle against my restraints, it took me a few seconds to realize that I wasn't going anywhere due to the tightness of the ropes. I frantically searched around the room in an attempt to figure out where I was.

A dark chuckle bounced off the cement floor and walls. "Don't worry, Jagger Whitlock, it's all a part of the plan," the disguised voice said. He peered at me through the holes in the skull mask as he paced a circle around my chair. I recognized him from the society invitation video. *Fuck, what the hell did I do?*

"What do you want?" Despite the chilly air against my bare chest, beads of sweat formed on my forehead. The bastards knocked me out, drug me out of the field house, and tied me to a chair. Apparently, it would have been too much for them to grab some sweatpants for me. Instead, I shivered in nothing more than my boxer briefs. I had no idea who I'd pissed off, but I mentally skipped down that long list.

"You're one of the chosen. Try to relax and enjoy the ride." The fucker laughed even more.

My blood boiled in my veins. The familiar feeling of fury and hatred reawakened the beast inside me.

The masked and cloaked person didn't speak, but I felt the power bubbling beneath his skin. He might be crazier than I was. I wasn't sure if it was a good or a bad thing.

I attempted to control my breathing, but I had no fucking clue who was behind the mask and had taken me prisoner. If I bargained for my freedom, it would tickle his ego, and I would leave wherever I was in one piece.

"A brotherhood will fight for each other, but only if they have something on the line. Something to lose. In your case, you want a pro football career. I can make that dream come true, but why should I if you have no skin in the game?"

I blanched at him. "You can get me a pro ball contract?" A sense of foreboding enveloped me. This wasn't good. Whoever was talking to me was fucking with my head, and I strongly suspected I knew who it was. *Shit. This is bad. Real bad.* Until I found his weak spot, I had to play his sick game.

"If you can get me a deal with the Eagles, I'll give you my damn soul." Even though I realized it wouldn't serve me well, I gave him a disbelieving snort. "What are you, the devil's right hand?" What he didn't know was that I was the devil's left hand. Maybe we could work together and solve a big problem I had that refused to leave me alone.

The figure stopped in front of me and bent over, the nose of his skull mask a mere inch from mine. "I can make it happen, Jagger Whitlock, but what will you give me in exchange? I have no use for a wasted, dark soul like yours." He straightened, staring a hole right through me.

"Name your price. Hell, I've done a lot of dark shit in my life. I'm pretty sure I can offer you something you'll find valuable."

I shivered, sweat drying against my skin and making me even colder. Minutes ticked by without another word from him.

"What should I call you? Skull? I mean, you know *my* name. That doesn't seem fair, does it?"

He folded his arms in front of his chest. "You can call me Black Widow. I am the leader of a secret society, and if you pass the test, you'll join us."

I barked out a laugh. "Sorry, man. You should have led with that. You're wasting your time. I pledge to no one. This shit show wasn't what I signed up for." If he wasn't lying, it wasn't who I thought it was, which meant this situation wasn't as bleak as I first assumed.

A spotlight blasted through the darkness and I shrank away, trying to shield my eyes until my vision adjusted.

"It's easy, really. I'll make sure you have everything you want in exchange for your deepest, darkest secret."

My heart skidded to a stop, and I reminded myself to breathe. "No fucking way," I said quietly.

"Are you sure? You're ready to walk away from all of your dreams?"

"I don't know you, asshole. How am I supposed to blindly trust you?" I tugged on my wrist restraints again, as if they had magically loosened.

The light dimmed and moved, illuminating the rest of the small area. Several people stood on the other side of glass walls, all of them wearing the same skull mask and robe as the Black Widow, arms crossed over their chests in what could only be called a power stance. They looked immovable.

A voice began to filter into the room.

"Jagger," a female said.

My throat constricted as she continued to talk. "I love you, baby. Promise me we'll never be apart."

"I'll never let that happen," I replied on the recording.

"What the fuck? How did you get that?" I yelled over the recorded conversation. Her voice sliced through me like hot knives carving out my heart and tossing it on the cold ground.

"If our parents find out, they'll separate us," she said.

As hard as I fought against it, tears pricked my eyes. It had been years since I'd heard her speak.

"Tell us your secret, Jagger, then all of this will disappear. You can finally move forward. I'm doing you a huge favor."

My body trembled as the recording continued, with the sounds of us kissing and moaning as we made out. I remembered every sound, every breath. Even though I'd promised her, it had been our last night together.

Agony twisted my stomach into a million knots as I was overcome with grief—the soft lilt of her tone wreaked havoc on me.

"What happened, Jagger? What did you do?" the Black Widow asked.

I sucked in a huge breath, trying to clear my head.

"If you tell us, then you'll have everything you've dreamed of: a family, a career, and more women than you could imagine at your fingertips. Most of all, I can grant you hope. All I ask is for your darkest secret in return. Pledge your loyalty to each man here and they will do the same."

Frowning, I looked around the room at each person staring at me. I could have sworn a few of them nodded. Had they already talked about their pasts?

"Who are they?" I gestured to the strangers on the other side of the glass.

"Members. Each have shared their secret and now have successful lives and careers. They will forever be a part of the brotherhood. You can have the same thing. Once you tell us yours, they will share with you as well."

I swallowed hard, wishing I had some water. Closing my eyes, I listened to the recording continue to play. She had sent me the video later that evening. It was still on my phone, but I couldn't bear to watch it. Now, I was listening to it and so were the people in this room.

"You're a perfect fit for the society, Jagger. Name your price. We need someone like you."

"I want the pro deal. Nothing else matters. I have nothing left except football."

Moans of her pleasure filtered through the speaker, and it took everything inside me not to break down and sob.

"Then you'll have it. Don't misunderstand my intentions. I've hand-picked every member. You have skills and value. Let the society give you the world. All I need is something that proves to us that you're all in. Betrayal of the members is punishable by death, so are you willing to pay the price to make all your dreams come true?"

The recording finally stopped, and a heavy silence hung in the room as the others patiently stood and waited for my answer. I had nothing to lose. Whoever the Black Widow was, he realized what I would say, or he wouldn't have the recording. He was one clever son of a bitch. I had to give him that. If he could deliver on the pro deal in exchange for dirt that he already knew, what the hell was I really losing? The others had to share too. We would all be on an equal footing. I was familiar with the pledge process since my uncle was the president of an MC, the Dirty Bastards. I understood how that loyalty worked—a secret for a secret.

Taking a deep breath, I realized that if this asshole knew, anyone could find out, and that knowledge left me vulnerable. Hell, I would need some friends to help me bury it. All this time, I thought I was protected. As soon as I was finished here, I would need to find a way to erase my past once and for all. Maybe the Black Widow had done me a favor and saved my ass.

I squared my shoulders, ready. "I . . ." My voice cracked. "My biggest secret is—"

Grab Illicit Obsession on Amazon or **FREE** in Kindle Unlimited! **Click Here!**

Forbidden, A Whitmore Elite Prequel

J.A. OWENBY

Edited by: David Steele

Cover Art by: Blushing Romance Designs

First Edition ISBN-13: 978-1-949414-84-4

Also by J.A. Owenby

The Beautifully Damaged Series

Beautifully Damaged

Beautifully Broken

Beautifully Shattered

The Whitmore Elite Standalones

Forbidden, A Whitmore Elite Prequel

Illicit Obsession, coming Fall of 2023

Ruthless Obsession

Sinful Obsession

Toxic Obsession

The Love & Ruin Series

Love & Sins

Love & Ruin

Love & Deception

Love & Redemption

Love & Consequences, a standalone novel

Love & Corruption, a standalone novel

Love & Revelations, a novella

Love & Seduction, a standalone novel

Love & Vengeance

Love & Retaliation

Love & Betrayal, a standalone novel

The Wicked Intentions Series

Dark Intentions

Fractured Intentions

The Torn Series, inspired by True Events

Fading into Her, a prequel novella

Torn

Captured

Freed

About the Author

International bestselling author J.A. Owenby grew up in a small backwoods town in Arkansas where she learned how to swear like a sailor and spot water moccasins skimming across the lake.

She finally ditched the south and headed to Oregon. The first winter there, she was literally blown away a few times by ninety mile an hour winds and storms that rolled in off the ocean.

Eventually, she longed for quiet and headed up to snowier pastures. She now resides in Washington state with her hot nerdy husband and cat, Chloe (who frequently encourages her to drink). She spends her days coming up with ways to torture characters in a way that either makes you want to throw your book down a flight of stairs or sob hysterically into a pillow.

J.A. Owenby writes new adult and romantic thriller novels. Her books ooze with emotion, angst, and twists that will leave you breathless. Having battled her own demons, she's not afraid to tackle the secrets women are forced to hide. After all, the road to love is paved in the dark.

Her friends describe her as delightfully twisted. She loves fan mail and wine. Please send her all the wine.

You can follow the progress of her upcoming novel on Facebook at Author J.A. Owenby and on Twitter @jaowenby.

Sign up for J.A. Owenby's Newsletter:
BookHip.com/CTZMWZ

Like J.A. Owenby's Facebook:
https://www.facebook.com/JAOwenby
J.A. Owenby's One Page At A Time reader group:

https://www.facebook.com/groups/JAOwenby

A note from the author:

Dear Readers,
If you have experienced sexual assault or physical abuse,
there is free, confidential help. Please visit:
Website: https://www.rainn.org/
Phone: 800-656-4673

This book may contain sensitive material for some readers. Gemma and Hendrix's story is considered a dark romance with language, sex, and violence.